I0761905

LEFT TO HUNT

(An Adele Sharp Mystery—Book Nine)

BLAKE PIERCE

Blake Pierce

Blake Pierce is the USA Today bestselling author of the RILEY PAGE mystery series, which includes seventeen books. Blake Pierce is also the author of the MACKENZIE WHITE mystery series, comprising fourteen books; of the AVERY BLACK mystery series, comprising six books; of the KERI LOCKE mystery series, comprising five books; of the MAKING OF RILEY PAIGE mystery series, comprising six books; of the KATE WISE mystery series, comprising seven books; of the CHLOE FINE psychological suspense mystery, comprising six books; of the JESSE HUNT psychological suspense thriller series, comprising nineteen books; of the AU PAIR psychological suspense thriller series, comprising three books; of the ZOE PRIME mystery series, comprising six books; of the ADELE SHARP mystery series, comprising thirteen books; of the EUROPEAN VOYAGE cozy mystery series, comprising six books (and counting); of the new LAURA FROST FBI suspense thriller, comprising three books (and counting); of the new ELLA DARK FBI suspense thriller, comprising six books (and counting); of the A YEAR IN EUROPE cozy mystery series, comprising nine books); of the AVA GOLD mystery series, comprising three books (and counting); and of the RACHEL GIFT mystery series, comprising three books (and counting).

An avid reader and lifelong fan of the mystery and thriller genres, Blake loves to hear from you, so please feel free to visit www.blakepierceauthor.com to learn more and stay in touch.

ISBN: 978-1-0943-9148-9

BOOKS BY BLAKE PIERCE

RACHEL GIFT MYSTERY SERIES
HER LAST WISH (Book #1)
HER LAST CHANCE (Book #2)
HER LAST HOPE (Book #3)

AVA GOLD MYSTERY SERIES
CITY OF PREY (Book #1)
CITY OF FEAR (Book #2)
CITY OF BONES (Book #3)

A YEAR IN EUROPE
A MURDER IN PARIS (Book #1)
DEATH IN FLORENCE (Book #2)
VENGEANCE IN VIENNA (Book #3)
A FATALITY IN SPAIN (Book #4)
SCANDAL IN LONDON (Book #5)
AN IMPOSTOR IN DUBLIN (Book #6)
SEDUCTION IN BORDEAUX (Book #7)
JEALOUSY IN SWITZERLAND (Book #8)
A DEBACLE IN PRAGUE (Book #9)

ELLA DARK FBI SUSPENSE THRILLER
GIRL, ALONE (Book #1)
GIRL, TAKEN (Book #2)
GIRL, HUNTED (Book #3)
GIRL, SILENCED (Book #4)
GIRL, VANISHED (Book 5)
GIRL ERASED (Book #6)

LAURA FROST FBI SUSPENSE THRILLER
ALREADY GONE (Book #1)
ALREADY SEEN (Book #2)
ALREADY TRAPPED (Book #3)

EUROPEAN VOYAGE COZY MYSTERY SERIES
MURDER (AND BAKLAVA) (Book #1)

DEATH (AND APPLE STRUDEL) (Book #2)
CRIME (AND LAGER) (Book #3)
MISFORTUNE (AND GOUDA) (Book #4)
CALAMITY (AND A DANISH) (Book #5)
MAYHEM (AND HERRING) (Book #6)

ADELE SHARP MYSTERY SERIES
LEFT TO DIE (Book #1)
LEFT TO RUN (Book #2)
LEFT TO HIDE (Book #3)
LEFT TO KILL (Book #4)
LEFT TO MURDER (Book #5)
LEFT TO ENVY (Book #6)
LEFT TO LAPSE (Book #7)
LEFT TO VANISH (Book #8)
LEFT TO HUNT (Book #9)
LEFT TO FEAR (Book #10)
LEFT TO PREY (Book #11)
LEFT TO LURE (Book #12)
LEFT TO CRAVE (Book #13)

THE AU PAIR SERIES
ALMOST GONE (Book#1)
ALMOST LOST (Book #2)
ALMOST DEAD (Book #3)

ZOE PRIME MYSTERY SERIES
FACE OF DEATH (Book#1)
FACE OF MURDER (Book #2)
FACE OF FEAR (Book #3)
FACE OF MADNESS (Book #4)
FACE OF FURY (Book #5)
FACE OF DARKNESS (Book #6)

A JESSIE HUNT PSYCHOLOGICAL SUSPENSE SERIES
THE PERFECT WIFE (Book #1)
THE PERFECT BLOCK (Book #2)
THE PERFECT HOUSE (Book #3)
THE PERFECT SMILE (Book #4)
THE PERFECT LIE (Book #5)
THE PERFECT LOOK (Book #6)

THE PERFECT AFFAIR (Book #7)
THE PERFECT ALIBI (Book #8)
THE PERFECT NEIGHBOR (Book #9)
THE PERFECT DISGUISE (Book #10)
THE PERFECT SECRET (Book #11)
THE PERFECT FAÇADE (Book #12)
THE PERFECT IMPRESSION (Book #13)
THE PERFECT DECEIT (Book #14)
THE PERFECT MISTRESS (Book #15)
THE PERFECT IMAGE (Book #16)
THE PERFECT VEIL (Book #17)
THE PERFECT INDISCRETION (Book #18)
THE PERFECT RUMOR (Book #19)

CHLOE FINE PSYCHOLOGICAL SUSPENSE SERIES
NEXT DOOR (Book #1)
A NEIGHBOR'S LIE (Book #2)
CUL DE SAC (Book #3)
SILENT NEIGHBOR (Book #4)
HOMECOMING (Book #5)
TINTED WINDOWS (Book #6)

KATE WISE MYSTERY SERIES
IF SHE KNEW (Book #1)
IF SHE SAW (Book #2)
IF SHE RAN (Book #3)
IF SHE HID (Book #4)
IF SHE FLED (Book #5)
IF SHE FEARED (Book #6)
IF SHE HEARD (Book #7)

THE MAKING OF RILEY PAIGE SERIES
WATCHING (Book #1)
WAITING (Book #2)
LURING (Book #3)
TAKING (Book #4)
STALKING (Book #5)
KILLING (Book #6)

RILEY PAIGE MYSTERY SERIES
ONCE GONE (Book #1)

ONCE TAKEN (Book #2)
ONCE CRAVED (Book #3)
ONCE LURED (Book #4)
ONCE HUNTED (Book #5)
ONCE PINED (Book #6)
ONCE FORSAKEN (Book #7)
ONCE COLD (Book #8)
ONCE STALKED (Book #9)
ONCE LOST (Book #10)
ONCE BURIED (Book #11)
ONCE BOUND (Book #12)
ONCE TRAPPED (Book #13)
ONCE DORMANT (Book #14)
ONCE SHUNNED (Book #15)
ONCE MISSED (Book #16)
ONCE CHOSEN (Book #17)

MACKENZIE WHITE MYSTERY SERIES
BEFORE HE KILLS (Book #1)
BEFORE HE SEES (Book #2)
BEFORE HE COVETS (Book #3)
BEFORE HE TAKES (Book #4)
BEFORE HE NEEDS (Book #5)
BEFORE HE FEELS (Book #6)
BEFORE HE SINS (Book #7)
BEFORE HE HUNTS (Book #8)
BEFORE HE PREYS (Book #9)
BEFORE HE LONGS (Book #10)
BEFORE HE LAPSES (Book #11)
BEFORE HE ENVIES (Book #12)
BEFORE HE STALKS (Book #13)
BEFORE HE HARMS (Book #14)

AVERY BLACK MYSTERY SERIES
CAUSE TO KILL (Book #1)
CAUSE TO RUN (Book #2)
CAUSE TO HIDE (Book #3)
CAUSE TO FEAR (Book #4)
CAUSE TO SAVE (Book #5)
CAUSE TO DREAD (Book #6)

KERI LOCKE MYSTERY SERIES
A TRACE OF DEATH (Book #1)
A TRACE OF MUDER (Book #2)
A TRACE OF VICE (Book #3)
A TRACE OF CRIME (Book #4)
A TRACE OF HOPE (Book #5)

CHAPTER ONE

Wide-eyed, Lorraine Strasser watched the masked woman float over the water. The *Carnevale di Venezia* was in full swing, and the thin wire attached to the floating woman's costume was nearly invisible against the dark skyline over the Grand Canal of Venice.

Lorraine witnessed the flying woman loop from one building across the water towards another. A passing gondola beneath shone multi-colored lights into the air, illuminating her frilled dress and reflecting off the porcelain characteristics of her Venetian mask. Two golden horns twisted out of a lily-white face covering, blossoming with red and blue flowers.

Lorraine stood at the edge of the small marble bridge looping over one of the channels, her eyes fixated on the spectacle above the city.

Beyond the floating woman and her flowered mask, other floats and spectacles made their eerie way down the waterway, bobbing on the canal. Jugglers and jesters danced about a small flotilla, and—beyond them—illuminated by a spotlight, a woman in a giant see-through bubble spun around and around with dizzying speed.

Crowding the walkways facing the waters, pedestrians, Venetians and tourists alike, all gathered to witness the displays of talent and beauty in the falling evening. Fireworks exploded in the distance and stray sparklers in the hands of mimes danced through the crowds of spectators.

And this was only the second day of the week-long festival.

Lorraine's eyes shimmered in delight at it all. However, she'd misplaced her friends—and now, as night continued to stretch later and later, she supposed it might not be safe to remain on her own in these crowded streets.

Beauty and youth were both appreciated in Venice. But beauty and youth such as Lorraine's often attracted the wrong sorts of attention when the sun dipped its head.

A couple of men, leaning against the opposite bridge rail were watching her and making no qualms about it, their eyes hazy and blinking, their cheeks stained red. The culprit of such facades lay in the discarded brown bottles at their feet, and the ones still gripped in their hands.

One of the men with an unwashed face and untrimmed beard burped, winked at her and took a long swig. His friend leaned in, whispering something in the unruly man's ear. This seemed to embolden the fellow and he nodded once, pushing off the bridge's railing and beginning to move through the assembled spectators in Lorraine's direction.

She winced, heading hurriedly the opposite direction.

“Lady!” the man called in American English after her. “Hey! Stop!”

But she pretended she couldn't hear, her heart hammering now, leading quickly down the marble bridge and along the wharf on the other side. She could feel her heartbeat rising, echoing in her ears. At the same time, the flying lady passed on the invisible wire above, accompanied by multi-hued spotlights chasing after her.

The crowd *oohed* and *ahhed*, but now Lorraine was beginning to wish she'd had the good sense to stay with her friends. She glanced through the crowds, still moving and trying to keep her head low to avoid further harassment.

She hastened quickly along the waterways and glanced back.

The bleary-eyed man was still following her. And his drunk friend was now with him, waving after her and calling loudly while making kissing noises.

Other spectators on the streets and paths lining the waters shushed the men or avoided them completely. Jugglers wearing Venetian masks were tossing flaming batons back and forth, women with darts were spinning on rotating wheels while tossing the darts back and forth to each other, hitting only wood.

All of it had seemed so lovely, so wonderful and marvelous, but now Lorraine felt like Alice, lost in Wonderland. She felt the urge to break into a jog, but decided this would only communicate fear to her pursuers.

She ducked past a stand where masks and art pieces were being sold, using the blockade of culture to disguise her trajectory. Then, quickly, she stepped into a slim alley between two rigid buildings, the scent of concrete mingling with the ever-present odor of moisture in the Venetian air.

Her breathing came soft and quick in shallow gasps as she continued along the slim alley, hastening away from the walkways and paths. Had the drunks seen her? She glanced back, but the alley mouth remained empty.

She smiled to herself, nodding quickly and moving even faster. She didn't quite remember this location but supposed if she made her way back towards the floating parade, she'd be able to find her friends soon enough. They were all supposed to meet at one of the small theaters. A masked production by *Compagnia dei Cielo* was taking place... Where was that theater again?

She reached into her pocket, fiddling for her phone as she arrived at the opposite side of the slim alley, stepping out onto a wider street witnessed by windows and buildings and tall structures. She felt another flutter of relief in her chest.

At the same time, she glanced up and down the sparse paths. No spectacles here, no masked balls, or sale of art or jugglers or actors or mimes or anything. This was a simple, quiet, residential path. No drunks to chase her either.

Lorraine Strasser paused a moment, grateful for the respite as she scrolled through her phone to the text chain her friends had sent. The theater... ah, there. Only five minutes away. Not bad. She hadn't gotten *too* lost.

She stowed the phone and looked up.

A man in a Venetian mask was strolling towards her along the street. She smiled in the man's direction, wondering if perhaps he was a tourist joining in the fun or another local. She didn't smile *too* long, though. Another curse of youth and beauty. Any affirmation could often warrant entirely wrong sorts of attention. Perhaps she ought to have bought a mask herself.

She shook her head, though, considering the directions from her phone in her mind and then moving up the street.

The man with the mask continued along towards her... But was it her imagination or had he altered his trajectory a bit?

She cleared her throat delicately, making a show of looking at the street signs before moving quickly between a barrier of two bronze benches and heading to the opposite side of the street.

The man crossed the street as well.

"Excuse me," she muttered quickly, her heart skipping again. Where were her friends? She turned and began to hurry in the opposite direction of the approaching man.

But all pretense faded in that horrible moment.

A sudden flurry of rapid footfalls.

She spun around, panicked, and glimpsed the pale porcelain mask flash by as the man fell on her. Another flash, this one harsher, colder in the moonlight above. Something metal. A blade.

And then sudden pain.

CHAPTER TWO

In the chill of the earliest part of morning, Adele shivered at the thought of someone spying on her. She glanced at her phone again, watching the feed of her apartment building from where she stood in the alley across the street from her old childhood home. It had taken her two weeks of bereavement leave, and more than one favor with the more technically savvy agents at the DGSI, but now she had managed to trace the origin of the video feed.

A stroke of luck she had found the hidden camera at all.

Two days into her break from work, Adele had wanted to think like the killer. Think like someone always one step ahead. Strategy required information. Information required surveillance. At first, she had combed her own apartment from every tile to every electrical outlet, to every light fixture. No stone left unturned. Then, she had tried the rest of the building. And finally had she started looking at the structures across the street.

There, hidden in plain sight, a rogue camera, under the awning of the small sundry shop.

She shivered again. It would be just like the Spade killer to taunt her by living this close.

She stared up the fire escape, her eyes tracing the grooves in the brickwork as she acknowledged the fourth floor. An external air conditioning unit whirred and rattled, two fluttering blue ribbons whistling from the small window unit's fan.

"Someone's home," she murmured to herself.

She was off duty and, technically during a leave of bereavement, carrying her service weapon in France wasn't strictly by the book. But now her fingers traced beneath her jacket, falling on the rigid grip of the gun. Both cold and reassuring against her fingertips.

She exhaled slowly, her nostrils flaring and blinked a couple of times against the stray cloud of dust drifting through the alley. Could it really be so easy?

Her DGSI friends had traced the video feed to the fourth floor of the building across the street from her own apartment.

What were the odds the Spade killer was brash enough to rent *this* unit?

Even as she thought it, she shivered.

A month had passed since Robert's death. A month of focused work, outside the bounds of legislation and bureaucracy that would only tie her hands with yellow and red tape.

Now on her own, for the first time in a decade, she felt like she was drawing near.

Could it be so simple? Someone was home. The running air conditioning unit said as much. She couldn't just go through the front doors, though. Announcing her presence would be a surefire way to get anyone watching those cameras aimed at her apartment to run. Rather, now was the time for caution, and a quiet approach.

Hence the alley. Her fingers brushed her weapon once more, but then retreated, lifting towards the fire escape.

She tested the sliding ladder against the brick structure. This building was old, just like her apartment, and as such didn't boast the normal security features of more modern constructions.

She rattled the stairwell, stretched to her full height, and then spotted the two interlocking pins holding the thing in place. Of course, she'd come prepared for this too.

Two weeks of preparation, of hunting, of impatient nights while waiting for reports from her colleagues. She wasn't about to let some stupid fire escape get in her way.

She grabbed the orange extension wire she had picked up from the hardware store the previous day. She lifted it from where it rested against the plastic lid of the dumpster. Then she pulled the rigid black metal attachment from the front of the circular orange device. The extension wire protruded up, like an elongating finger towards the pins on the fire escape.

In the past, Adele had seen the same device used to run wiring and electrical lines through the outlets in her building. But while she wasn't running wire, the extending mechanism would have to serve on the old, poorly maintained fire escape.

The black wire tapped against the metal frame of the lowest level, sending flakes of rust fluttering towards the ground.

Adele looked away, coughing, trying her best not to inhale too deeply. She ran the extended black wire towards the nearest clasp, poking it up and under the latch.

Wincing, sweat beading on her forehead, Adele's heart hammered.

Bleeding... bleeding.... always bleeding...

Old images bobbed to the surface of her mind, attempting, it seemed, in her subconscious to try and distract her from the task at hand. But Adele refused the intrusion.

She redoubled her efforts, tongue in cheek, eyes narrowed, arm trembling from the strain of trying to keep the extension wire on track.

And then, a soft *click*.

She nearly yelled in victory. The wire had slipped between the clasp and the ladder. The lowest rungs were jutting just below the slots in the bottom of the fire escape.

Again, Adele glanced up, staring at the fourth floor. The two blue ribbons attached to the air conditioning unit continued to flutter.

She hadn't taken the normal route through the front doors and the stairs because she had little doubt that the Spade killer would have been prepared for that. But now, her tongue lodged in her cheek, her face stretched and stiff with focus, she paused briefly, wondering perhaps that she was underestimating her opponent.

Would he have cameras in the alleyway as well?

What if he was watching her that very moment? What if, while she fiddled with the fire escape, he was already escaping out the front?

She shivered at the thought, and glanced frantically around, keeping her arm extended, sweat still beading on her forehead, but her eyes tracing the alley walls, the many different metal balconies of the apartment units on either side. At the base of the wall, a few steps from her, settled a green exit door to the small building.

No sign of cameras, no winking red lights.

Maybe she was missing something.

Or maybe, even killers sometimes had blind spots.

She redoubled her effort, un-clasping the first latch, and feeling the wire go taught as the entirety of the ladder's weight was now wedged by the final clasp beneath the lowest rung. It took her a bit longer on the second one, and she was now breathing heavily as if she had been running.

She cursed a couple of times, the wire slipping both times from the extension.

She could feel her frustration mounting. The extra weight from the single clasp made it impossible to wedge the wire between the clasp and the scaffold.

There wasn't enough space.

"Come on," she murmured. "Come—"

The rusted latch snapped.

Adele yelped, darting back just in time as the extension ladder slammed into the alley floor with a reverberating *clang*.

She gritted her teeth, feeling horror pulse through her, and her eyes darted up towards the fourth floor window, watching carefully, frozen in place, one hand still gripping the orange handle of the extension wire tool, and her other darting towards her weapon.

No movement. No shouts. No eyes glancing into the alley from the street either. She looked through the path between the buildings, watching as a bus chugged by, and a pedestrian on the very opposite side of the street hefted two brown paper bags.

Adele let loose a small whisper of air, and then, lowering the extension tool back onto the lid of the trashcan, she reached for the nearest rung.

The rusty metal was cold beneath her fingers. But in that coldness, a frigid certainty also fell across her. She was getting closer.

Even killers had blind spots it seemed.

She pulled herself hand over hand, rising up the fire escape, and then up to the second floor, the third, and, finally, rust flecking her fingers, her hands reddened from the powder, she pulled herself onto the small, cramped balcony of the fourth floor.

Her heart pounded. Perhaps she should call for backup...

What backup, though? Technically, until tomorrow morning, she was still on leave.

Besides, if the killer was in there, she wasn't sure she wanted other agents around.

Why not? A small voice probed at her. *What are you going to do to him?*

Adele felt a lance of guilt, followed equally by a cold, unyielding sense of righteous fury.

The killer had gotten away for more than a decade. One way or another, she was going to end it.

He had made it clear he could get to her. He had killed her mother. Killed Robert. He had gone to the length of installing a camera across from her apartment.

She paused, one hand reaching towards the balcony door.

She frowned, her expression flickering. What if the killer wasn't the one who'd placed the camera? What if it was someone else? What if the camera had nothing to do with her?

Her lips pressed together and she gave a nearly imperceptible shake of her head.

No. It couldn't be. Who else would be the target of surveillance across the street? She had already checked with local police, with Interpol, with DGSI, with federal agencies that reported through her headquarters. No one knew anything about a surveillance tab on her building. No one had a clue what the camera had been there for.

What about some weird peeping tom?

Again, she shook her head. The camera itself had been too high-end, too expensive. No, whoever had used it came from means and had a purpose besides lechery.

The killer had put it there. She felt certain. And it was just like him to rent the property across the street from her. Taunting her without her even knowing it. Playing with her, without her even realizing she was in the game.

"Through the gates of hell," she muttered to herself, and then pushed hard against the balcony's door handle.

CHAPTER THREE

The door didn't budge.

She huffed in frustration, pushing harder.

Still no movement.

The air conditioning unit next to her was still whirring, the fan churning along, the two bits of blue ribbon fluttering on the breeze.

She glanced at the ribbon, frowning in thought for a moment.

The door was locked. The window was completely covered, too, blocked by thick drapes. For a moment, she stood on the balcony outside the fourth floor. What if the killer wasn't home?

No risk no reward, she decided.

She extended a hand, hesitantly, her fingers probing towards the two blue ribbons, which looked like painter's tape of all things. She spotted a couple of paint splotches on top of the air conditioning unit.

For a moment, she hesitated, glancing between her feet. A line of beige paint, encircling the small balcony and up the wiring box, seemingly trying to blend into the wall, then made its way to the air conditioning unit itself.

Her eyes trailed from the blue paint strips, which looked like they'd been used to keep the paint within bounds. And she trailed her gaze along the electrical wiring sheath, around the balcony, up, and beneath the fifth-floor balcony.

Her eyes stopped, fixated on some small, black device in the corner of the base of the fifth floor.

She stared, and it stared back.

The blinking red light of a camera fixated on her.

A chill shot down her spine. She cursed, suddenly, slamming her foot hard into the electrical sheath, crushing it where it circled the edge of the balcony. Gray and blue wires exposed, and then the weapon met her hands, whipping up. Hard, she slammed the butt of the gun into the window.

A shattering sound.

No more time for subtlety. Someone was watching.

"DGSI!" she shouted. Not for the sake of the killer, but just in case she had missed it. Just in case there was someone inside who deserved to live.

The glass scattered, and she reached desperately in, feeling the shards scrape against the back of her thumb. She ignored the sudden pain and gripped the door handle on the inside. She suddenly yelped, yanking her fingers back. Something sharp had been embedded in the handle.

Two things were realized in that moment.

She hadn't taken him by surprise. But also, whoever was inside this fourth-floor apartment had gone to great lengths to guard their back entrance.

All of it was coming together now.

He was here. He had to be.

She snarled, gun still raised, using the edge of her shirt now to protect her fingers, as she reached for the inside handle again. She felt the rigid edge, as if someone had soldered razors there.

She yanked the door handle open from the inside, and it spun in. She took a second, allowing it to careen forward just in case the door was wired.

No explosion. No alarm.

Whoever had booby-trapped the door hadn't gone too far, it seemed.

She didn't shout; she didn't announce herself. The certainty was now rising in her. An inevitability. What was she walking in to?

For a moment she went still, breathing in, out, all too aware of the sound of her own ragged gasping. *He* was in there. She knew he was. The devil himself.

She swallowed, pushing back her rising sense of worry. Then, Adele stumbled in through the door, and found herself in a dark room.

Across from her, a sealed door and a painted smiley face in pink and blue colors stared at her. The walls were covered with other painted things. Some of them childlike drawings of houses, others like the sorts of art a proud parent might display on their refrigerator. None of them particularly good. None of them looked like they had been done by anyone much older than a six-year-old.

She stared at a sun, with brutish and blunt yellow lines extending away from a blotted circle. A black smile had been drawn into the yellow center as if watching her. She snarled, slamming her shoulder into the opposite door, and it banged open into a hall.

And then...

... she heard a flurry of footsteps.

"Stop!" she screamed.

She heard a gasping sound but no words.

For a moment, Adele stayed half concealed in the doorway of the strangely painted room. If she burst forward, and the killer was armed, she would be shot. But if she waited too long, he might make good his getaway.

Suddenly, Adele heard a gunshot.

She cursed, ducking back out of sight. Breathing heavily, she waited, her shoulder pressed hard against the oddly painted wall. The paints were dry, suggesting the killer had been here for a while.

"Show yourself!" she yelled. "I know you're there!"

For a moment, there was no sound. And then, another loud *bang!*

Adele realized her mistake. Those weren't gunshots.

She poked her head back around the door, growling. A third *bang*. This time, she realized.

Someone was using a hammer.

She wrinkled her nose in confusion, gun raised, heart pounding, breath coming in ragged gasps. She now stepped into the hall, her weapon pointed towards the opposite end of the dark entrance. She spotted movement all of a sudden. A small, shadowy form, darting across.

Had it been her imagination, or had the person been no larger than a child? Bony, rail thin, with gaunt, ghoulish features. It had only been a brief glimpse, but more than she'd ever had before. Was this the killer? A victim?

"Stop!" she yelled. Now, her fear was replaced by fury. With reckless abandon she broke into a sprint, gun still in her hand as she raced up the hall.

After a few footsteps, she careened out into an entryway.

And then she saw him. Hammer in one hand, whipping forward and slamming into the final plank of wood that had been nailed across the door. The wood ripped, splinters scattered. And then, the killer reached out, tearing the door handle down and flinging it open.

Adele raised, fired twice. But the killer was quick, darting forward.

She'd been aiming for center mass. But he was small. Very small.

For a moment, as she stared at the doorway, gasping, aiming at where the man had disappeared, she glimpsed a head suddenly dart back into the room, like an odd whack-a-mole, staring back at her through the frame of the door.

Two eyes didn't quite match. One of them didn't reflect light, nor did it move or twitch as if perhaps it was a painted marble.

The man was missing hair. No eyebrows, no hairline, nothing on his face, no eyelashes even. Adele stared at the strange face, and it stared back. And then, where it was half jutted through the doorway, it smiled once and winked with its good eye. But didn't say a word, as he turned, and ran.

Adele heard the clap of feet against the stairwell outside. She growled and sprinted forward.

She supposed she should have realized he'd been goading her. Why come back at all?

To get her to chase, obviously.

She landed on what she thought was solid ground directly in front of the door, but her foot slammed through the floorboards.

Adele yelled in horror as wood splintered around her, and in a shower of debris and dust and splinters, she plummeted from the fourth floor through the ceiling of the third floor.

Gasping, groaning, she tried to push to her feet, and found her arms, while aching, still worked. Breathing heavily, she sat up, blinking, dust still swirling about her.

Groaning, and shaking more dust from her blonde hair, she looked left and right, and spotted three old men sitting around a small table with a backgammon board between them. All of the men had small tea glasses in their hands, and they were staring at Adele, wide-eyed. Two women, behind the men, were standing next to the television, with children hidden behind them, sheltered. One of the women was rattling off something in a language Adele didn't understand.

Adele blinked, blearily, groaning. *He's getting away...* a small, focused part of her tried to speak to her more dazed self.

A groan and grimace and she tried to reach her feet. Her ankles weren't sprained, her elbows were bruised, but all she had really hurt in her fall, it seemed, was her pride and her knee.

"Sorry," she said, rattling off. "Sorry." She held out a placating hand.

And then, the men saw the gun.

One of them yelled in horror and started chucking backgammon chips at her face. Another threw his tea in her eyes.

"DGSI!" she tried to scream, but then the hot liquid reached her, and she had just enough time to look away before it splashed across her cheeks.

It hissed, and it hurt; she yelled, scraping at her face, but this only rubbed the dust from her fall into her eyes. And now, she was blinking both hot tea and dust. She heard more shouting in a language she didn't understand. She felt hands, old, frail hands shove at her, trying to push her away.

She could hear screaming now. The children were crying.

"Stop!" she said, desperately. "Please. Stop."

And then, something which felt suspiciously like a frying pan struck her across the back.

She was sent tumbling.

"Don't!" she yelled, trying English now. And then German. "I'm a friend! Stop. I need water. My eyes."

But then, she heard a whistling sound, the pan swinging again.

A loud *thunk* across the back of her head. It all went black.

CHAPTER FOUR

Adele woke slowly, wincing and blinking and pushing up from her couch, propping on one elbow. Back in her apartment? Strange... How had she gotten here? She rubbed the back of her head, probing gingerly where her neighbors had clocked her with the heavy saucepan, and made a mental note to learn Turkish at the first chance possible. She did her best to suppress the rising tide of ill will towards the unfortunate family whose early morning tea party she'd accidentally dropped in on.

As she pushed off the couch, she glanced towards the clock over her microwave and groaned softly to herself.

Three hours of recovery time. Now nearly nine AM. She was almost late for work.

Adele rubbed at the back of her head again, pulling her fingers away and glancing down to make sure there was no blood. Given how things had gone, falling through the floor and getting assaulted with the skillet, she had come out relatively unscathed. She was especially thankful the tea hadn't been hot enough to scar, though her eyes were somewhat ringed in red; she was lucky she didn't look like a raccoon version of Renee...

But the Spade killer had gotten away.

Her mood darkened further, and she glared through the windows. She nibbled on the corner of her lip, considering what she might have done differently earlier that morning.

She should have called in backup sooner...

"Agent Sharp?" A voice said.

Adele jolted, glancing towards her front door. It was ajar. She swallowed, staring. "He—hello?"

A uniformed police officer poked his head through the door, giving a nervous little wave. "Umm, sorry, hello," he said, quickly.

She stared, blinking. "Do I know you?"

He winced and shook his head. "No, so sorry, Agent Sharp. Just, only," he swallowed, "the Executive of the DGSI told us to bring you here after..." he winced delicately, "after we found you tied up in an old lady's nylons across the street." He flashed a would-be comforting smile.

His words, though, only caused Adele's stomach to sink even lower. She glanced sharply at her wrists, then towards the door. Her hand moved to her pocket, where she normally kept her apartment key. It was missing.

She felt a jolt of worry, but then spotted the key placed delicately on the kitchen counter. So that explained how she'd woken back in her apartment...

She glanced back towards the officer. "Foucault told you to bring me here?"

"After the EMTs, checked you, yes!" he said, quickly. "They said you needed rest."

"What did Foucault say?" she asked, still staring uncertainly towards the officer who'd been assigned to babysit her.

"He said you should come into the office the moment you wake up. How are you feeling?" The officer added.

Adele ignored him though, growling, getting to her feet, striding towards the door and slamming it shut with her foot, in the face of the peeping officer. She paused for a moment, feeling a flash of guilt, then calling through the door. "Thank you, officer," she said. "Have you cordoned off the apartment upstairs yet? It belonged to a person of interest."

"Yes, agent!" called the voice through the door. "We have! Still sweeping it for bugs right now! Your boss—er, the Executive mentioned we should keep the unit under wraps."

"Find anything?" Adele said, her heart skipping a beat.

"A camera in the shower," the officer said, hesitantly. "Another facing the front door. Say, do you have a moment to give your statement?"

Adele groaned, closing her eyes, but then popping one open. "Classified," she said, speaking the first word that came to mind. "Sorry! Just photograph the unit. Send me anything you find! Fingerprint it too!" A long shot, but all she had left at this point.

She turned away from the shut door now, frowning and shivering at the thought of being dragged into her apartment, unconscious, at the Executive's orders.

Still, Foucault wanted to see her first thing? Was she in trouble? She winced... wondering how she might explain this morning's escapade to the hawk-nosed DGSI boss...

Bludgeoned by skillets, assaulted with tea, then dragged across the street by unfamiliar officers, though, was the least of her worries.

Far worse by a country mile...

The killer had gotten away.

She'd been so close. So very close. And now, she'd seen his face. He hadn't spoken a word to her. He'd simply winked. That had been enough. Clearly the killer had been using the rental as a stakeout alone. There were no signs of it having been lived in. No fridge she'd seen, no bedding or sheets. The strange paintings on the wall would be photographed, the apartment swept for bugs.

Still, Adele was determined, now more than ever, to return to the small apartment, and go through it once more with a fine-toothed comb herself after the locals had processed every inch.

"I'm coming for you," she muttered out loud. If only to make herself feel better.

The killer had winked. Taunted her. He'd set up a camera and had rented the apartment across from hers. He had killed Robert.

But now, she'd looked beneath the mask. She had kicked over the stone and revealed the creepy crawlies beneath.

She had seen his face.

And she had to believe that he was now feeling some of the pressure she'd been living under for the last decade.

She wasn't the only one being watched. Now he had a target as well.

She closed her eyes again, picturing the face she'd glimpsed as it had darted through the doorway before she'd fallen through the floor.

A dull, dead eye. Every hair shaved free. Cold, pallid skin. Some sort of growth or hormonal deficiency, no doubt, given the frail, bony nature of the fellow. He had even moved, it seemed briefly, with a mild limp.

A strange looking man and Adele felt certain she would find him again. What had once seemed such an elusive goal was, once more, close at hand.

But for now, the trail had gone cold.

She groaned as she pushed away from the door, massaging her neck, forcing herself not to probe at her head again.

No sense making the Executive wait... She grabbed her apartment keys, then double checked she had her wallet, her firearm still, and then stepped out into the hall, locking the door twice behind her, with a significant look towards the babysitter posted outside her door.

The man stared ahead, his hat tilted back, looking awkwardly across the hall.

“Agent Sharp,” the officer said. “Is there anything else you could tell us about—”

“Classified!” she insisted, sweeping past the policeman. She ignored the babysitter and paused at the end of the stairs for a moment, glancing up and down the hall, looking into the shadowy corners and behind the fire alarm, just in case. She paused beneath one of the sprinkler heads. No cameras.

A new habit, perhaps, but she couldn't afford to stick to her old habits. Not now that the killer knew she was coming for him. He was on his game, so she would have to be twice as careful.

Still, he was in the wind again, and Adele's leave of absence had come to an end.

She needed to talk to the Executive anyway. For the first time in the last two weeks, she was looking forward to going back to work. She could convince the Executive to give her manpower on this case. Now that she'd closed in, he certainly would see it her way. He would want to help find the killer just as much as she did, wouldn't he?

She picked up her pace, circling the banister, looking towards the local policeman and pointing a finger. “Don't enter my apartment again,” she snapped. Then, feeling bad, she added, “Thanks for looking out for me.” She took the stairs two at a time as she moved down towards the lobby once more.

Once she was out of earshot, she tried to rehearse in her mind how the conversation would go.

"Yes, Executive, I totally understand, sir. I know you don't pay me to chase cold cases. But this one... is so close. I was able to see him, sir."

She scowled, mimicking the Executive's usual expression, and lowering her voice, she muttered as she took the stairs, "Now, Adele, we both know we don't have the resources."

"But sir," she said, voicing the scene in her imagination. "I know I can find him. I just need some more time. Some resources."

"Now, Agent Sharp, don't get ahead of yourself," she continued muttering. She reached the bottom floor, strolling past the mailboxes, smiling, despite herself, at her own play-acting.

She felt a bit of a weight had lifted from her shoulders.

She would convince the Executive. It was the only way. And so, she pushed out of the front doors, and took the final steps down to the sidewalk with a skip in her step, excited to return to the office, and make her case.

"What's got you so cheerful?" a voice called from the curb.

Adele looked sharply over, and spotted the tall, handsome form of her old partner, John Renee, leaning against the hood of a Jaguar.

She stared at the sport sedan and inched an eyebrow up. "No more Cadillac?"

"Totaled it."

"Ouch."

John shrugged his large, muscular shoulders. "Not as ouch as the guys I rammed into."

Adele hid a smile, taking the final step in approaching her old partner, with tentative motions.

It was good to see John again. He reached up, beneath the collar of his untucked shirt, and scratched at the burn mark stretching over his neck up to the underside of his chin. He reached the same hand and pressed back his slick hair, pushing it over and out of his eyes.

Those same, dark eyes now fixed on her, unblinking, as if trying to take in every motion and movement.

"I'm okay," she said, almost reflexively.

"I didn't say anything."

"What are you doing here?"

He shrugged and patted the hood of his Jaguar. "Was in the neighborhood. Heading to work. Figured you might need a ride."

She frowned. “Did they radio it in?”

John grinned now, wagging his head giddily up and down. “Hit with a skillet, right?” he said, still grinning. “Tied up in nylons? I hear you were knocked out by a little old granny.”

Adele glared ahead. “I don't want to talk about it.”

“What were you doing beating up old women, Sharp?”

“I *don't* want to talk about it.” Adele crossed her arms for a moment, and shook her head briefly, but then winced from the gesture.

John glanced at her. "Still hurts?"

Almost in synchronization, the two of them glanced across the street, towards the apartment building. Adele spotted a police officer stationed out front, and caution tape crisscrossing over the alley. She shrugged. "It was a close thing."

John whistled beneath his breath. "Working a case? I didn't get the details."

She glanced at John and cleared her throat. For a moment, she considered telling him what had happened. John was the only other agent who had ever gotten close enough to see the Spade killer. He'd gotten away then too. But at the same time, Adele wasn't sure she wanted to live through the questions. And questions would be inevitable. How? What? Why? How do you feel?

If she had to weather another storm of questions about her feelings, she was certain she'd explode. Adele briefly thought back to the previous month. They had buried Robert Henry. They had said their goodbyes. Adele had gone to the funeral, and then she'd been given a case chasing a mentally unstable serial killer.

And in all of it, people had questioned her feelings, her emotional state.

If she was honest, she had questioned much the same.

In her mind's eyes she pictured the small raincoat closet next to her front door. The package that had been sent by Robert's niece. The items he had left her in the will. She still hadn't opened it. For two weeks the box had sat in the darkest corner of the closet, collecting dust. Whatever Robert had given her, she knew she didn't deserve. Some things were best left taped and hidden, though perhaps other things had to be shown the light of day.

She glanced towards John again, looking him up and down, and muttering, "You're looking good," she said.

"I've taken up running," he replied.

She raised her eyebrows. "Really? You? Running?"

"That's a lot of question marks for three words."

"It's all in the inflection my friend."

John quirked a smile, his lips rising slowly. "Are we?" He said softly. "Friends again?"

Adele winced, hesitating, trying not to think of how she had treated John. She had thought by keeping her distance she would keep him safe. But now...

Now what? Had anything changed?

She had seen the killer. Seen his face. That lumpy, misshapen, shaved face with the missing eye.

He hadn't seemed a threat so close.

She shivered at the thought. But she had found him. That counted for something. Something, at the very least, had changed. *She had found him.*

She swallowed and gave a sheepish smile and a single shoulder shrug. "I mean, your sense of fashion is hard to be seen with."

He watched her, but then smirked and shook his head, rolling his eyes. "And you? Those suits you wear scream middle-aged businessman."

"Sexist pig."

“Feminist harpy," he replied, with a good-natured nod.

"One of these days, I'm going to report you to HR."

"They already have a cabinet filled with files on me, my dear." He tapped his nose. "It's all about the connections. Anyway, do you want a ride or not? I'm having half a mind to leave you here."

Adele sighed, considering where she had parked the rental she was using. But then, she looked at John. They'd left things strange. Well, more accurately, she had. Which meant, perhaps, it was up to her to endure a bit of awkwardness to restore what they had.

Which was what exactly?

Her eyes traced John's handsome features, landed on the scar over his chin, and then moved up to meet his eyes.

She'd missed him. She hadn't realized how much until this moment. She shrugged again, and then moved around the side of the car. "I won't challenge your fragile masculinity by asking to drive."

John grunted. "The only fragility here is going to be your tolerance for high speeds when I hit the highway. Buckle up Sharp."

Adele had half a mind to take the warning and take her own car, but then, trying not to smile, she slid into the passenger side and buckled as John slid into the front of the leased vehicle.

He revved the sport sedan, and then peeled away from the curb before she had even settled, his fingers gripping the steering wheel, tearing down the Parisian roads, and heading to the highway which took them to the headquarters.

"Don't get us killed," she muttered, as John picked up pace.

"I wouldn't be able to see the look of horror on your face if I did that."

"You never were the most perceptive sort."

John snickered. "Nice to see someone back on their game."

Adele didn't give him the satisfaction of a smile, but instead just crossed her arms, refusing to wince as her bruised head pressed back against the headrest, and she settled in for the drive back to the headquarters. It was nice to be back with John.

Back with?

Whatever that meant. At the very least, nice to be next to him. She'd missed it.

She'd nearly caught the killer. Now, by bringing others close, she wasn't putting them in danger. She couldn't think that way anymore.

No, she was the hunter, and he was the prey.

He was the one who should fear her; he was the one who should be terrified of ever going after one of her friends again. She would have to double her attention, think like the killer. Maybe even set up surveillance of her own. But now, for the first time, she felt like she had a head start.

John continued to rev the engine, flooring the pedal and testing all manner of speed limits as he zoomed away from the city.

Adele leaned back in her chair, quite relaxed, trusting herself next to the old military helicopter pilot.

It would be her first day back at work in nearly two weeks. She wondered how Executive Foucault would react. Would he immediately grant her the leeway to start an investigation again into the Spade killer? Or would he have something else entirely?

She would just have to convince him.

CHAPTER FIVE

"Absolutely not," the Executive snapped, glaring at her across his desk. "You're lucky I'm not firing you!"

Adele leaned in, feeling her stomach twist in frustration, her eyes fixed on the hook-nosed leader of the DGSI. His dark, deep, bushy eyebrows were low over his piercing gaze. The window in the back of his office was open. The space smelled less like cigarette smoke than it ever had. But the packs of nicotine gum were piling up in the wastepaper basket.

Already, the Executive was chewing on his seventh stick, judging by the evidence of the remnants in the basket. In between chomping on the gum, he was shaking his head firmly side to side. "No new cases. What do you think you were even doing at that apartment Agent Sharp? You were on leave, might I remind you! You broke into the apartment of an innocent family!"

"I fell in," she said, primly. "It was an accident."

Foucault massaged the bridge of his nose, shaking his head and inhaling softly. When he spoke again, he seemed to have calmed a bit. "You already had two weeks off, Agent Sharp. Be reasonable. We have something else."

"Sir," she said, insistently. "Look, I understand. But the Spade killer, I *saw* him."

The Executive pointed at her and then pointed at John who was sitting quietly in the chair next to her. "Did you see anything different than he did?"

Adele winced. She glanced at John, who was staring at the back of his knuckles. His eyebrows had gone up when she'd revealed to the Executive exactly what had transpired back at the apartment. But he hadn't said a word since.

At the Executive's redirection, Adele tried to shake her head firmly. But her heart wasn't in it. She knew John had already worked with a composite artist. He had spent hours giving detailed descriptions. Some of the same things she'd seen. Small, weak. No larger than a child. A bit of a limp. A pallid, ghoulish face. One dead eye.

What was there to add?

"He was bald," she said, quickly. "That's new. That wasn't something we had written before!"

"I'll be sure to pass it on," Foucault said. "But Adele, as you know, there's no trace of him. Nothing. He didn't leave any evidence in that apartment."

Adele growled. "Those security cameras. They're expensive. Military grade. There's got to be a way to figure out where he got *those*."

John though cleared his throat and grunted, "Probably stolen. A lot of those sorts of things earn you a nice buck on the black market. Something the military is clamping down on, but not perfectly. My guess is that's where he got it. A guy looking like that, small as he was, he definitely didn't serve."

Adele gritted her teeth in frustration shaking her head, and looking back from John to the Executive. "Sir," she said, "you know this case is important."

The moment she said it, she wished she hadn't. Trying to leverage personal preference with Foucault was a venture in futility.

He was glowering again and tapping his finger against an ashtray which hadn't been used in months. He just seemed to keep it nearby, like a security blanket. He twisted the ashtray a couple of times in his fingers, and said, "I'll make you a deal. I'll have someone look into those cameras, if you help me out on this case. Also, this time, Agent Paige isn't available."

Adele glanced at John. "What sort of case?"

Foucault frowned. "Does it matter? Or did you forget that you work for us?"

Adele leaned back in her chair in frustration. "You'll have someone look at the cameras?"

Foucault crossed a sharp finger over his suit pocket. "Cross my heart," he said, grimly. "And Agent Sharp, this is the last leeway I give you. You're either back for good,or need to find another job."

Adele blinked in surprise at the harsh words. Blunt though he was, the Executive wasn't normally one for such ultimatums. Vaguely, she wondered if Agent Paige had perhaps said something behind her back after their last case together. But then she shook her head. Perhaps the Executive was just stressed.

"Sir," John said, interjecting, and sensing the tension. "What's the case?"

Adele allowed her silence to serve as acquiescence. She waited patiently now, deciding that the promise to have the lab techs look at those cameras would have to be good enough. Who knew, maybe they'd get lucky and find a fingerprint. Either way, that would take time.

She supposed it wouldn't be the worst thing to solve another case to keep her mind off things, and more importantly, to keep herself sharp when it mattered most.

"Right," the Executive said, firmly, "two dead. One American two days ago, and one German, only last night."

John frowned. "Tourists? Where?"

"Venice."

John cursed. Adele glanced at him.

The tall agent was shaking his head. "I hate Venice."

"Keep it to yourself," Foucault snapped. "You're going. Both of you. And look, that first victim, she was a fashion model. High amount of press will cover her death if it leaks. The second, not as well-known, but a young woman working to become an actress. Both of them were found with their throats slit."

"Throats slit? Is that the only connection?" Adele said, frowning.

"No." Foucault reached behind the table, slid open a drawer and pulled out two white, glossy photos. He slid them, roughly across the desk, twirling them with his fingers, the same way he had twirled the ashtray, so they were facing the agents.

Instinctively, Adele and John both leaned in, peering at the photos.

"They were both wearing those," Foucault said, tapping the pictures.

Adele couldn't tell the victim in frame was a woman. The photo was close, cutting out most of the torso. But more importantly, the victim was wearing a mask. A beautiful, ornate mask, that reminded her of the inside of a porcelain cup. Small flowers, blue and red were painted up the side of the mask. The eyeholes were dark, and the mouth had a streak of lipstick crossing over it like a big red X.

Adele stared at the lipstick X mark, and then scanned the rest of the photo. She regarded John, who was also staring at a second photo with another woman wearing a similar mask.

This second mask had a mesh of silk coming out of the back and looping over the top. Instead of painted flowers, the porcelain surface of this one was pure black, with pale butterflies etched into the face. Instead of two eyeholes, this one had two slits in the shape of stars.

Adele glanced from one photo to the other, "They were both found with their throats cut wearing those?"

"Even more strangely," the Executive said, "those masks don't fit them, and weren't actually strapped to their heads. More like laid on top of their faces."

As he said it, the Executive just shrugged, signaling that he realized how strange this might sound.

"Laid on them?" John said, wrinkling his nose. "What do you mean? Like the masks weren't theirs?"

"The killer put them there?" Adele asked. "We're sure it's the same person?"

"We're not sure of anything at this point, agents," said Foucault firmly. "That's why we pay you."

"Not enough," John muttered beneath his breath. Adele resisted the urge to kick him. They weren't back to that level yet.

If he had heard the jibe, the Executive didn't show it. "Flight is booked. Just keep in mind, these girls have followings. Lorraine Strasser," he tapped an indicating finger on one of the photos, "was quite popular because of her Instagram, and Rebekah James," he tapped the other, "like I mentioned, was a fashion model. She was making waves. Which means her death is going to make waves the more people find out."

"Her identity hasn't leaked yet?" Adele asked.

"Not yet. One thing those masks help with, I suppose. But just keep in mind, the moment that's released, you're going to be working with a lot of scrutiny." He glared, clasping his hands beneath his chin and leaning forward, resting his face on his knuckles as if they were stone. "And what reflects badly on you, reflects badly on me. The more eyes, the better the behavior, yes?"

Adele and John both shared a look. A lot passed in that flickering glance. She wasn't sure if the Executive knew exactly who he was hiring to work this case. If there was one person he didn't want to stick in front of a camera, it was Agent John Renee. In fact, the last time they'd tangled with a camera crew, he thrown expensive equipment off the edge of a cliff.

She sighed, and John smirked. "That all, sir?" John said, chipper.

"Yes. The rest of the information can be sent to you while you're in the air. Get going. We want to stay ahead of this, try to catch the killer before the names of the victims are released to the public. At least that way we will have something to stem the tide of questions. Oh, one last thing."

John and Adele, who'd been in the middle of rising from their chairs paused, half out, but also frozen. They both looked at their boss.

"Venice is currently having a festival. A masquerade festival. It's going to go on for the next week."

"Hang on, masks?" John groaned. "Are you telling me we're going to be surrounded by a bunch of fruitcakes with hidden faces? How are we going to find the killer in all that?"

"What's the phrase again? Needle in a haystack? You'd better bring a magnet," Foucault said.

Adele wasn't sure if this was meant to be clever or cutting. Either way, the Executive seemed quite proud with it, and nodded to himself; he turned away from them, deliberately, and returned his attention to his computer.

John continued muttering darkly about how much he hated Venice. Saying things like, "Too much water. An ungodly amount of water."

For her part, Adele was more troubled by the prospect of the masks. It would be hard to hunt down witnesses, to find culprits, and to interrogate suspects if everyone was anonymous. Not to mention, during a Venetian festival, there would be crowds, all of them in the cafés along the river walks and the waterways. Crowds upon crowds. The perfect cover for a murderer.

She shivered, and then turned, following John out of the opaque door to the Executive's office. It wasn't ideal, as far as silver linings went, but killers aside, Adele had always wanted to see Venice...

CHAPTER SIX

"Come on, it's not so bad," Adele said, standing by the Giudecca Canal, her hands on her hips as she surveyed the crowds on one of the lower roads below.

In her honest opinion, it was really quite beautiful... Wild, too, for sure. Already, though it was still early—nearly noon, some of the festival participants were drunk, and tossing their bottles at the prow of a passing gondola.

John surveyed this with mild approval and amusement, but as his gaze moved across the rest of the scene throughout Venice, his eyes took on a reproachful, if not queasy quality.

"So much damn water," he muttered, his eyes tracing the old lagoon and the more than a hundred small islands upon which the entire city had been constructed. "And such tight spaces," he added, glancing at the Venetian callettes behind them—streets so small, someone of John's size would have to turn sideways just to walk through.

"Is it true there isn't a damn road in the entire place?" the large Frenchman muttered beneath his breath.

Adele patted him consolingly on the arm. "Just think of it as being hugged by a building and kissed by the Adriatic. You'll be fine. Come, the crime scene is this way."

Adele turned her back on the rousing spectacle in the early afternoon of the festival. Already, many jugglers and mimes and magicians were moving about the walkways between the canals and flows. She spotted a small troop on a low balcony performing some unfamiliar play, all of them wearing porcelain masks. Many of the tourists along the waters or floating on boats in the canal also wore masks which, likely, they had purchased from the many stalls lining the entrances to the calli.

John tried to follow Adele's lead as she headed towards the tiny, cramped alleyway. But before he could catch up with her, Adele watched as a group of acrobats appeared at the top of the street, flipping over each other and singing as they passed. Another group of spectators laughed and cheered, following along after them, with streaming green ribbons fluttering in the air over their heads.

The spectacle of joy and beauty and energy put John Renee in a sour mood.

"I hate Venice," he muttered, facing the tiny alley.

Adele rolled her eyes before side-stepping into the small callette, gesturing John to follow. "Good you've taken up running," she called. "Might still need to suck in that gut of yours."

"Gut? I don't have a gut. What gut?"

"Pay attention, you might see it," Adele replied, stepping through the alley, beneath the large shadows of the buildings on either side.

"Can't see anything with your giant fat ass blocking the view," John muttered, wrinkling his nose.

"My ass might be fat, but at least my belly isn't. Santa, come on!"

John cursed after her, taking twice as long to slide through the tight space, and scraping his shirt along the edge of one of the windowsills as he followed.

Adele turned, hands on her hips, watching him approach and beaming at his dark muttering and discomfort. There was nothing like John's sour mood to remarkably improve her own.

Given where they were headed, of course, she could use all the mood boost she could get. It was rare to find the scene of a murder that was anything but dour.

Then again, if she were to find such a thing, she imagined it might be in the swing of festivities during the *Carnevale di Venezia*.

***

"She was staying nearby, yes?" John murmured, dusting off his shirt and leaning in to examine the portion of the street where Lorraine Strasser's body had been discovered. The body itself had long since been taken to the morgue. But the blood stain from the knife wound could still be seen leaked into the dusty ground beneath a bronze bench.

Adele leaned in, one hand brushing the arm of the bench, feeling the chill extend up her fingertips from the cool metal. The clustered Venetian buildings, crowded as they were, prevented much of a breeze from swooping through the pathway between the structures. The air smelled of the canals and, in the distance, she could still hear the revelries of the festival attendees.

The noise and festivities would increase in direct proportion to the darkening skies. For now, though, the sun was still high, beams reflecting off the staring windows around them. A few of the windows had drapes brushed aside, with locals watching the police do their work. Still other witnesses to the scene had exited the front doors of their homes—few porches or steps to speak of. The crowded nature of the city only allowed the doors to lead directly to the pathways themselves. Leaning against the walls and ignoring pointed looks from the police, various denizens watched the morbid scene with curiosity.

Adele felt her spine prickle, remembering the Executive's warning about this particular case. Once the names of the victims became public knowledge, more eyes would be on them all. She glanced towards where John was still frowning at the blood stain, his dark brow low over his even darker gaze.

She could only hope no one—names unmentioned—caused too much of a public spectacle once they were being watched. If Executive Foucault was going to follow-through on his promise and send those military cameras in for inspection, she knew she'd have to be on her best behavior and make sure John was as well.

One of the best ways, of course, to please the Executive was by solving the case.

She tapped her fingers, one at a time on the metal arm rest, murmuring. "The first victim was American, yes?"

John grunted.

"The second was German."

"Tourists," he said as if it were a nasty word.

"Perhaps. Venice does attract a lot of tourists this time of year. The thing the victims most had in common..." Adele glanced at her phone, scrolling to the information provided by the office. "Lorraine Strasser was only twenty-three," she said, softly, feeling a lance of regret. She couldn't do anything about it now, though. So young to die so violently. Still... there were others out there counting on her. She couldn't let her emotions sidetrack now.

She shook her head. "And the American, Rebekah James..."

"She was twenty-five," John said, frowning even more deeply and sighing as he leaned back up, straightening, his large shadow casting across the bronze bench.

Behind them, Italian police officers were muttering to each other and scrutinizing the surrounding alleyways, scanning for anything that might catch their attention.

Adele turned though, now looking at the single item that had been left behind at the scene of the crime.

The mask. The beautiful, porcelain craftsmanship reminded her of old plays she'd once read back in German school. The delicately hand-painted flowers along the edge of the white caught her attention and she leaned in even closer. Most jarring, though, of the entire piece was the slashing red mark of lipstick over the mask's mouth.

"What do you think that means," she murmured, pointing at where the mask had been left when the body was taken.

"Means she wasn't wearing it," John grunted. He tapped a large finger to the ground just next to the right eye-slit. "Cracked, see? Wasn't like that in the photos."

Adele frowned, leaning in and noting where John had caught a small spiderweb of a blemish. "Damn it," she muttered. She glanced towards the local police moving through the buildings, sighing as she did. "Think they dropped it when moving it?"

"Her body? Probably. Too much time skating about on water—clumsy clogs on land no doubt."

"It's just water, John. Let it go."

He growled further, but didn't reply, occasionally shooting askance glances at the buildings around them as if worried they might sink into the lagoon before his very eyes.

Adele took her phone and took a picture of the slight crack on the edge of the mask. It wouldn't have been secured to her face, in that case. According to Foucault, it had been too big for her as well.

"The killer must have left it," she said, quietly. "The red lipstick—what do you make of that?"

John frowned more deeply. "Maybe he's silencing them... Say, when's our Italian liaison getting here? I want to know which numskull cracked the mask."

He looked up and around, his furious gaze shifting from one local to another. As if somehow sensing his indignation, the three police officers who'd been waiting at the scene redoubled their efforts, scanning the alleys and beneath the windowsills in search of anything the killer might have left behind. One of the officers was moving from onlooker to onlooker, checking to see if anyone had seen anything.

At first, Adele had thought this promising; now, though, as she watched the fifth apartment-dweller shake her head and shrug, she felt an icy lance of frustration shoot through her. No one seemed to have seen anything or heard anything. Likely, most had been involved in the festivities. The killer had struck at night, beneath a sky showered in vibrant streaks of fireworks.

Just then, a voice called out from between one of the small

pathways through the buildings. A handsome man with perfectly sculpted features stepped beneath an arching stone loop topped with red shingle. He called out, “Adele! John! What a pleasant surprise!” He spoke nearly perfect English, with a mild Italian accent; his tone inflected delight, and the sound of his footsteps increased as he hastened over to them, his smile matching the rest of his features, perfectly maintained and displayed with an easy confidence.

Adele blinked in surprise, feeling a flush of excitement immediately beset by a flurry of discomfort. “Oh—ah, Christopher!” She declared, swallowing and straightening over the cracked mask. She beamed as he approached, matching his smile, but she felt John's glower level on her and she quickly dialed back the smile a couple of notches, feeling an odd cavalcade of emotions make their presence known.

“I—Christopher,” she said, trying again. “Good to see you. I didn't know you were our liaison!”

The Italian winked and in a teasing voice, said, “Maybe if you'd ever answered some of my calls, I could have told you.”

Adele winced at the jibe, but Agent Leoni was still smiling, so she decided not to comment.

Agent Leoni had worked with Adele on a couple of separate occasions, both times proving to be an excellent partner and even better agent. Not to mention he was quite easy on the eyes. Which also, perhaps predictably, meant John disliked everything about the Italian.

Already, John's arms were crossed, and he was shooting annoyed looks through hooded eyes at Agent Leoni. If Christopher noticed this, he didn't show it. Rather, he gave a little laugh, slapping John on the back in a genial fashion but then stepping deliberately past him and gripping Adele's forearms, looking her in the eyes.

“How are you?” he said, everything in his tone and gaze suggesting an earnestness that was often off-putting.

Adele didn't think Leoni had a deceptive bone in his body. Still, she could sense John's discomfort, could sense the shift in atmosphere, and she coughed delicately, giving Leoni's hands a quick squeeze of greeting, before glancing towards the mask.

“It's good to see you,” she said. “I'm glad,” she hesitated on the word, considering amending it, but then allowing it to stay, “yes, glad you're here to help. On the case.” She didn't mean to emphasize these last few words, but Agent Leoni responded quickly with another congenial chuckle.

“Don't worry Agent Sharp, we're here to catch a killer. All of us, yes?" He glanced from John, back to the mask.

"If that's the case," John said, clearing his throat and pushing back some of his open distrust, "What can you tell us about the mask? Why is it cracked?"

"Cracked? Where?"

John's toe jutted out, his black shoe pointing towards the spiderweb imperfection.

Leoni leaned in, frowning, his single superman curl of hair darting over his eyes. He reached up, brushing it aside and straightening as he did. "The killer, perhaps?"

"No," John said. "Crack wasn't in the crime scene photos. Happened after."

Leoni frowned at this, turning and waving towards one of the policemen moving between the apartment-dwellers. He called out in Italian, rattling off a question. The police officer called back, wincing as he did and waving towards one of the other officers who was searching beneath an old metal trash can soldered to the brick floor.

Leoni turned back, some of his chipper attitude having faded to mild frustration. "Ah, well," he said, delicately. "I guess one of the workers with the coroner accidentally dropped the body. They thought the mask was attached, but rather it had only just been laid across the victim's face."

"They cracked it," John said.

"Yes. They cracked it, I'm afraid."

"Anything else we should know?" Adele asked, frowning at Leoni. "Anything about the victim in particular."

Christopher turned to her, his suit sleeves straining as he crossed his arms over his chest. He wasn't as well built as John, but was in excellent shape, nonetheless. Something, Adele desperately wished she didn't keep noticing. *Focus Sharp,* she thought to herself. *Get your head in the game, damn it.*

Still, there was a part of her that was glad she was noticing such simple, superficial things again. It felt like stepping from a shadowed room out into a sunbeam. For nearly a month there, she had cut off all contact with her friends, with anyone who'd attempted to get close. A strange thing to find solace in the recognition of a beautiful man. And yet, she hoped such things hinted at a return to some normalcy. At the very least, she wasn't trying to avoid John or Christopher.

If only to spite her inner critic, she took another long look at John's biceps where they also crossed his suit and then, coughing delicately, returned her attention to Leoni as he answered, "We're looking into details," he said. "Apparently, she was staying in a small hotel only a few minutes' walk from here. She came with friends."

"Understandable," John said. "Given her age. Anything else? Was anything stolen?"

At this Christopher frowned so deeply his eyebrows nearly met over the bridge of his nose. "I—I'm afraid not. That is to say, no—the killer took nothing."

"Nothing at all?" Adele said. "You're sure."

"Yes, very much. Ms. Strasser had over two hundred euros still on her person. She was carrying a small purse which was left, along with a room key and an expensive cell phone." Leoni shook his head. "Whatever the motive, it was not theft."

Silence fell after this declaration, with each of the agents frowning now. John's eyes traced the mask, still looking towards the crack. Agent Leoni was watching the police move about the alleys. Adele, though, stared directly at the blood stain beneath the bronze bench, her eyes fixed and unblinking.

A slow chill crept up her spine at Leoni's words.

No theft. No signs of sexual assault.

Which meant the killer, whoever he was, was hunting for some other reason entirely. Normally, crimes could be traced to one of three motives: sex, money,... or power.

The third was often the most violent of the three.

Killers who did so to simply sate their bloodlust never found the satisfaction they were after. It only increased their appetite for pain and death.

A sadist was one thing... Predictable in a way.

Consummate killers, though, who were fascinated by the simple act of murder—these tended to be the most careful, the most meticulous. And the least likely to leave a trace.

Adele gritted her teeth, looking away from the blood stain and glancing towards John. In a soft murmur, she said, "Perhaps we'd best go see the bodies now."

CHAPTER SEVEN

Adele saw that the entrance to the coroner's office was in the base of a canal-facing office space strangely centered across from a dock surrounded by all manner of vessels and even small, luxury craft. The boats rocked on the water, swishing softly back and forth as other vessels traveled up and down the wide channel. A small clearing on the opposite side of the canal, accessible over a looping bridge with a grey stone railing, cradled a small dance troupe, all wearing masks, who were moving in time with the music from a live band.

As the agents moved towards the entrance of the coroner's office, following Leoni's lead, Adele spared a glance towards the strange amalgamation of art, music, and costume. Briefly, she wished she'd had a chance to come to such a festival on her own time, simply to enjoy it.

But while she was noticing the music and dancers, John kept staring at the boats and the water.

This, in turn, had seemed to cast a greenish tinge across Agent Renee's face, which he quickly hid by glancing into the darker, shadowed portions of the awning above the office-entrance.

"This it?" he said, turning his back fully to the water now and staring—rather pale-faced—at the office entrance.

In answer, Leoni pushed his way through, allowing a little brass bell to jingle above as he entered. The bell reminded Adele of *Gobert's,* a small shop back in Paris. To have a joyful little tinkling bell above a door that led to a morgue seemed a strange and morbid contradiction.

She followed Leoni into a cold hall, with John squeezing in behind her. The halls *in* the buildings seemed smaller too, similar to the alleys outside. John even had to duck as he took a step down into a lower portion of the office complex and moved along the dim hallway towards a glass door at the far end. Other doors, sealed and without illumination, lined the hall on either side.

"We're low," John murmured, shooting a glance towards the two steps that had dipped down from the entrance into the hall. "Very low."

"It's not going to sink, John," Adele said.

"I didn't say that. I just observed."

"You observed with a squeak in your voice."

“Did not. Shut up. I didn't.”

Adele patted the muscled man on the arm. “I used to swim, you know,” she said. “Back in high school. If you fall in, I promise to jump in after you.” She smiled in a would-be comforting way, and then, picking up the pace, muttered, loud enough for him to hear, “Big baby.”

John muttered as well, seemingly more for his sake than hers. “It's all fun and games until Renee drowns in Venice.”

Adele smirked, reaching where Leoni was pushing open the only illuminated glass door at the far end of the cramped, lower-level hall. Briefly, she considered John's aversion to the water. She supposed it made sense; he'd been a helicopter pilot during his service days. The further from the water, the better, it seemed.

Leoni was waiting patiently but as she neared, he led the way into a small room. Immediately, Adele was assailed by a frigid breeze and the scent of cleaning fluids like from a hospital floor. She wrinkled her nose at the offending odor, glancing around the small morgue.

“Hello?” Leoni called. “Dr. Fazio?”

A voice called from out of sight behind a supporting pillar of concrete, shouting something in Italian.

Adele took a moment to further scan the room, her eyes darting from the expected metal cooling closets to the two gurneys against them. On the metal platforms, two pale sheets were draped over the unmistakable forms of bodies.

Adele felt John nudge her from behind, pointing.

“Yes, I see,” she said. “Let's wait. I prefer the guided tour.”

Adele watched as an old, stooped man moved from behind the pillar, zipping up his pants, and wiping his hands off on the sides of his white lab coat. Adele frowned, watching the old fellow limp towards the bodies.

He shot a glance towards them, his eyes surrounded with bright liver spots, staring over the top of the spectacles perched on the bridge of his large nose. The coroner's hair was dyed pitch black, which contrasted sharply with his aged and wizened features.

He waved again, saying something in Italian, which Leoni translated, "He says to follow him.”

Adele fell into step behind Christopher, and shot a glance behind the pillar, towards a urinal built into the floor, without a door to speak of.

She uncomfortably adjusted her sleeves and approached the two bodies beneath the white sheets.

The coroner waved a hand over the nearest form, murmuring something which Christopher translated as, "He says both of them were killed rather quickly. No defensive wounds to speak of."

"Nothing at all?" Adele asked. "Has he checked thoroughly?" She wasn't sure why she asked it this way but supposed the older gentleman's demeanor didn't exactly scream *professionalism*.

Leoni waited for a response, and then translated back, "He's double checked. Nothing beneath the fingernails, no wounds on the hands. Nothing suggesting a struggle at all."

"And both of them died from throat wounds?"

In answer, the old coroner pulled down the tops of the sheets.

Adele stared at the two pale faces staring at the ceiling. One of the women had dark hair, pulled back. The other's was blonde, and cut short.

The coroner lowered the sheets just a bit more, displaying the slits across their throats. The cuts were no longer bleeding, like gouge marks on a hunk of meat. Adele shivered at the thought, trying to dislodge the comparison.

Both women looked like they'd once been quite beautiful, but now lay lifeless in the dim, cold room, across from the urinal. Adele felt a twist of sadness flutter up in her chest, but quickly looked away, inhaling softly.

"Any fingerprints?" Adele said, quietly, leaning in, but not too close.

John was glaring, and something about his posture had gone more aggressive, as if he were taking it even more personally now that he'd seen the victims. Adele knew he always had a soft spot for young women. Some might have called this propensity chauvinist, but she thought it more of an evolved instinct. John was a warrior, through and through, and the best of those types were always the sort to go to battle on behalf of someone. John would never have called himself a gentleman, but he sometimes behaved like one, despite his best efforts to the contrary.

"The second mask?" John said, stiffly. "Is it here?"

Agent Leoni didn't need to translate this time, and instead moved over towards a portion of counter, next to a row of sinks. He pulled past a red towel, upon which another porcelain, Venetian mask had settled.

This one, Adele recognized from the second crime scene photo the Executive had shown them back in the office.

Grateful to turn away from the morbid scene behind her, Adele approached, glancing at this newest face covering.

It was even more beautiful in person than it had been in the picture. The same silk mesh extended past the top, and the two star-shaped eyeholes stared out, with the crimson towel beneath it adding a veneer to the gaze. Again, the lips were crisscrossed with a lipstick X.

Adele shivered, staring at the mask.

"Can you ask him if he found any fingerprints?" Adele murmured.

Agent Leoni repeated the question, and the old Italian coroner brushed a gnarled hand through his pitch-black hair. Leoni translated, "He says there were no fingerprints. No signs of the killer at all. That, with the lack of defensive wounds, makes it difficult for him to say anything about the nature of the attacker, except that they were shrewd. To be able to cut someone's neck, that quickly, would require speed and surprise."

Adele blinked, picturing a nighttime stroll through the Venetian alleyways, with someone crouched, hiding just out of sight. She shivered, wondering if the women had even seen their killer coming.

"Is there anything else you can tell us?" She asked, still staring at the beautiful mask.

Leoni translated, and then said, "Nothing currently. He's running some tests on the blood, just in case. But in his words, he's not finding anything unusual. They were killed with single cuts across the neck."

Adele frowned at Agent Leoni. "So the killer is practiced? He knows how to wield his blade."

"Seems like it. Yes. And *strong,* very strong, to kill with a single stroke."

Adele crossed her arms, her back to the gurneys, grateful as she heard the rustle of the sheets being pulled back over the young, bloodless faces. She stared at the porcelain mask, considering her next move.

"Both those masks are really quite beautiful," she murmured. "Pieces of art even."

"I was thinking the same thing," Leoni said.

"There's no autograph is there? A painter signing their work?"

"I can try and check," Christopher said, with an apologetic shrug. "But I can try to find something."

She turned to him, looking away from the mask and nodded once. "Perfect. If you could, I'd be obliged and indebted."

"While he's tracking down the mask maker," John said, "What should we do? It isn't like we have any witnesses to the murders."

"No," Leoni replied, quickly. "But we did have a roommate for Ms. Strasser. The second victim, the German. She too was staying with an Italian girl in the city. We haven't had a chance to interview her yet. We had to call her back from activities in the city. She should be at their shared hotel room within the next hour or so."

Adele paused, considering this. The young woman's friend might have heard something. It wasn't like they had anything else to go on. Besides, again, they were running against a clock. The moment the identities of the victims made the rounds, it would be a lot more difficult to move without gaining unwanted attention.

"All right, Christopher, if you don't mind, track down what you can about those masks. See if we can trace them to a seller. John, you and I can go speak to this young woman. She's not another actress, is she?"

Christopher winced, and scratched at the back of his head. "Actually, she is, after a fashion." He swallowed delicately, and to Adele's surprise, his cheeks were turning red.

"What?" she pressed.

"Ella Onio is," he said, trailing off, "an actress involved in more adult entertainment."

Adele blinked. John tried to hide a cough, but ended up choking on it and turning, coughing into his hand.

"A porn star?"

"No, not exactly," said Christopher quickly. "More of an erotic actress, in the style of Edwige Fenech."

"I have no clue who that is."

John said, "She started in a couple of movies like *All the Colors of the Dark* or, a personal favorite, *My Sister-In-Law.*"

Leoni and Adele both looked at him hard, and John coughed again, looking away. "At least, I think so."

"Nice cover," Adele grunted, rolling her eyes. "All right, so she's an erotic actress. Just tell me where she's staying. Hopefully she might know something about the killer."

CHAPTER EIGHT

As Adele and John took the final flight of stairs to the address Leoni had provided, Adele marveled at the view over the open-air balcony next to the door of the hotel. The scene overlooked much of the city, staring down the Grand Canal itself, witnessing the horizon against the Adriatic as if suspended above the water. For a moment Adele just stood, enjoying the sights, and then she allowed the more analytical part of herself to catch up with her thoughts. "Imagine how much this has to cost per night," she grunted.

John, next to her, shook his head. "Too much for the Executive to ever lodge us."

Adele wrinkled her nose, shaking her head. They hadn't yet stopped off at the small hotel that Executive Focault had stationed them in. But according to the pictures she'd been sent, there wasn't a window in the space. Which, she supposed, was the sort of thing in Venice that suited John's tastes. Still, as she marveled at the display across the Grand Canal, she reached up, knocking delicately on the door. Even the wood grain, and the inlay of silver and brass suggested the door itself might've cost an entire month's salary.

"Come in!" a voice called out in English.

Adele frowned. A second later, there was a *click*, followed by the rattle of a chain, then another *click*. Then, the door opened.

"Sorry," said a voice as the door swung in, "you can never be too careful."

The woman speaking couldn't have been much older than Lorraine had been, and she carried a youthful vibrancy that exuded in her words and the way she moved, gesturing at both of them to enter the small apartment overlooking the Grand Canal.

"Come, come," the young woman said, gesturing. "I saw you two walking up. DGSI? That's what the police said. They mentioned you were coming by."

Adele blinked, trying to keep track of it all. On one hand, the woman had locked her door multiple times; on the other, she was just inviting the two of them in. The strange juxtaposition of youthful caution and trust.

The woman was beautiful; there was no doubt about it, but not in the way Adele had expected. In her mind she had envisioned a large, silicone injected blonde bombshell, with lips twice the size of normal, and eyes streaked with blush. Instead, the young, 23-year-old had dark hair, cut nearly to her scalp. She had two simple diamond studs in both her ears, and a perfectly framed nose across sharp cheekbones. Her eyes were rimmed in a dash shadow, and the way she moved caught even Adele's attention. Almost like a dancer, every motion and step as she entered the apartment and beckoned at them, seemed rehearsed, confident, almost like the gestures of a charismatic politician, trying to ensnare the public.

John was determinedly staring anywhere but in the woman's direction, likely unable to jolt the phrase "*erotic actress*," from his mind. Adele resisted the urge to roll her eyes or kick his shin.

The young women settled on a large, leather couch beneath a floor-to-ceiling window, which overlooked the canal itself. A Turkish rug extended in front of the couch, with a small ottoman upon which a plate of cheese and crackers had been set.

The woman waved a hand towards the crackers, "Refreshments, if you'd like. I know hoofing it around Venice can be a bit bothersome for people who aren't used to it."

Adele blinked, shaking her head. "You're Ms. Onio?"

"Ella, please. One and the same. Agent Sharp, yes? That makes him Agent Renee. Hello." Her eyes lingered on John for a moment, and Adele frowned. John nodded back, giving a little wave. He crossed his arms, leaning against the door frame. "Do you mind closing that?" Ms. Onia asked, her voice musical and playful.

Adele wrinkled her nose. John shut the door with a thud, latching it, and then returning to his post by the doorway, his arms crossed, staring across the well illuminated hotel room.

"We have a few questions, if you don't mind," Adele said. "Would you like to see some ID?" She added as an afterthought, again, a bit taken aback by the sudden trusting nature of the young woman.

But the actress shook her head. "No, that's fine. One of my friends at the station sent me your pictures ahead of time. John and Adele, right? Do you prefer I call you agent or by your first names?"

"You have a friend at the station?"

The woman just smiled.

Adele cleared her throat and continued, "Agent Sharp is fine."

"John's okay," Renée added.

Adele shot him a look, and he shrugged.

For a moment, Adele glanced deeper into the apartment. A couple of framed pictures lined the wall—movie posters. After a moment, she realized these were posters displaying Ella's face. Well, not *just* her face. Adele's cheeks reddened, and she looked away again, trying not to spend too much time dwelling on a poster with the title, "Heartless Love *in HD!*"

"I'm not sure what I can tell you," Ella said, biting her lip, somehow even making this gesture sensuous. Even the way she sat, shoulders back, hips angled, knees folded up against her, chin high, all seemed practiced, intentional, communicating a thousand words with posture alone.

Or maybe, Adele was just being jealous.

The thought made her frown, and she crossed her arms, matching John's posture and stepping closer towards the tray of crackers. "We just have a couple of questions. Nothing about what you didn't witness."

"And that's just exactly it," Ella said, shaking her head. "It was all so horrible. When I heard the news about Lorraine, I cried. For a full hour, it was awful. My cheeks puffed and everything."

John clicked his tongue, shaking his head with grievous sympathy.

Anything but puffed cheeks! Adele thought to herself in mock sympathy. But out loud she said, "I'm very sorry for your loss. How did you know the victim?"

"Oh, please, Agent Adele, don't call her that. Her name was Lorraine. I don't think I could possibly think of her as anything else."

"All right. How did you know Lorraine? Are you from Venice?"

"No, actually. I live near Rome. But Lorraine and I often met up, renting this room during the festival. It is really quite lovely, isn't it?"

Adele shrugged. "It's nice."

"Very beautiful," John chimed in.

"I'm glad you agree," said Ella, nodding and smiling in a thoughtful sort of way. The sun shining through the open window reflected off her short hair and caressed the slope of her sculpted nose along her cheekbones, sending shadows towards her small chin. She angled her face in just such a way, suggesting again, she was all too aware of the effect the lighting had on her. This was a woman who knew her way around perspective.

"So she's a friend of yours. How did you make friends with a German actress?"

"The Shine conference," Ella said, nodding once. "When we were just young, nearly eight years ago. It's a festival for up-and-coming actresses and models in Rome. Lorraine came through for that, and we hit it off right away. We spent every summer together since." She shrugged. "I'm going to miss her; I already know that. I don't think the full weight of it has even hit me yet."

"It can take a while sometimes," Adele said, nodding. "Were you with her last night?"

"I was, at first. Me and some of our other friends. They also came here for the festival. But," she said, biting her lip again, "I hate to say it, but we got separated. Lorraine didn't like being babied and walked around. She wanted to see some of the sites for herself, while I was more interested in a play one of my friends is in. We split up, intending to meet back at the theater, but she never showed. And that's when," Ella winced, closing her eyes for a moment, and said, "that's when I heard the news. Like I said, it was very upsetting."

"I bet. Well, is there anything Lorraine might've told you? Something that might suggest who did this?" Adele paused, realizing perhaps she was being too hard on the woman. She paused, gathering herself, trying not to glance at John. “I'm sorry,” she added. “I know how hard this all must be.”

Ella shook her head quickly. She gestured a hand towards the plate of cheese and crackers. "Please, if you're hungry."

"I'm fine," Adele said.

John, though, stepped forward, over the ottoman, and grabbed a cracker, popping it in his mouth. As he did, he pulled himself to his full height, crossing his arms over his chest in a way that emphasized his biceps.

Ella looked at John, smiling. "You're very tall," she said. "That's a horrible scar. How did you get it?"

Adele blinked at the forward nature of the question. John, though, didn't seem offended at all. "I'm a war hero," he said, sighing as he did as if weary to admit his own greatness. "Just one of the little badges of courage I was given during service."

"Oh my," Ella said, shaking her head. "That's incredible."

"It is, isn't it?" John said, nodding solemnly. Adele resisted the urge to throw up in her mouth as John continued, "You don't happen to know anything about a mask, do you?"

Ella paused, nibbling her lip. "Mask? You mean like the masks everyone's wearing outside?"

"Yes, but specifically Lorraine's. Was she wearing a mask when she left the apartment?"

"Oh, no. She still needed to pick one out for the ball. But she hadn't yet."

"The ball?" John and Adele said at the same time.

Ella nodded quickly, and pushed off the couch, with an energetic balance, moving to the opposite side of the apartment, and opening a door to a closet. "The *Masque Cielo,* yes, look, see, I already have my own dress picked out. A mask too." She waved a hand into the closet, where a single item was dangling from a hook.

The dress had blue lace and ribbons and was missing portions that might have suggested any effort at decency. There was also a mask, settled on a cushion in the base of the closet.

Delicately, like lifting a child, Ella picked up the mask, and held it up to her face so the agents could see.

Bright blue threads, and peacock feathers jutted out the top of the mask. Instead of pale, the texture was crimson, streaked with patterns of swirling yellow and green.

"Do you like it?" Ella said. "It took me hours to find the right one."

"It's lovely," Adele said. "And Lorraine, she didn't have a mask yet?"

"Not that I'm aware of. And she promised to shop with me for one." Ella paused, frowning. "Why?"

"Your friend was found with a mask. We're trying to figure out where she might've gotten it."

"She was? She *promised* she'd wait to shop for one with me!" Ella said, sounding scandalized briefly, but then, catching herself; she winced, glancing off with a flash of guilt. "I mean, that's horrible. I'm sorry. But I don't know where she got it."

Adele sighed through her nose, considering their options. The killer made the most sense. Who else would have given a mask to the victims? Both of them had one.

Which meant Christopher's ability to track down the mask maker would make all the difference. But it also meant, if they weren't able to find a connecting point between the face-wear, they would be back to square one.

Ms. Onio smoothed her sleeves, and said, "I don't have any idea who might've done this. I promise. I swear it. That mask, whatever it was, wasn't mine, and it wasn't Lorraine's."

"I believe you," Adele said, sensing the flustered tone of the young woman. "Is there anything else we need to know? Anyone Lorraine might have gone to see? Anyone who might've recognized her? We know she was a bit of an up-and-coming actress."

Ella declared, "She was marvelous! She was going to have a big break soon too, I could tell. I always could tell. I was trying to convince her to star in one of my films, actually. Did you know that I did films?" She tilted her head in just such a pose to match one of the movie posters closest to the window.

"I could tell," John said quickly.

"Good for you," Adele said, shooting a nasty look towards Renée. She coughed delicately and continued, "So some people might've recognized her—is that what you're saying?"

"Well, perhaps not in Venice. She was still small time. She could have done wonderfully. But she had, well, standards. Quite judgmental standards I might add." Ella sniffed. "But there was a man that Lorraine would see whenever she came to Italy. Every year for the festival, she would take some time to go meet with him. Very secretive though, and she would never tell me his name."

Adele perked at this, glancing at John again, who nodded, prompting her to continue the line.

"A secret lover?"

"Perhaps. Maybe just a friend. She wouldn't tell me, and I'm not sure why. I sometimes wondered if maybe it wasn't a man at all." Ella inclined her eyebrows significantly, but then glanced out the window once more.

Adele sighed softly, considering this new angle. "Any idea where they might have met each other? Or where they would meet up during the festival?"

"No, sorry. Nothing like that at all. I mean, you have her phone, don't you? You could check? I'm sure there's something there. Not that I'm trying to tell you how to do your job."

"All right, thank you Ella," Adele said, nodding. She waved at John, who was reaching for another cracker. "Please stay in Venice for the week, in case we have any more questions."

"Oh, I'm going to see the festival anyway. For Lorraine—she would've wanted that." Ella nodded, sniffing in a sort of theatrical way. And Adele turned, moving back towards the door.

She saw more movie posters on the opposite wall, and paused, trying to consider the next move. The roommate hadn't been much help, but this information about the secret lover, perhaps that would be useful.

At just that moment, her phone began to ring. Adele answered, "Yes?"

"Adele," came Agent Leoni's voice on the other end. "I have a lead on those masks."

Adele felt a tiny jolt of excitement. "Yes? Did you find who sold them?"

"Better," said Leoni. "I found who *made* them. I'm texting you the address. I'll be waiting here when you're done interviewing the witness."

Adele paused, glancing towards where John was still talking with Ella, pointing at his scar and leaning in to give the actress a closer look.

Adele cleared her throat. “You coming?” she called.

Sheepishly, John looked up, winced and gave a quick farewell to the beautiful, young woman. For her part, Adele tried not to glare too hard at the side of John's face as he rejoined. Into the phone, she said, “Already done with the interview. We're on our way."

CHAPTER NINE

Adele ducked under a row of dangling beads and glass baubles which created a sort of half curtain over the entrance into the cramped shop facing the Grand Canal.

The presumptuously titled *Michelangelo's Masks* was about a mile from the hotel where Lorraine and Ella had been staying. Not that this meant much, as Venice was a crowded city near the more touristy destinations.

Michelangelo's Masks had prime real estate, right on the Grand Canal, surrounded by a small movie theater on one side and a museum and gift shop on the other. Wedged between the two rectangular buildings, the curio shop had vibrant neon signs in the windows, but the lights, instead of flashing from glass bulbs, reflected off shards of crystal and resplendent beads in strange swooping patterns. Inside, the shop itself was similarly decorated and ornamented. As Adele moved beneath the bead curtain and entered deeper into the cramped store, she was confronted by a grizzly bear carved from a pure block of reflective tiger's eye, the semi-precious stone.

The grizzly bear of tiger's eye looked to be nearly four feet tall; Adele leaned in, glancing at the price tag, and nearly swallowed her tongue.

$50,000.

"Shopping for souvenirs?" John murmured behind her. The tall agent had to duck even lower than her, and now was busily trying to extricate one of the strands of crystal from where it had landed behind his ear. He brushed noisily at his face and scanned the small space of the artisan shop. Besides the carvings, the beads, and the fragments of crystal out front, Adele spotted the source of the shop's title.

Rows of masks lined the wall behind the glass counter. For a moment, it almost felt as if she were staring into a crowd, and they were staring back. The suspended faces on the wall, dangled from metal hooks with bright flowers and hand-painted patterns on the surface, were made of porcelain, and others mesh and ebony. Still other, more exotic, masks were made of varnished wood, and a row beneath a small wooden sign read Hawaiian Koa and Sinker Redwood.

These masks were dark and coffee stained. There were feathers tucked behind the frames, and gold dust sprinkled in intricate swirls over the eye-sockets.

Adele glanced around from one mask to the other, in equal parts admiration and mild unease.

"You like?" called a heavily accented voice from the back of the shop, behind the counter. "You like, discount, two-for-one." The voice boomed in the small space, immediately attracting Adele and John's attention.

First, Adele noticed Agent Christopher Leoni, where he stood by the glass counter, next to a full-figured mannequin wearing a ballroom dress and red mask with what looked like bats' wings sprouting out of the top.

Christopher gave a little wave, and then nodded surreptitiously towards the man behind the counter who he had been speaking. Christopher's small notepad, which Adele remembered from their previous missions, was resting on the glass counter, and his right hand scribbled furiously on the pages, nodding quietly as he did.

"We're not here to buy," Adele said, glancing at the shopkeeper.

The man was three sizes larger than Christopher. He had a double chin, and a wild, bushy full head of hair. His eyes were vibrant blue, and he wore red sunglasses perched so low on his nose that they didn't serve his eyes.

The enormous man carried his weight well, like an opera singer, and gesticulated wildly with a hand towards the masks behind him. "Hand-painted," he declared, "each one masterpiece!"

"They are quite beautiful," Adele returned as she covered the final distance between the carving of the bear and the mannequin by the glass counter. She pulled up next to Leoni, glancing at what he was scribbling.

She read the words, *alibi? busy season.*

"I'm with the police," Adele said. "We're here to ask you some questions."

She looked up from the notepad, and realized the mask maker and shopkeeper was now frowning.

"You scare customer," he said, tapping a finger hard against the glass. He frowned from Adele to Christopher and over to John. On this third glance, his expression flickered hopefully again, but John grunted, "I'm not buying either."

Now, the bluster of the shopkeeper melted completely, to be

replaced by a frown and a weighty sigh. "Waste time," the Italian said, glumly. "Nothing to say. No help."

Christopher shook his head, though. "That's not quite true. Tell them what you told me," he said.

The Italian glanced over, frowning and wincing. "Ha?"

Christopher repeated the question, this time in Italian.

The shopkeeper wagged his head quickly and glanced to Adele. "Yes. Mask. I know. What's of? I sell to mask. I know."

Adele glanced at Christopher who said, "He recognized both the masks when I showed him. One of the wooden stalls selling the masks recognized the paintwork, directed me towards Mr. Angelo here."

"Nice to meet you Mr. Angelo," Adele said, curtly. "And? So he recognizes the masks?"

Christopher folded back the top sheet of his notebook, revealing two pictures of the masks that had been found with the victims. He tapped both of them again, and said, "Tell me again how you know these."

Mr. Angelo coughed, looking furtively from Adele to Christopher and back again. He was beginning to look uneasy, and a thin bead of sweat formed on his brow. He wiped at his thick neck and shrugged. "Maybe I wrong. Maybe mistake."

"Maybe," Leoni said. "But weren't you just telling me that you take great pride in every mask you make?"

"Yes. Beautiful."

"Very beautiful, I agree. And these two, they're beautiful also. One of your friends, who works down the wharf suggested that you had made both of these. They said they recognized the paintwork—it really is quite eye-catching. Is that true?"

The shopkeeper looked hesitantly from Adele to John to Christopher, and if anything, despite his large frame, he almost seemed to shrink in on himself, as if he were trying to become smaller and disappear. Adele had often known that the more touristy types could sense trouble a mile away. Perhaps because they spent so much time causing it themselves with the exorbitant prices and underhanded dealings they had with unsuspecting visitors.

"This masks, may be mine, but sold, years ago," he said quickly, nodding for emphasis.

"So these are yours," Adele asked, leaning in now and tapping the photos as well. She scanned the wall behind the counter, trying to match any of the masks with the ones in the photos. But there was no perfect match. In fact, there were no two alike.

"So what?" the mask maker said, grunting. "I painted. My mask. I sell. I sell many mask. So what?" He repeated.

"So," Adele said, delicately, "both those masks were discovered on the faces of two murdered women in the last week."

She left the time frame sufficiently vague to try and see if the shopkeeper might fill in details she hadn't yet offered. But the shopkeeper seemed too stunned by this news to get bogged down in the details. "Murder? Dead?" He said something in Italian to Christopher, who nodded.

The man cursed, wiping a hand across his sweaty forehead. "No, no no. I sell mask. Years ago. I no kill. I here all night."

Adele glanced at Christopher. Who shrugged back at her. "That does mesh with what the other shopkeeper was saying. He says Mr. Angelo here works until midnight, especially during busy season."

Adele frowned, shaking her head. "You have any idea who you sold those masks to?"

The shopkeeper shrugged his large shoulders. "No. Years ago."

Adele closed her eyes hard in mild frustration but opened them just as quickly. "You don't keep records or anything?"

He waved this away with a flourish of his fingers. "Years ago," he said, repeating the two words with emphasis. "No records. You sure you don't want mask?"

Adele began to shake her head, but ever the persistent businessman, Mr. Angelo tapped a pudgy finger against the photos. He spread an arm towards a section of the masks on the wall behind him, saying, "17th-century French," speaking those words with a surprisingly small amount of accent, suggesting perhaps they were a practiced spiel.

Adele said. "I'm not shopping. Thank you though."

Adele glanced around the shop once more, frowning as she did. "You don't happen to have proof you were here late last night, do you?" she said, hesitantly.

Mr. Angelo didn't look like he had the physique to go chasing after young women in the dark and executing them without a fight. But looks could always be deceiving, especially where masks were concerned.

In answer, though, the Italian shopkeeper ducked behind the counter, and he emerged with a small iPad. He waved fingers towards the ceiling, pointing, and Adele followed his gaze, spotting, there, behind an ebony mask, a blinking red light from a security camera.

For a moment, she jolted, her mind taken back to Paris, to the small apartments. But then, she focused again as Angelo tapped the small screen, and then turned it so she could see. John and Christopher both leaned in as well.

Still without a word, the shopkeeper pressed a button, and the screen began to display a video feed. It showed Angelo himself, moving about the shop, and he sped up the image, pointing with a finger towards the date in the top right.

"Last night," Christopher said, softly.

Adele had already discerned this. She watched, as Angelo fast forwarded through the video. There wasn't a moment where he disappeared from behind the counter. Every time a customer come in, Angelo himself would greet them, and walk them through the different masks. He sold a surprising number in the short period between 9 and 11 PM. Even until midnight, though the trickle of tourist traffic diminished somewhat, the large mask maker remained in his position behind the counter, like a lion waiting to pounce.

"You were here all of last night?" Adele said, softly.

Angelo again instead of answering, just rewound the video and pointed at the date.

"I get it," Adele said, with mild annoyance. "Thank you," she added, hoping to offset her tone. She turned away from the large shopkeeper, glancing at John and raising an eyebrow. John coughed delicately, and then in French said, "Probably not him."

"He doesn't seem the type," Adele said, also in French.

"So now what?"

Adele considered it for a moment. Sex, money, or power.

The killer was after the third, in part... But perhaps a lack of one of the other two?

For what end, and why, she couldn't be sure.

Why was he hunting tourists? Was it a nationalistic sense? Pure hatred?

A racial motive, perhaps?

Angelo might have sold the masks in question, but if he didn't have records, it didn't matter. For all she knew, the masks had traded hands many times before ending up with the killer. Or, even more likely, he had stolen the masks to use for his kills.

She sighed and shook her head. Still in French, she said, "Maybe we should start working on phone records. It's like Ella said, we can't forget about that strange boyfriend Lorraine was going off to meet.

Maybe he's involved."

At that point, the shopkeeper cleared his throat, and wiggled his fingers, saying, in equally accented French, "Are you sure you don't want to mask? Especially you," he said, nodding to John. "A mask would look very good on you."

John frowned. Adele tried not to chuckle. She said, beneath her breath, "You'd look really good with your face covered."

John waved away Mr. Angelo a final time, turning to Adele and muttering, "Funny, really funny. Look, whoever's hunting these girls, there's no way he's done. He's already killed two and has the taste for it. The festival is still on for another few days."

Adele winced, nodding and sobering at this. "All right, well, we're going to have to try to track down this boyfriend then. And in the meantime, we can talk to the American victims' friends." She turned, slowly, switching from French. "Christopher, I have another favor to ask."

CHAPTER TEN

He faced the small gathering before the elevated wooden platform and puffed his chest, feeling the mask cold and smooth against his face. He stood beneath the dipping sun, the shade from the buildings behind him cast over his form as he adjusted his suit, raised his voice, and began to sing, powerfully at first, belting the lines, allowing the music to swell.

A few of the tourists were clapping already and others were smiling, pointing at each other and then to him.

He ignored the attention at first, singing louder, deeper, his voice piercing across the canal, attracting more attention.

The anonymity of beauty was his favorite part. No one knew his face. No one knew his name.

Most of the tourists thought he was just another commissioned artist, part of the act. But he hadn't reserved the spot. The musicians who would use it later that night didn't know he was here.

Beautiful anonymity.

Of course, he hadn't chosen this particular spot randomly.

He watched, his eyes flickering through his mask, as the young and gorgeous Fiorella paused where she had been exiting from her apartment. She glanced over towards where he was singing, and then, frowning in curiosity, began to move in his direction.

This only emboldened him. He sang even louder, belting the lines, breathing in deeply, and holding the high note until another round of applause swept through the onlookers.

He dipped his masked face in a sort of bow, and then with a final flourish, ended the Venetian boat song.

The applause pattered throughout the audience, and he felt a flicker of frustration.

Fifteen maybe twenty spectators. Hardly what a man of his talents deserved. Fiorella Lettiere, the 23-year-old Venetian, stared at him. She was smiling, her blonde curls bouncing as she clapped too.

He smiled behind his mask, bowing at the waist now, and receiving his just due of praise.

Fiorella Lettiere, twenty-three—the only facts he knew about her.

Her name and age. And where she had been staying. That was it. He didn't need much else.

She would fit perfectly into what he was planning, of course. She would have to, as like a musical note in any composed song, she had been chosen, fitting perfectly between the other notes. They were all the same anyway. He sneered behind his mask, but the facial covering hid the twisted lip.

Like the conductor he was, the maestro, every composition required creativity and improvisation at first.

He already knew the climax, the ultimate crescendo, but leading up to it, he was delightfully surprising even to himself. Yes, now that he saw her, he knew she would do just fine.

Fiorella was beginning to turn away, and she began to move down one of the small paths between the buildings. Where would she head to now?

He took another bow, and then skipped off the wooden platform, humming to himself. Beneath his breath, his voice hissing in his mask, he murmured, "Where are you going my dear?"

He didn't say it loud enough for anyone to hear; some music was just meant for his own ears. Not all creations needed to be displayed so gaudily.

The beautiful of Venice didn't understand this. Those moving statues, with the features they had, would often flaunt them. The Internet had ruined art. Now, art was dying, music was fading, and it took the truly courageous, those with iron wills, to bring back and resurrect the painful crafts once more.

Without pain there couldn't be creativity. Without determination, beauty would be forgotten.

He followed after Fiorella, whistling beneath his breath, strolling along through the gathering crowds who were preparing for the rest of the night's festival.

He was in no rush.

One couldn't rush such endeavors.

CHAPTER ELEVEN

Adele glanced around the large, nearly empty theater. This was the widest building she had yet to see in Venice. There were nearly five hundred seats, facing a small wooden stage, with a red curtain pulled back on either side and tied with a crimson sash like two bathrobes.

There, in the front row, she spotted a police officer waiting for them, standing by the seats.

Reclined in the cushioned chairs, three girls were glancing nervously at each other, whispering, and then turning sharply as the sound of Adele and John's footsteps reached their ears. The police officer nodded once, gesturing at the agents. Adele stepped down the walkway, leading to the VIP seats facing the empty stage.

Her footsteps, in the acoustics of the room, echoed in a strange, ominous sort of way. She offset the sound by clearing her throat, and murmuring to John, "What was the first victim's name again?"

"Rebekah James," John replied. "She was the American."

"I remember *that*."

"I don't know what you remember. Say, that underwear model of yours, is he going to follow through on that phone?"

Adele frowned at John, continuing towards where the nervous girls were waiting. "He's not an underwear model. And yes, Agent Leoni is excellent at his job. He'll be able to tell us if Lorraine's phone has anything about that strange and secret lover she was going off to meet."

"We still don't know it was a lover," John said, firmly.

"Oh, well maybe he was just an underwear model then," Adele said. Before John could offer a rejoinder, they reached the first row of seats, and Adele nodded in gratitude towards the stationed officer, who moved off to the side, giving them space.

Adele cleared her throat, glancing at the three women who were sitting uneasily in the otherwise expensive chairs.

None of them could have been much older than mid-twenties.

"Can we go yet?" said the woman closest to Adele, her one hand gripping the seat rest, and twisting at the felt. "We've been here for hours," she said.

"If I'm correct, you've only been here for thirty minutes," Adele murmured, softly. "My name is Adele Sharp; this is John Renee. We're with DGSI."

The middle girl glanced at both of them, shaking her head. "DGSI?" She said in an American accent. "What's that?"

"French FBI," Adele replied, and then pressed, "I don't mean to take up much of your time, and I'll make this as brief as possible. I'm sure you know, I'm here about Rebekah."

The moment she said the name, all three girls reacted.

The quiet one, who hadn't yet spoken, furthest from Adele, stared at her hands, hunching her shoulders, her bangs draping past her face to shield her eyes.

The girl who'd spoken loudest and first, closest to Adele, let out a soft little sob. The one with the American accent, looked like she'd stepped on a nail, her face twisting in pain, and she glanced off, blinking, reaching up to wipe at her eyes.

"I'm very sorry for your loss," Adele said, delicately.

"I don't want to be here anymore," said the American. "Please, we just want to go home. Everything is ruined. This whole festival was a terrible idea."

Adele nodded sympathetically. "You can leave after just a couple of questions. Look, I just need you to tell me about your friend. Anything you might have seen, anything that stood out."

The first girl, with a loud voice said, "We had only just arrived."

"You were only here one night with Rebekah?"

"Yes," said the first girl crossing her arms over a pink sweater with a small, stenciled heart over the sleeves. "We were celebrating. She had signed a contract with *J.P Azienda*. You know who that is?"

"No," Adele said.

"Yes," John said. "The fashion studio. I love their commercials."

Adele shot John a long look, then glanced back at the girls. "So you were here to celebrate."

"Yes. All of us go to a school in California. You know where that is?"

Adele blinked, unsure whether the girl was being sarcastic or not. She looked sincere enough, though, so Adele nodded slowly. "Yes, I know where California is."

"Yes, well, we came here for the week. We were going to be here for the festival. We were excited, Rebekah most of all."

The girl on the far end, whose hair was still hiding her face, began to shake once more, sobbing, her shoulders trembling. Adele felt a jolt of sympathy, and in a gentle tone, murmured, "All right, and then she got separated from you? What happened?"

"Not separated," said the American girl. "She went off on her own; she wanted to ride one of the gondolas. The rest of us were too tired from the airplane. She was always the most energetic of us. It was one of the reasons she got hired so quickly. She was only twenty-five."

"It's very rare for someone so young to be hired by *J.P. Azienda*. They're unique in that way. They don't just prey on teenagers and the like. They actually look for talent."

At this, all three of the girls nodded their heads. Even the one who was still shaking in the corner.

"All right, so she went off on her own. Does she know anyone else in the city?"

"No." The American girl shook her head. Adele glanced towards the third woman who was still shaking.

The loud one said, "She doesn't know anyone else. None of us do. We haven't been to Venice before. It was going to be our first time. And now, I never want to come back. Please, we just want to leave. They've been keeping us here for so long."

Adele sighed. "I am very sorry. Just another question. Is there a chance that your friend was going off to see a boy? Anyone like that?"

The American girl blanched at this, and the first one said, "Definitely not. She had a boyfriend back in California. They loved each other. There was no way she cheated on him. Why, are you saying she did?"

Adele quickly shook her head. "No, I'm just exploring all options."

John had moved around the front of the chairs and now he sat on the edge of the stage, facing the girl who hadn't looked up yet. He crossed his arms, frowning slightly, and clearing his throat as if to catch her attention.

Everyone else fell silent for a moment, looking towards the large Frenchman. He cleared his throat again, a bit more emphatically this time, but still the girl in question kept her head ducked, her bangs shielding her eyes.

At last, John said, loudly, "Excuse me, young lady!"

She looked up now, tears streaking her face, her eyes baggy and red. She looked like she might have been the youngest of the group.

"What's your name?" John said.

The girl coughed and then murmured, "Izzie."

"Right, Izzie, good to meet you. What can you tell me about your whereabouts on the first night of the festival?" John said, firmly.

The girls all looked stunned for a moment, considering the implications of the question while staring at Renee. Adele's brow flickered into a frown. And then, at once, they all began to talk the same time.

"Never, I wouldn't—"

"—We were all in the same room. All of us."

"—Talking about the ball. Talking about boys."

"—We were there. We didn't see anything."

John frowned even more deeply. He glanced at Adele and back at the girls. "One at a time please. Where were you that night?" He spoke a little bit more firmly now, his scowl deepening.

The girls all seemed to sense they were now being questioned in a different manner. The American was crying now too. Izzie sniffled, and, in a shaky voice, said, "We were trying to get some sleep. We just got in on the flight. None of us saw her, sir. I promise. None of us saw her. I wish I had. I wish I'd gone with her."

John didn't seem moved by the tears, though. He said, even more firmly, "You were sleeping? Can anyone else verify that?"

Adele, though, had heard enough. She cleared her throat, and stepped next to John, placing a hand back against his leg, as if to withhold him. "What my partner means to say," she said, softly, "is there anyone else who might have known where Rebekah went? Anyone who might've seen where she'd gone?"

Each of the girls was shaking their heads now, though. The first one was saying, even more insistently now, "I'm too tired. Please, let me go. We don't know anything. We didn't see anything. Please, that's *your* job."

John looked ready to question even further, still scowling, but again, Adele tapped a hand against his leg, and said, delicately, "I'm very sorry for your loss; the police over there will escort you back to your hotel. If you can think of anything, please, contact me." She pulled out a business card, handing it to the first girl, and watching as she shakily put it in her pocket. The three girls, with an air of extreme relief, slowly rose from the chairs, turning away from the theater.

As they filed out into the aisle, Adele said, quickly, "One last thing; you mentioned you've been talking about a ball. Which one?"

All three of the girls glanced back at her. The American said, "*Masque Cielo*—the one hosted by *Compagnia dei Cielo.* That was what we were most excited about. It's tomorrow, now that we're nearing the end of the festival. Why? Is that important?”

Adele gave a quick shake of her head. "Just asking, I'll let you know if we find anything."

The girls filed one by one out of the seats into the aisle and began to follow after the Italian officer up towards the exit to the theater. Adele stood by the stage for a moment longer, in the acoustically reverberating room. Beneath her breath, she said, "That's the same ball Lorraine was going to go to," Adele said softly.

John frowned, crossing his arms and just nodding once.

Adele closed her eyes a moment, ignoring the stage behind her, and the empty audience forum. She ignored the three bereft women walking up the aisle, relieved to escape the pressure from the questioning. She considered the two young victims. Both of them beautiful, both of them with friends both of them wearing masks they hadn't bought. Both of them intent on visiting *Masque Cielo* towards the end of the festival.

A pattern was emerging—she just wasn't sure exactly how to connect the dots.

And if she didn't figure it out soon, someone else was going to pay a heavy price. On top of it, though, what had John been thinking? She frowned as she opened her mouth to speak, her expression darkening as she turned to her partner, feeling a jolt of frustration shooting through her chest.

CHAPTER TWELVE

As the last of Rebekah's friends filed out of the theater, following the police officer, Adele snapped, “What was that?”

John blinked, leaning on the edge of the theater, and scratching one ear. “Huh?”

“You were grilling those girls. They're not suspects.”

“I... We're supposed to question them, Adele.”

“Yeah, but you were giving them the third degree. What gives?”

She crossed her arms, facing where his long legs stretched from the edge of the stage to the well-swept floor. He scratched at his jaw for a moment, shifting so that his weapon revealed beneath the edge of his jacket, holstered on his hip. Somehow, as if given a bit of confidence by the reveal of his sidearm, John found his voice and said, quietly, “Maybe you're right.”

She blinked, expecting almost anything but this. “I—yes... I am?”

John rubbed his chin, closing his eyes for a moment and sighing. “I hate it, Adele. I hate this whole damn business. But especially when young women are concerned. It... It gives me the creeps.” He shivered, glancing off and trailing one large finger along the edge of the stage.

Adele watched where her partner reclined, his feet still loose beneath him, facing the empty audience seats. For a moment, it struck her how odd of a setting this was, in the heart of an old theater in Venice, facing John Renee, without a witness around.

Her eyes traced his scar, up to his deep gaze which was fascinated, it seemed, by the extending crimson drapes framing either side of the stage.

“God damn it Adele,” John said, closing his trailing hand into a fist and slamming it against one of his knees. “It's just not right—it isn't... I... I hate it is all.” He shrugged, his fist still clenched.

Adele felt her annoyance flit away, watching the tall Frenchman grapple with his emotions. John was no stranger to loss and pain, but he was also a gentleman of a sort—hidden beneath more quills than a porcupine—though he hated to admit it, and though there were some who might belittle him for it.

Adele wasn't such a person. She approached her old partner, sitting on the stage next to him, her shoulder brushing his as she also stared out across the red seats facing the stage. An empty audience, and yet, as she witnessed the expensive sitting area and her eyes traced up to the second-floor balcony, jutting over the back portion near the fire-escapes, Adele felt a flicker of unease in her stomach.

Not a strong sense, but a brief reminder.

When she'd first found herself at the DGSI, nearly a decade ago, she'd had a similar sensation stepping onto her first crime scene. The same feeling had returned the previous month, when she'd been investigating a killer that was hunting wealthy women who owned homes in Southern France.

Now, though, sitting on the stage, her shoulder against John's, she found the sensation ebb and flow away, as if somehow fleeing her presence. Or, perhaps, fleeing the two of them.

"I get it," she murmured. "I do... trust me. But they're not suspects. I can guarantee that."

"We don't know, though, do we. Just another damn part of the job. The constant second-guessing. You never really know, do you?" He sighed, and then glanced at her. "Was that bastard really across from your apartment? He had a camera?"

Adele didn't react at first, considering how much she wanted to bring him in on. John was an ally, a friend... more.

But at the same time, while she'd decided she couldn't protect everyone from the Spade killer, did she really want to drag him into this? It felt somehow... personal now in a way it hadn't before.

Because you're not approaching this as an agent. The words echoed in her mind, loud like an internal voice.

Perhaps it was true, though. What would she have done if she'd managed to get her hands on the small bastard back in his apartment? Would she have called anyone at all?

It scared her that she didn't know the answer.

"He set up a camera," Adele said, quietly. "Watching my apartment. I was able to track it back to the rental unit. He got away before I could grab him. I fell through the floor."

"Trapped?"

"Yeah. He's a slippery one. I'll give him that."

"I should've killed him," John muttered. "That one time. I almost had him. Small little monkey got away."

"Yeah—he slipped me too. It is what it is."

Adele sighed, glancing off. She felt something warm against her hand, where it trailed on the edge of the stage. She looked down, to see John's large hand was now next to hers, his finger grazing hers, trailing for a moment, as if afraid she might jerk back.

She smiled softly, and left her hand where it was, staring out at the empty theater—a welcome juxtaposition to the mayhem, and crowds of the Venetian roads during the festival. No loud sounds, no wild music, no laughter or cheering, no hullabaloo... Just quiet; a large, expansive quiet.

And John at her side.

"Adele," he said, softly.

"Hmm?"

"I wanted to tell you something," he murmured. "Something... something I've been thinking a lot about. A *lot.*"

"You're not going to propose to me, are you?"

"Psh. You wish. Marriage is death."

"Nice to hear the romantic in you."

"I'm romantic. I am. What? Don't look at me like that. No—hey, don't roll your eyes. Remember that time I saved your life?"

"Psh. That's not romantic. You shot a man above me. Some of his blood got in my hair."

"Romantic," John said, nodding. "True romance. You just don't appreciate the arts."

Adele snorted, leaning against John's shoulder. She realized he hadn't said what he'd been about to. She also realized she wasn't sure she cared too much. Whatever it was, it could wait. In that moment, in the heart of the empty theater, surrounded by the waters of Venice, she was simply glad to be next to him.

As these thoughts rose within her, her phone suddenly began to ring.

Adele sighed and she felt John's hand jerk instinctively away from hers, the warmth leaving, allowing her to reach into her pocket. He looked at her as she pulled her phone and answered, "Leoni?"

"Adele?" said the voice on the other end. "Hey, I've got bad news I'm afraid."

Adele winced. "Lorraine Strasser's phone records?" she guessed.

Leoni's voice carried chagrin. "Unfortunately, nothing. Whoever our second victim's mystery man was, they must have communicated some other way."

"Email?" Adele guessed.

"We'll look into it, but it's going to be harder than the phone records. Sorry Adele."

"It's fine...." Adele paused, clearing her throat briefly. She frowned. "Say, Christopher, put a pin in that. I had another thought."

John was watching her with interest now, studying her as her brow furrowed and she said, "I—I actually think we found a connection between the two victims. We were just speaking with Rebekah's friends... Both victims, it seems, were intent on visiting the same masquerade ball. Know anything about it?"

"Which one? There are usually a few towards the end of the festival."

"Oh. Well, they said it had something to do with the theater crowd. Both victims seemed to be interested in the performing arts in fact."

"Right, that'd be the *Masque Cielo*. What about it?"

"Any chance we could get a guest list for it?"

There was a pause. Adele winced. Nothing good ever followed such a pause. Leoni hesitantly said, "I—I suppose. But Adele, these things are attended by *hundreds.* Some anonymous."

"There has to be a front end, though. Somewhere they purchase the tickets, no? Who could we contact about that?"

"Well... Yes, I think so. If I remember correctly, that particular ball is actually being coordinated by one of the more prestigious acting troops in Venice. Name of *Compagnia dei Cielo*. They're a bit of a big deal in Italy. Deep roots, some still patronized by big money, if you catch my drift."

"So this *Compagnia dei Cielo*, can we get the records of their ticket purchases? Anyone who has a ticket to attend their masquerade ball."

"The ball isn't for a few more days, from what I remember," Leoni replied. "But I can check. Just keep in mind—they're a big deal. They're not going to appreciate the prying. And like I said, they have wealthy friends."

"And wealthy means powerful," Adele said, supplying the unspoken contingency. "Great. Well, if you can do it on the quiet, I'd be obliged."

Another pause and another sinking feeling in Adele's gut. But then, Leoni replied, "I'll see what I can do Adele. Hang tight, keep your phone on."

"Thanks, Christopher."

Adele hung up, glancing at John.

"Was that *Christopher*?" John said in a would-be innocent tone.

"Agent Leoni," Adele said, without taking the bait, "is looking into a guest list for the masquerade ball both victims were going to attend."

"I see. He seems like he'd be good going through files."

"What does that mean?"

John shrugged. "Nothing."

Adele frowned at the Frenchman, but then again refused to push the point. "The killer might have access to the guest list," Adele said, shrugging. "Or maybe he's choosing them some other way. Whatever the case, it's the only connection we have right now."

"Good thinking. At the very least perhaps it will help us narrow down our suspects by determining who has access to the list."

"That..." Adele said, frowning and then pushing off the stage, dusting the back of her pants. "Or it might help narrow down our list of potential victims. Guaranteed, one way or another, this guy isn't done dropping bodies."

John pushed off the stage as well and brushed past her, moving up the aisle. "Well, while Leoni is doing that, did he tell us who *has* the list for the ball?"

"A *Compagnia dei Cielo*," Adele said. "Some acting troop with deep pockets, apparently."

John wrinkled his nose. "Sounds pretentious."

"That's a big word."

He tapped his nose, pointing at her. "I'm not just a pretty face, Agent Sharp. Don't you forget it. Speaking of pretty, let's see if we can beat that underwear model of yours to the punch." Still pointing at her, he backed up and then turned, marching towards the exit without waiting for her to follow.

"Beat him to the—what?"

John shrugged, and without glancing back, called, "If they're an acting troop, they have a theater or office. Like this one, maybe. How hard can it be to find them?" He paused next to the exit and frowned at her. "You coming?"

Adele supposed it made sense. There was no point waiting for Christopher to track down his own information. What could it hurt, anyway?

She'd never investigated the organizer of a masquerade ball before.

CHAPTER THIRTEEN

It turned out, the organizer of the *Masque Cielo* wasn't to be found in a theater, but rather lodged in the top floor of a dusty, molding old building overlooking a row of dumpsters somewhere, in Adele's opinion, that was likely the armpit of Venice.

The interior of the office for the *Compagnia dei Cielo*, though, seemed a venture in opposites. Where outside, the building had water damage and black mold growth, inside the halls were pristine and lined with marble and smooth limestone.

Where outside, Adele and John had moved past a row of small mopeds—two of them missing wheels—inside, a large, bright chandelier illuminated the pristine and polished space.

Outside, someone had been peeing in an alley, while inside, two butlers in immaculate black and purple suits were standing on either side of the room, next to honest-to-goodness statues of marble lions facing the doorway.

Adele slowly stowed her identification under the scrutiny of one such attendee who cleared his throat delicately, spun on a perfectly polished shoe and gestured a white gloved hand for her to follow, wiggling his fingers like someone summoning a puppy.

Adele shared a look with John as she followed after the man.

He led them to a pure glass elevator. Surrounding the elevator, a floor to ceiling, chambered aquarium stretched from the ground.

The immaculately dressed attendee pressed the button, waiting patiently. As the elevator arrived, he said something in Italian lost on Adele.

She just nodded and followed him into the elevator, waiting for the same white-gloved hand to tap the button to the top floor.

Then, the elevator began to rise, smoothly, lifting through the chute of water and fish swimming about in the rectangular aquarium around them.

"*Pretentious*," John said, hiding the word in a sneeze.

"Shut up," she whispered.

"Just saying," he muttered.

The attendee said something else as the elevator dinged and again,

Adele just nodded. The attendee repeated the Italian phrase, a bit more insistently this time.

Adele winced and tapped her ear. "English?" she said.

The butler stared blankly at her.

"German?" she tried.

More blank, and now mildly judgmental staring.

"French?" she attempted finally.

At this, the butler actually sneered and gave a little roll of his eyes before wiggling his gloved fingers in a shooing motion towards the door as they slid slowly open.

"Hang on, what was that?" John said, frowning. Adele grabbed at him, tugging his arm and leading him out of the elevator. "Wait, why did he make that face at French." John raised his voice, though he did allow Adele to guide him away. "Right back at you!" he said. "Better France than this water-logged hellhole! Hear me? Hey—you, glove-boy, learn a real language!"

The elevator doors closed again, and the light above began to blink, suggesting it was lowering once more. John stood seething now, Adele gripping his forearm.

"John," she said, pressing her lips. "Could you calm down, please?"

"Calm? I am calm. You calm down."

John yanked his arm away from her and marched towards two pristine silver doors etched with gold filigree, again flanked by two marble statues—this time of tigers instead of lions. Adele stared at the sealed doors, feeling like she'd been ushered into a boardroom instead of a small office for an acting company.

She remembered Leoni's admonishment. *Compagnia dei Cielo* had connections... and wealth.

"Into the lion's den," she murmured beneath her breath, reaching for one handle.

"Tiger's," John said, grabbing the other.

Together, they pulled open the door.

If they'd been intending to catch the occupants off guard, the effort would have been an abject failure. The attendees downstairs, no doubt, had already warned the occupants of their arrival.

And now, at the end of a long, glass table, beneath a black, sixty-inch television, five figures were staring directly at them.

Adele went stiff, clearing her throat slowly.

All five of the onlookers looked like they'd wandered off the pages of a Hollywood's "Sexiest Alive" list.

Two men and three women were sitting in padded leather chairs. One of the women in particular sat at the head of the table, in a chair just a smidgen larger than the others. Though perhaps this was just Adele's imagination.

"Do any of you speak a real language?" John called out in French, completely unaffected, it seemed, by the severe attention of all five figures.

Adele winced, resisting the urge to elbow her partner. "What he means to say, is does anyone speak English? French?"

The woman who sat furthest from them in the largest chair, directly beneath the television above was frowning over steepled fingers. She had sheets of paper in front of her, and two of the other people in the room seemed to be presenting her a photo book of images that Adele couldn't make out from so far away.

One of the men, a silver-haired fellow that looked a bit like George Clooney, leaned in, whispering something in the seated woman's ear.

"What is DGSI doing here?" the woman at the front of the table said in English, still peering over steepled fingers. She spoke like a queen addressing her subjects, all impatience and ice.

Adele shivered against the tone, trying to remember exactly why they'd come.

"We're sorry for bothering you," Adele said. "But we're investigating and need a second of your time... Mrs..."

"You can call me Harmony," the woman said without batting an eye. If she had, Adele suspected the glued-on eyelash extensions might have reached to her cheek. The woman's hair was dyed pure silver and the suit she wore matched with, of all things, stenciled snowflakes circling the collar and a scarf like white silk draped over her shoulders. The other beautiful people in the room kept glancing towards the snowflake woman and back, waiting, it seemed, for her reaction and looking for their cue.

"Mrs. Harmony," Adele said, trying again.

"No," the woman cut her off with a quick shake of her head. She didn't add anything further.

"Ms. Harmony?" Adele said, raising a questioning eyebrow.

"No," the woman replied, her eyes narrowing, her eyelash extensions fluttering again like the bars on a cage sliding back into place. "Just Harmony."

John coughed again, but this time, to Adele's relief, hid the word well enough.

“Right, Harmony,” she said, hesitantly. “We're here about—”

“I know why you're here,” the woman said, cutting Adele off again, and this time folding her hands in her lap. She moved, causing the silk scarf to shift about her shoulders.

“You just asked—” Adele tried to finish once more, but again the woman cut her off.

“We don't have time for this. Do you know who we are? Hmm? Of course you don't. The French never do. We are *Compagnia dei Cielo.* Have you heard of us? Of course you haven't. In a day's time, we'll be hosting one of the most prestigious masquerade balls in all of Italy. And right now...” She pressed a long finger straight down, bending it against the glass table. “You. Are. Interrupting.”

Adele blinked, too impressed by the sheer audacity to be much offended. John was trying to hide a snicker as a cough, holding his hand up to his lips, and Adele felt an urge to join him. She glanced off to the side, towards a golden tray beneath a second T.V. screen where a small little remote—spray painted silver—rested on a tasseled cushion.

“I...I'm not trying to interrupt,” Adele said. She raised her voice as Harmony's lips twitched, it seemed, to speak over her again. “And I ask you don't either for a moment. We're here about the murder of two women who were going to attend this ball of yours.”

At this, the other four pretty faces at the edges of the table all begin whispering, muttering to each other and shaking their heads. The two men who'd been presenting the photo book closed it swiftly, frowning from Harmony to the two agents and back.

“Ridiculous!” Harmony said, though, cutting off the mutterings and worried glances. “Absolutely ridiculous. No one is murdering girls attending our ball. No one!”

“I'm afraid the evidence suggests—”

“No one!” the woman slapped a hand against the glass table, but the sound seemed a bit hollow now. Everything about the spectacle seemed just that—spectacle. Adele could feel her patience being tested, but at the same time she remembered Leoni's admonishment. *Compagnia dei Cielo* came from money. They clearly also came from ego.

But she wasn't here about big-headed theater stars. So she swallowed her own pride and said, “I'm sure you're right. And I imagine we'll look through the guest list and conclude as much, and your party can go on without a hitch.”

“It isn't a party,” Harmony snapped. “It is crowning moment in the *Carnevale di Venezia.*”

“Certainly,” Adele said. “Well, this crowning moment will still take place. We have no interest in intruding and we certainly don't want to get the press involved in any way.” She didn't blink an eye at this last part and pushed smoothly on. “I imagine that would be horrible for business, which is why it is the very last thing I want to do. I'd far prefer to solve this quietly. If you would be so kind as to supply us with the current guest list for your,” she swallowed, “crowning moment. We can be out of your lovely hair.”

Harmony stared at Adele, as if she'd been slapped. Slowly, her cheeks turning crimson above her silken scarf; she rose to her feet, revealing the full extent of the dress she wore. Icicles dangled from the edges of her sleeves, tinkling like crystal.

“No one is murdering guests,” Harmony repeated, firmly. “And if we hear a whisper of it in the papers, I will personally sue you and your agency. Agent...”

John interjected, “Melody,” he said in his heavily accented English, without batting an eye. “She just goes by Melody.”

Adele had never felt such an urge to stomp on a man's foot before. She exhaled slowly, trying her best to keep as respectful a posture as she could manage.

The coordinator for *Compagnia dei Cielo*, though, didn't seem to realize she was being mocked. “Agent Melody, this had best *not* reach the media in any way. It could prove disastrous for our ball, and even more for the Venetian economy. Do you understand? Damages alone will be worth a hundred times what you will possibly be able to compensate. Do you understand?”

“I understand that we need to handle this delicately,” Adele said, side-stepping any desire to get in a back-and-forth barking contest. “But the best way for us to do this is without getting judges or legal teams involved, right? Which means if you supply us with the guest list, quietly, you have my word we won't speak of it to the press or anyone. Why would we? We're just trying to catch a killer. Besides, if the violence escalates...” Adele trailed off, shrugging. “Who knows, the authorities might decide to shut down portions of large gatherings. For the sake of safety. At the very least, we may have to place a large police presence throughout the city.”

“Buzz kill,” John supplied, nodding.

Harmony sighed, her long eyelash extensions fluttering again. She muttered darkly to herself, shaking her head, and then glanced towards the standing man who looked a bit like George Clooney, and whispered something beneath her breath.

The man nodded once, and then circled the table, marching towards where John and Adele stood, his eyes frowning, it seemed, but his eyebrows painted on his forehead.

"Come with me," he muttered in English, waving a hand.

"You'll give us the list?"

The man said, "It's in my office. Yes. Come. Please. Harmony is very busy. Come, come."

Again, feeling like a dog following the orders of its owner, Adele sighed and fell into step behind eyebrow Clooney.

John coughed delicately again, seemingly enjoying himself far too much for Adele's comfort as they exited through the ornate, swinging doors. On this side of the room, though, the doors weren't nearly so impressive as they'd been on the way in.

Following would-be Clooney from the impressive board room to a smaller office hidden behind a row of potted plants felt like stepping from Narnia into a dreary cubicle. Behind a thin wooden door, a simple desk and two filing cabinets ornamented an otherwise unimpressive room with a window facing the alley.

"Nice décor," John murmured, sidling in after Adele and Clooney.

"I'm the accountant," the man said as if this were an explanation. "Hang on, give me a second." His English was nearly perfect, but Adele could trace the faintest of accents in the vowels. She waited patiently by the door and the man coughed, wiggling fingers. "Mind closing that," he said. "Some of the even coordinators aren't part of *Compagnia dei Cielo* and we're going for a bit of a... well *impression.*"

"It's a very impressive impression," said Adele.

Eyebrows shrugged sheepishly as he hunched over his computer, and muttered, "It pays to keep us afloat," he said. "Don't judge Ms. Herrera too harshly."

"Ms. Herrera, that's Harmony?"

The man pressed a key on his computer and then, swallowing, turned to a printer. For a moment, they all stood in silence, listening to the whir of the machine. Then, he turned, presenting two sheets of paper to Adele and John.

"There you are," he said, simply. "That," he pointed to the sheet he'd handed John, "is the event organizers, caterers and employees." He pointed to the paper he'd handed Adele. "And those are our guests. It goes without saying, but Ms. Herrera is very serious. If either of those lists end up in media hands, she will invoke legal. I don't mean that as a threat, but our business is a competitive one. I hope you understand." The man shrugged, glancing from John to Adele.

Adele, though, was too busy reading the list to reply. As her eyes scanned down the rows of names, flitting from one column to a second, to a third, to a fourth, her frown only deepened.

"What is it?" John murmured beneath his breath.

She continued to scan the list, feeling a prickle along the back of her neck. Her cheeks felt warm and her frown was now a full scowl. "Hundreds of names," she murmured.

"It is a very popular ball," Clooney supplied.

"Yes, but also this," Adele snapped, tapping one finger against the paper and causing it to crinkle.

John leaned in, reading the indicated row.

"Mr. Amos?" he said. "What about him?"

Adele lowered her finger and John read, "*Mr. Amos...*"

She lowered her finger to *another* line again. "Mr. Amos," John said a third time. "I don't get it."

"Ah, well, some of our guests buy multiple tickets," Clooney said, clearing his throat. "For friends, family, events. In fact, it's quite rare to only have a single ticket purchase. The event is more of a social gathering."

Adele's eyes skipped across the list of hundreds. Every few lines, she found a block of names with tickets ordered by a single person. On one row, between numbers three hundred and three hundred and twenty-eight, nearly thirty rows were occupied by the same name. A Cleo Iadanza.

Adele shook her head, looking away from the paper and glancing at the accountant before regarding John. She shrugged. "No way to know who these tickets are for..." She glanced at the accountant, adding, "Is there?"

He winced, shaking his head. "All the information we have is there."

She sighed, looking back to John. "Well?"

He frowned past her. "Who has access to this list?" the tall Frenchman said, pointing insistently. "Hmm? Who can read it?"

Clooney crossed his arms now. "Well, I suppose there's me... Ms. Herrera *and,*" he said, emphatically, "any number of people coordinating the event. Caterers, and their entire staff. Performers, and their staff. Decorators, the theater staff..." he trailed off, shrugging. "Not just people organizing the ball, but also other event organizers of the Venice festival. We all use the same ticketing platform and tend to share information pertinent to audience capacities. It's a one-week event, so it's important everyone knows how many employees to hire, how much merchandise to order... And the like." He winced, shaking his head. "At least a hundred people have seen that list. Maybe more. It's the reason Ms. Herrera was so willing to give it to you."

Adele frowned, folding the copy of the guest list and sliding it into her pocket. "Thank you for your help," she said. "We'll see ourselves out."

She turned, still frowning, trying to think through the information.

The guest list was too long, and the names hidden beneath the ticket purchasers. There would be no way to track that many people in such a short amount of time. Already, Adele knew they were on a clock. The killer was hunting tourists, and time was rapidly running out.

At the same time, John had been right to question access to the list. It was a smaller number of people... Maybe there was an angle that way.

John reached the elevator before her, jabbing a finger against the descending arrow and looking past her, over the potted plants towards the accountant's door where he watched them through the gap in the frame.

Frowning, and turning as if to hide his mouth, John lowered his voice and said, "Think we split up?"

"Might be the only move," she replied. "No way we can cover that ground teamed up. You want guests or employees?"

John wiggled his own piece of paper. "Fewer names on mine—I'll keep it."

"Great," Adele muttered. "I'm not going to be able to make it through all these names," she said. "I need a way to narrow it."

"Might be good to look for the victims' names," John said. "Maybe narrow it that way." He shrugged as the elevator dinged and opened above the aquarium. The two of them stepped into the compartment, turning to face the ornate hall as the doors slowly slid shut once more.

Adele didn't relish the prospect of splitting up, but John was right. There was no way they'd be able to cover enough ground together.

She'd just have to hope one of them got lucky or... better yet... that the killer made a mistake before it was too late.

CHAPTER FOURTEEN

Fiorella Lettiere stretched like a cat in sunshine, moving through the motions of the exercise, her hands passing over her knee to her toes. At the same time, she curved her other leg back, slowly, feeling the tautness of her muscles, the way in which her body obeyed her intention.

She shifted across the vibrant green yoga mat, arching her back, putting both hands on the mat and then lifting one leg up, high, over her head, pointing it at the ceiling.

She held the pose, breathing in, out, slowly, her abdomen muscles clenched, her teeth similarly braced.

She counted in her mind, using her breathing pattern to keep track before lowering her leg again and then lifting the next one. She tilted her chin, carefully, avoiding a rush of blood to her down-turned face.

She then lowered both feet, lifted her hands off the mat and stretched, pulling herself to full attention. As she did, her eyes glanced to the mirror above the cabinet in the corner of the small living room she shared with her roommate.

In the reflection of the mirror, she spotted her dress for the masquerade ball hosted by *Compagnia dei Cielo*. Her eyes lingered on the lacework and oddly shaped butterfly buttons—made of actual silver. Of course, the dress would have been *far* out of her price range if not for her new boyfriend.

Her lips turned slightly as she paused, upright on the yoga mat, considering the last few dates she'd gone on over the intervening weeks leading up to the festival.

In fact, she'd only just returned from a dinner date. Perhaps he was more than a decade her senior—something her roommate Drina never failed to point out. But Drina was just jealous... especially after she'd seen the stream of gifts. Who knew Germans, even Germans on prolonged vacations in Venice, could be so generous with their new girlfriend.

Not that Fiorella was complaining.

She paused before resuming her exercise, glancing at the clock above the mirror. Her roommate was due to return home following a late work shift. Tourist season of all things. As a Venetian herself, Fiorella didn't *love* the crowded streets or the loud city, but the festivals alone were well worth it—plus, those without wealthy German boyfriends benefited from the influx of commerce.

Her eyes flicked towards the mirror again, glancing at her dress draped carefully over the couch. She still hadn't picked out a mask for the ball, but already she could feel the rising sense of excitement.

Compagnia dei Cielo were hosting a new masquerade. She'd been to the others over the last few years. But this new one, put on by the famous theater troop was bound to be a noteworthy affair. Everyone was talking about it. Even her boyfriend, who'd bought the dress, seemed to have heard of it.

At that moment, she heard the front door to the apartment open and shut.

She'd left it unlocked for her roommate. Drina was back.

"How was work?" she called out, then bent over again, hands placed on the mat once more. Her foot raised behind her, stiff now, extended like a plank. She winced against the throb in her stomach, but kept the position, breathing in, out, slowly, feeling sweat prickle across her forehead.

She heard her roommate's footsteps, the soft sound of breathing.

"Drina?" she asked, still upside-down. "How was work? Did Adamo bother you again?" She caught her breath, exhaling once more.

When her roommate didn't answer, she frowned, twisting just a bit to glance in the mirror which reflected past her in the direction of the small apartment door.

She glimpsed a flicker of motion in the mirror, someone crossing in front of where her dress draped over the couch. Someone approaching her.

The breathing grew louder... A familiar sound. The same sort of intentional, quiet puffs of someone uncomfortable in the Venetian masks.

Masks?

Her eyes flicked along the mirror where she maintained her pose, her body still tremoring with the effort.

Her roommate glanced into the mirror.

Except...

It wasn't Drina.

This person was wearing a pale mask—a man, standing directly behind her.

Her heart collapsed and her lungs loosened a horrible scream. She dropped the pose, scrambling over the mat and tripping in a desperate attempt to spin around, to locate the threat. For a brief moment of cognitive dissonance, as she spun, she desperately hoped perhaps she'd just been mistaken. Maybe Drina was pulling a prank.

But as she rounded and her vision adjusted, sweat slipping down the corner of her eye, her gaze landed on a *large* figure, a tall, barrel-chested man wearing a simple, unadorned Venetian mask.

In one hand, he had something glinting—something sharp. A knife?

In the other... almost more horrifying, he held a second mask. This one he waved in her direction as if offering it to her.

"Please," she gasped, breathing heavily, her back to the window, feeling the cool glass against her sweaty skin. Her eyes darted to the apartment door behind the intruder. "Please—who are you? Drina!" She screamed again.

The man seemed in no rush. He moved towards her, cutting off any attempt to flee towards the door.

Behind her, Fiorella heard the soft sound of a chugging engine. The moped Drina used to go to and from work. Her roommate was back...

"Drina!" she screamed again.

But Drina would have to park, first. In the sparsely available spots outside the building. She'd have to then reach the buzzers. Enter the code. Take the stairs... Reach the door.

Far, far too late.

The man in the mask descended on her. She tried to bolt past him, but fingers caught her curls, yanking, hard. Her head snapped back in pain, her chin angled up, her neck exposed.

She tried to yell again, but the man jerked her hair again and she let loose a sob of pain instead.

The pale, inexpressive mask stared down at her as the man's hand whipped forward, and a blade flashed in the dimming light.

She could still hear the chug of her roommate's moped before she died.

CHAPTER FIFTEEN

The smell of flowers wafted on the air, intermingling with the overbearing scent of the canal behind him. John had given the waterway a wide berth as he'd strolled to this particular outdoor stall. He glanced up at the title of the small, river-side shop, and double checked the list he'd been provided.

Marotta Flowers.

He glanced at the stall once more. The same name painted in curving, flowing green and pink and purple letters, matching the wares displayed beneath the small umbrella. An older woman was sitting on a small stool, smiling up at John and displaying a row of pearly whites with more gaps than teeth.

"Flowers?" the woman said in English.

"No thank you," John replied, tiring once again of the foreign language. He had to resign himself to the inevitability of it though, especially given the tourist nature of this case.

"Are you Margherita Marotta," he asked, consulting his list of festival employees again.

"Yes," she said, nodding. "Flowers?"

John frowned. "No, thank you. I had a couple of questions. I was sent to you by Mr. Fazio." He waved a hand across the canal towards the edge of a bridge where a man was walking along a thin wire from the middle of the bridge to a boat tied off at the dock. Crowds were watching, clapping. The man made a big show of almost losing his balance, before doing a front flip, and landing on the bouncing wire.

He spread his arms and bowed, still over the canal and everyone clapped again.

"Damn fool," John muttered. He glanced back at Mrs. Marotta. "Fazio said you were having trouble recently with one of the festival employees. Is this true?"

"Flowers?"

John nearly bit his tongue.

"No, flowers. Are you having trouble with an employee, Mrs. Marotta?"

She winced, shaking her head apologetically and shrugging.

John resisted the urge to scream. His hand hesitated, nearly moving towards his phone, but then he froze. He refused to do it. He simply wouldn't. Christopher Leoni might have been willing to translate, but John didn't need anything from that underwear model. He'd been working cases long before that toothpaste commercial had shown up on his doorstep. He could still remember the last case they'd worked together. The man had nearly snapped his ankle repelling from a helicopter onto a moving train because of a faulty harness.

"Amateur," John muttered. "Mrs. Moratta," he said, slowly, pulling up his phone and shifting to Google translate. He pressed French for the first box, and then Italian for the second. He cleared his throat and spoke into the microphone. "Trouble with an employee."

He waited for a moment... Then, words appeared in the second box... He frowned. The words were in English, not Italian. He gritted his teeth.

Now, Mrs. Moratta was watching his hands. She leaned in, peering at his phone.

"French?" she said, suddenly, spotting the box over his thumb.

John's heart skipped. "Yes," he said, quickly, in the best language ever invented. "Yes, please. Do you speak French?"

She smiled at him, nodding. "Yes, a bit, yes." She had an accent, but still, John had never heard anything so clear and sweet.

He resisted the urge to lean down and kiss her. "I'll buy flowers," he said, gratitude welling in his chest. "As many flowers as you'd like. Just first, I need to know," he said, slowing down a bit and enunciating precisely, "Fazio over there, the one playing fast and loose with the canal—he mentioned you'd been having trouble with one of the festival employees. Is that true?"

Mrs. Moratta leaned back, folding her arms over her stomach, smiling at John. "Flowers?" she said in French.

He nearly yelled, but then, his eyes narrowed at the shrewd look in the woman's eyes.

"Alright," he muttered. "Have it your way." He pulled his wallet out, peeling off a crisp hundred euro note—his entire spend for the day. "How many flowers will that get me?"

She beamed at him, pulled out two red roses and handed them to him.

"Fifty per flower," he muttered. "Steep." For a moment, John considered the flowers, wondering if perhaps he could give them to Adele... Even as he thought it, though, he snorted and shook his head.

She'd just spent a month ignoring him. No sense tossing more ammunition on to her side of the line... Then again, Adele was anything but petty. Not where important things were concerned. He sighed softly, returning his attention to the florist who was speaking again.

"For the flowers *and* information," she said, in French. "Yes... I've had some trouble. Normally, the stalls are opened by the festival. But last few days I've had to open myself. No help with the flowers. No help with the stand." She shook her head, wagging a finger impatiently. "Not good," she said in English.

"No, not good," John replied.

"So one of the employees just ditched? Know his name by any chance?"

"I know more than that," she said, smiling widely. "Flowers?"

John pointed a finger at her. "I like you, lady, but don't push it or I'll take my money back and chuck your bloody flowers in the canal."

She frowned a bit now but seemed to decide the large Frenchman was being serious. Which he was.

"Normally," she said, treading the words carefully, picking them out with a frown of concentration as she translated them in her mind. "Little Jacopo."

"Who's that?"

"No little now," she said, shaking her head. "Use to be. But now just Jacopo Siciliano."

The name slid off her tongue twice as fast and comfortable as the rest of the words in French.

"I see. Any idea why Little Jacopo has been missing work?"

The woman winced, shaking her head. But it wasn't denying knowledge, rather it seemed a commiseration. "Poor Jacopo," she said. "His heart bread."

"His heart bread?" John said, frowning.

"No. Sorry. Break. His heart break." she nodded once.

"Someone broke up with Little Jacopo? That's why he's skipping work?"

She nodded happily.

"Happen to have an address for Little Jacopo?"

"He young," she said. "No. She is young."

"She? The girlfriend."

The woman nodded, her eyes widening in the excited and scandalized way that only florists of a certain age could manage.

"Oh... So Little Jacopo was dating a much younger woman, is that what you're saying?"

She smiled again, nodding, tapping her nose. "Flowers?"

"Keep the rest of your flowers, lady. Thanks." John poked the roses into his jacket pocket. "How about an address?" he said, trying again.

She sighed, glancing at the money in her hand and the flowers as if wondering if she might be able to press further. But then, she conceded and said, "Yes. 13 Calle Basego."

John was already moving, glancing at his phone and nodding his thanks. He hastily typed in the address, following the purple line, and frowning as he began to move.

***

Little Jacopo Siciliano only lived about a ten-minute jog from the florist stand. John approached the apartment, wedged between two others, all of them tan, all of them at least four floors and all of them with even smaller alleys than the first one he'd attempted to enter.

John reached the front door, scanning the names on the buzzers. Siciliano was the third one up.

"There we go," John muttered to himself.

He glanced over his shoulder, towards the canal behind him, and then eyed a gathering of small children playing hopscotch on the sidewalk with multi-colored chalk. "Might wanna stand back," he said, nodding knowingly at the kids.

They ignored him completely.

He reached out, pressing the buzzer with Siciliano's name on it, then waited.

To his surprise, it buzzed nearly instantly. No voice, no questions, just a buzz. The door clicked open and, frowning to himself, John pushed into the building.

He wished he'd taken the time to look up more about Jacopo Siciliano... Surely the old lady would have mentioned if the man had a criminal record, wouldn't she have? Besides, how dangerous could someone named *Little* Jacopo really be?

John took the stairs up to the second landing, pausing outside the door marked with the big silver numeral 3.

He hesitated briefly, wondering exactly what sort of posture he ought to go for. Contain and control...

He nodded to himself, that would have to do. Leave the schmoozing to Adele. Sometimes even one trick ponies could win a race.

He cleared his throat, raised his large fist and then, in a booming voice, bellowed, “Jacopo Siciliano! DGSI! Open up!”

He pounded his hand *hard* against the doorway. And then, stepped back, one hand darting to his weapon, his eyes fixed on the doorway as he scowled.

No answer.

John frowned. The man had been quick enough to buzz him in, but now wasn't responding. He tried again, pounding his hand against the frame once more. “Jacopo Siciliano!” He yelled. “Open up! DGSI!”

Perhaps he wasn't yelling loud enough. He inhaled deeply, preparing for the best bellow yet...

And then, the door swung open *fast* and a large form came barreling out. A thick shoulder, like from an American linebacker, caught him in the chest and sent John reeling backwards. He slammed into the opposite door, watching a large blur burst down the stairs, racing.

John cursed... Little indeed. The man had to be as large as he was.

“Stop!” John yelled.

But Jacopo, perhaps, predictably at this point, didn't. He slammed into the door at the base of the stairs, tearing out into the streets.

John growled, keeping his gun holstered and breaking into a sprint himself.

“Stop!” he yelled.

Jacopo yelled something in Italian over his shoulder.

John supposed now wasn't the time to request for French. He continued chasing as Little Jacopo, who looked more like a *giant* Jacopo bolted in one large leap over the chalk outline of the hopscotch. A couple of the kids chucked chalk at his back, but the absent festival employee kept running.

“Stop!” John tried again. “You stupid lump! Stop!”

Jacopo was now making his way to a bridge, heading towards the angled structure. By now, though, the large man was wheezing, gasping as he did.

John, not for the first time, felt a flash of gratitude he'd finally decided to pick up running over the summer.

“Don't move!” John tried again.

Jacopo, winded now, spun around, fists raised. The man looked a bit like a cross between a grizzly bear and an oncoming train.

John's eyes narrowed. Jacopo's thick fists danced beneath his chin as he stood gasping at the front of the bridge, trying to regain his deflated breath.

“Bitch!” Jacopo said. A word that needed no translation.

John lowered his head, his chest still aching from where Jacopo had slammed into it. Instead of swinging a punch, John kept his head tucked and *dove* hard.

Jacopo had positioned himself in just such a way so his back was to the railing of the canal. John had noticed the posture. Perhaps the man had thought with water to his back, he'd be safe.

But if there was one thing John hated more than water, more than Venice's endless canals, it was being slammed in the chest by a suspect.

And so he collided with Jacopo, grunting as he did, feeling a lancing pain behind his ear as a fist collided and then, the two of them with shouts, toppled over the railing into the canal.

A mighty splash, followed by a mouthful of horrible-tasting water. John spluttered and kicked, dragging desperately at the large bean-bag who he'd tackled. For a moment, images flashes across his mind. John went stiff, like a plank of wood. His ears echoed with machine-gun fire, the shouts of men, and the sound of explosions. The heat of sand against his cheeks, the lapping of saltwater against a grainy shore. He blinked, shaking his head in the water, splashing it across his cheeks as he growled.

Even still, as he focused, forcing himself to snap out of it, the images and memories still played across his mind's eye. He heard the screams of his friends, the sound of shrapnel ripping through—

John clenched his teeth until a tooth hurt, gasping heavily now, treading water.

Jacopo, though, wasn't giving him a moment to recover. Instead, the large Venetian was kicking at John, hard, trying to shove him under. For a moment, they tangled, splashing around in the frothing water, neither speaking, both gasping and grunting in fury and frustration. John hated swimming—but even pilots had to go through basic training, so he could passably float. The memories were dull aches now, still resounding in his ears and playing across his mind's eye.

Jacopo kicked again and John kicked just to maintain his head above water. He was anything but a strong swimmer, and with the muscle mass he had, even floating was often optional.

Still, he wasn't about to drown because of a man named Little Jacopo. He'd never hear the end of it from Adele. Besides, John wasn't about to let a little bout of PTSD derail him now. So he reached out and gripped the man's throat, *hard.*

Jacopo began to wheeze, trying to kick away and swim, but John's thumb and forefinger pressed until the man was gasping desperately. A second longer, and the big guy went limp, unconscious.

Growling to himself now, hefting the limp form of the large festival worker, John kicked, desperately, moving towards the lowest dock at a slow, steady pace. Adele might have swum in high school, but John had survived in high school.

And this time would be no different.

He kicked a bit more, floating with the current, and dragging his suspect along behind him, using the man's own momentum to float them both back towards safety.

God, how he hated Venice.

CHAPTER SIXTEEN

Adele now found herself at an Italian precinct. She'd called in backup in the form of Agent Christopher Leoni who sat across from her.

Adele frowned in frustration, feeling the weight of the task before her creasing her brow in a frown. The expression was mirrored by Agent Leoni across the table. The handsome Italian was shaking his head, his lips moving silently as he read the names on the list in front of him. Every couple of moments, Adele would glance at her own list, her eyes searching the various columns of information, before returning to Christopher and watching him to see if he was faring any better.

At least the precinct was well illuminated.

"Anything?" Adele said.

"I'm not sure exactly what I'm supposed to be finding," he replied.

Adele shrugged helplessly. "Potential victims. Where the killer might strike next."

Agent Leoni sighed softly, moving his finger along the names again. "I can't help but notice," he said softly, "we don't have a date of birth for any of these."

Adele winced. This had become readily apparent on her first read-through of the list, and one of the reasons she'd asked for Leoni's help. She had been stuck for the last couple of hours trying to find a clue hidden somewhere in the list. But the names were often repeated by the ticket purchaser, and there was no way to tell how old the guests on the ballroom list were. Not only that, but the information contained didn't even tell where the guests were from. Tourist or Venetian, they were all listed the same. Adele could pick out a name here or there, judging by the familiarity of the region, but even this didn't help. There had to be at least two hundred names on the list that could potentially be tourists.

"I don't know what to do next," she murmured.

"Where's John?"

"Tracking another lead."

"Have you thought of running the names through any database?"

"I could, but something like that, with this many names would take hours. Plus, it doesn't help with the sections of guests who had tickets purchased *for* them."

Leoni sighed softly, which, for the good-natured, quiet man was akin to a growl of frustration. "Did you think of finding who might have access to the list? Try to find the culprit rather than the victim?"

Adele nodded. "Already did it. The vendors, employees, and participants at the ball are in the hundreds too."

Both of them leaned back, slumping in their chairs. Agent Leoni scratched at his chin, and finally put a hand over the list, as if trying to hide it from view. He sighed softly, and then with the air of a man changing the subject he said, "This is near where I live you know."

Grateful for the opportunity to look away from the list herself, Adele watched Christopher. "In Venice? I didn't know that."

"No, I'm about thirty minutes north of here. In Treviso."

"I've never been actually. I hear it's nice."

"Do you think the killer is targeting people outside of Venice? Or Italy? In the former case, our list of suspects is much larger."

Adele frowned at this horrible thought, but before she could reply, there was a sudden banging sound on the interrogation room door they had borrowed.

Adele heard yelling voices, growling, and she spun around, staring as the door was flung open.

A large man with blunt features, his hands cuffed behind him was shoved unceremoniously into the room. Behind him, the tall, lanky frame of Agent John Renee strolled in after, his bangs damp, his clothing, similarly, seeming wet. Adele could even hear his shoes squish as he marched the equally waterlogged civilian in front of him. The door slammed shut behind John.

"We need a seat for our guest," John growled.

Agent Leoni was already on his feet, moving quickly over to help secure the strange suspect, and guide the large, beefy man into the chair across from Adele. John swiped the list of guests' names, as the suspect was shoved into a chair, and then, with a sigh, he crumpled the paper, and tossed it at the man. It bounced off his nose, and rolled down his knee, onto the floor.

The blunt featured fellow blinked in surprise, but then his eyes narrowed in frustration, and he yammered something in Italian.

"Who is this?" Adele said.

"Jacopo," John said simply. "He ran."

"You're both wet."

"He smelled, so I gave him a bath," John said.

Adele shared a look with Christopher, who seemed to be doing his best to suppress a grin. Adele looked at Jacopo.

The man narrowed his mean eyes, staring from one to the other, and shaking his head quickly from side to side, muttering a series of dark words in Italian.

"Christopher," John said, with a growl in his voice, "Can you ask our princess here why he ran?"

A brief Italian exchange ensued. Jacopo looked reluctant to speak at all, but he kept shooting mean-eyed looks towards John. John glared back, spinning his finger around and around as if to say, *get on with it.*

Christopher leaned in, nearly imperceptibly, his eyes flashing in the poorly illuminated room. He reached out a placating hand, placing it on Jacopo's arm. The man stiffened as if he'd been shot, his eyes traced down to Leoni's fingers as if in a sudden horror.

Christopher gave the man's arm a reassuring pat and then released the grip, seemingly content he'd managed to redirect the large fellow's attention. Then, in Italian he spoke softly.

Adele blinked, watching in interest to see if Leoni's more comforting strategy might work. The definition of good cop, bad cop—but Jacopo didn't seem a connoisseur of late-night detective shows. He seemed to settle a bit, his expression less hostile as he shrugged once and glanced surreptitiously off to the side, murmuring briefly.

Leoni nodded as if in understanding and asked something else. Again, Jacopo paused, but again responded, nodding more adamantly now. Leoni's expression flickered with a frown, but he hid it quickly and continued. Now, the suspect's voice was getting louder, and he pounded an elbow on the table all of a sudden, unable to use his cuffed hands. The startling noise caused Adele to jolt.

“What's he saying?” she said quickly.

Leoni rubbed at his jaw, glancing over at her and shaking his head. “He says he ran because he thought Agent Renee was there about something else.”

“Else? What does he think he's here for now?”

Leoni winced. “He seems to have inferred, from the three of us, that it's something violent. He wants to give his most...” Leoni cleared his throat, adjusting his posture and shooting a sidelong glance towards the suspect, “sincere assurances that he is not a violent man. I told him I'd relay this.”

Adele stared at the blunt-faced fellow, glancing towards John and quirking an eyebrow.

"Seemed violent enough trying to drown me," John muttered. "Threw his hands up when he saw me coming."

"Ah yes," Leoni said, nodding hurriedly. "I think I might help there to." He nodded in a sort of placating way towards Jacopo to offset the forming expression of worry as he glanced between the agents speaking in English. "Our friend here recently broke up with his girlfriend. He says there have been some... *miscommunications* with her. Police have been involved."

John snorted, wiggling his phone and handing it to Leoni. "Miscommunications my ass," said the large Frenchman. "I looked up his rap sheet. Bastard's a stalker. Been stalking his ex—who's about ten years younger than him, I might add. Not a good look for a twenty-eight-year old," he continued, clearing his throat and leveling a harsh gaze on Jacopo. "Can you tell the princess that I don't believe him? Ask him where he was two nights ago."

Leoni turned towards the suspect, repeating the question. The man shook his head vehemently, glaring at John, but glancing at Adele, his eyes wide and imploring. He murmured something and then shrugged.

Leoni coughed delicately. "He says he doesn't know what you're talking about. He's lovestruck—not a criminal."

"Dumbstruck more like," John muttered.

"I mean, you *did* hit him," Adele muttered. She winced, remembering Executive Foucault's warning about John's behavior. For now, the media hadn't butted in, but if he kept taking swings at suspects, this anonymity wouldn't last.

John glared at her. "I don't get it," he grunted. Then he glanced back at Leoni. "Ask him about Lorraine Strasser. Use her name. Mention Rebekah James."

Leoni turned and complied with the request.

Here, Adele paid close attention, her eyes fixed on the Italian thug's face. But if the names registered at all, he didn't show it in the least. He simply shrugged, grunted without a word and gave a shake of his head.

"Says he—"

"Doesn't know," John cut off Leoni. "Right. Well, I don't buy it. Guy's lying. He probably killed them because he has it out for young, attractive women. I know the sort. Just look at his little pug eyes."

Jacopo seemed to realize he was being insulted now. He turned to John, sticking out his blunt chin and spitting a few choice words back of his own.

"What's he saying?" John demanded.

Agent Leoni blinked. “He... in so many words, suggests perhaps you are ill-suited to conclude anything.”

“Did he call me a dumbass? I heard it. I know some Italian. You're the dumbass!” John yelled, jamming a finger at Jacopo. “Hear me? I'll rip your ears off.”

Jacopo spat towards John and the tall Frenchman growled, stepping in, his fists balling. For a moment, as Renee's *long* shadow stretched over him, Jacopo's eyes widened and he let out a small squeak, seemingly realizing perhaps he'd taken it a step too far. The chair he was seated in scraped as Jacopo tried to inch away.

Adele, though, intercepted the large man, placing a hand against his chest and pressing against him. “Don't do anything Foucault will make you regret,” she said, firmly.

John glanced at her, shaking his head. “He did it, Adele. I can tell. Look at his stupid face. He *did* it.”

“Maybe,” she said, softly. “But what if he's telling the truth? What if he ran because of the stalking charges?”

“I... It's not...”

Before the words could form on her partner's lips, though, Adele's phone began to buzz. At the same time, John's went off, and a second later, Leoni's vibrated as well.

Adele frowned, and all three agents lifted their devices as one. Their countenances darkened in a near perfect sequence, their brows simultaneously furrowing.

“A third?” Adele murmured, the cold device to her ear. A similar, frigid sensation reached her belly, twisting it like a clenched fist. She swallowed, her back prickling. “When? Just now... You're sure? Alright. We're on our way.”

CHAPTER SEVENTEEN

Adele stared at the body. She wore pink workout clothes with a blue sweatband and lay on top of a green yoga mat, facing the window of the small apartment. The woman's colorful and crumpled form seemed like a wilted flower, and though the windows were closed, Adele felt a shiver up her spine.

Agent Leoni stood in one corner of the cramped space, speaking with the victim's roommate. The younger woman in question had a blanket thrown over her shoulders and was trembling, her eyes wide, her expression gaunt. She didn't seem to be answering any of Christopher's queries, and another police officer, standing next to the woman, was doing his best to hold off a paramedic, who was now speaking in louder tones, gesturing in frustration towards the woman, as if to say, *look at the state of her.*

Adele's sympathy didn't just linger with the roommate though. She glanced back towards the victim. Blood stained the yoga mat, the red liquid spreading across the green fabric and onto the carpet. The woman was laying on her back, and Adele could see the single, swift cut in her neck. Outside the window, she glimpsed the coroner and two assistants readying a stretcher and spreading clear plastic over it.

She looked away, glancing back towards what remained of Fiorella Lettiere. John was by the window, glancing over the coroner's head, into the distance, his eyes deep and troubled.

"Another mask," Adele murmured, softly.

John didn't look back, he didn't grunt, he just stared through the glass out into the fading night.

This new mask was a simple, plain, pale covering just for the eyes. The victim's cold lips could be seen pressed in a hard line just below the pale half mask. The coloring was a bit different, but the shape and style was the exact same as the first two masks. And again, as Adele leaned in, she realized the mask wasn't strapped to the woman's head, but rather just laid over her face. And this time, the red lipstick mark was over the woman's lips, crisscrossing down her chin and up to her cheek.

"He's taking one every day," Adele said, softly, "he's escalating."

"She was Venetian," John said, bluntly, still facing the window.

Adele looked up, frowning. "Excuse me?"

"The girl, she was Venetian. Not a tourist."

It took Adele a moment, but then she glanced around the rented apartment, glanced towards the Italian roommate. She winced, realizing the implications of John's words. "Shit," she said.

"Shit is right," John said, glancing back. His eyes landed on the body, and his face creased in pain. He gritted his teeth, looking away sharply. "Double shit. We're slow, Adele. Way too slow."

Adele felt a jolt of worry, anxiety swirling in her stomach. She felt grief wanting to settle across her shoulders. "I know," she murmured. Images flashed across her mind's eye. *Bleeding... always bleeding...* Always late. Just a second too slow. Adele wanted to shout, but she kept her temper in check, one hand balled at her waist. Vaguely, as she stood there, her mind wandered back to the raincoat closet in her apartment. Back to the little brown package Robert had left her, where she had hidden it out of sight in the little, dark corner of the space. Maybe it was her fault these killers kept getting away. Her refusal to accept help from others... Maybe she was overthinking it.

Adele watched the paramedic, who had now managed to extricate the roommate from Leoni, guiding her towards the door, but pausing, as the coroner with the stretcher tried to navigate around them.

Adele looked away from the body, her eyes scanning the sparse furniture for any sign of a weapon, any sign of *anything.* But the room was clean; even the furniture hadn't been knocked about.

Leoni approached from behind, murmuring, "She's in shock; the paramedics won't let anyone speak with her now."

Adele looked up, "Did she see anything?"

Leoni shrugged. "It doesn't sound like it. Sounds like she got back pretty close to the kill, though. Paramedic says the victim couldn't have been dead for more than two hours."

"From when she found her?" Adele asked.

"No. From when *we* arrived."

Adele's eyes widened at the significance, and John voiced the realization. "That means the girl found her roommate dead almost instantly after the kill," he said, quietly.

All three of them stood over the body, facing each other, but lost in their own thoughts.

For Adele, she knew the killer was escalating, and now they would have to rethink their approach. He wasn't targeting tourists. Venetians now too. Fiorella Lettiere was a native.

"How old was she?" She asked, looking to John.

"Twenty-three," he said, shaking his head in disgust.

"See anything by the window?"

John shrugged, glancing again towards the window, but then looking back at her. "Nothing. He's not gonna leave a clue. He's already done this three times, maybe more. He's getting better as he goes and picking up the pace."

Adele breathed slowly, glancing around the room. "Another young, beautiful woman. But a Venetian. He doesn't care about nationality. It's their youth, their beauty that seems to attract him."

"Sexual sadist?" Leoni asked.

But Adele shook her head. "Doesn't seem to fit. He's not doing anything with the bodies. He's not even posing them. The only adornment is the mask, which he provides. He kills them quick, mercifully, if such a thing could be said. He's not trying to exact pain. It doesn't fit with a sadist. Sex doesn't seem to be the motive."

"They're young and they're beautiful," John murmured. "Sex has something to do with it."

Adele wrinkled her nose, shaking her head. "Perhaps tangentially. But this is more about him than them. Something else is going on. It's not money, either. He doesn't rob them. Look," she said, nodding towards the television, and a laptop on the table. "He could have taken either of those but didn't. With the other victims, he left them with cash in their wallets."

"Alright," said Leoni, "so what's the killer after?"

Adele shivered as the coroner's two assistants rolled the stretcher towards them.

She didn't like thinking like this. There was no benefit to it. But what more could she do? Standing over the body as they were, discussing it in such callous terms, it was enough to turn her stomach. But then again, the killer was operating with cold calculation. There were no defensive wounds. He wasn't stalking people to try and scare them. He wasn't inflicting pain.

"I don't know," Adele said, quietly.

John growled and turned, brushing past the coroner, and pushing towards the door. "We damn well better find out," he snapped. "Or this is just the beginning."

Adele stared after her retreating partner as he slipped through the door into the night. She could feel Agent Leoni's gaze on her. "He seems to be taking it personally," Christopher murmured.

Adele shook her head. "I don't know why. He doesn't normally get like this. Something about their age, their youth, it bothers him." She shrugged.

"And perhaps it *should* bother him; maybe I'm just too use to it," Leoni said, shaking his head sadly. "I wish I could say this was the first young victim I've encountered, but we both know that to be a lie."

Adele looked at the Italian agent, forcing herself not to watch as the body was lifted from the ground and placed on a plastic sheet. For her, it wasn't a lie. And it did bother her. But for Adele, she'd learned to live with the bother, the pain, the grief. Live with it like a chronic pain in her gut. Some things couldn't be avoided; they simply had to be managed.

"The victim's roommate, is she going to the hospital?"

"*Giovanni e Paolo*, yes."

"Will we be able to speak with her in the morning?"

"I'll see what I can do..." Leoni trailed off, glancing at his watch, then back at her. "Say, it's getting late, and I know you two have rooms here, but I should warn you about the hotel you're at," he said, wincing. "John mentioned it. The *Bisanzio Flora Hotel* right?"

Adele frowned. "Yeah. What about it?"

Leoni scratched his chin. "The place is notorious for being frequented by lice and mold." He winced and held up his hands as if to prevent protest. "I'd hate to see you lose sleep, especially since in that part of Venice, there are often impromptu firework shows throughout the night during the festivals."

"You're serious?"

"Look it up online yourself; that hotel has a one-star rating with five hundred customer reviews. Mostly college students and young tourists use it because everything else is out of their price range," he said with a shrug. "Just warning you."

Adele massaged the bridge of her nose, then began to move towards the door, away from the body, and away from the stretcher.

Agent Leoni fell into step next to her. She exited the small apartment, back out into the streets, the scent of canal water wafting on the air. John was standing as far away from the railing to the river as he could, his shoulder blades placed against the brick wall of the apartment. His arms crossed, and he watched Adele and Christopher step out into the night.

"What next?" He called out.

"Sleep?" Adele countered.

John exhaled softly, but not in frustration. If anything, he seemed relieved she had said it so he wouldn't have to.

"Got the address for the hotel?" He queried.

Adele winced, looking to Christopher and back at John. "Apparently it's a hellhole," she said. "And I need my sleep. If we want to catch this guy, we can't be waking up in the middle of the night to lice and fireworks."

John stared. "Lice and fireworks?" If anything, he almost sounded excited, some of the glower in his gazer receding.

"Perhaps I have a compromise," Agent Leoni said, quickly.

Adele glanced at him.

He continued, transitioning smoothly, "As I mentioned, I do have a place nearby in the city. Both of you are welcome. I have a spare room, and the couch," he said, glancing at John with this last word. He shrugged, returning his attention to Adele. "Of course, it's completely up to you.

"That's quite all right," John said, before she could, "we have rented rooms."

Adele paused. She glanced towards Leoni, trying to study him. He'd assured her they would solely work on the case... Was he up to something? Did he think by getting her alone it would rekindle things? Or was she just being cynical? Perhaps a bit of both. Still, sleep sounded nice. Adele sighed softly, but then reached a decision and shook her head. "Hang on, if what Christopher says is right about this place I don't want to be worrying if someone's going to break into my room and steal my shoes, or if I'm going to wake up with rats nibbling my toes."

John grumbled, but instead of seeming frustrated at her, he was now shooting daggers towards where Leoni stood with his hands clasped behind his back, rocking on his heels and waiting with a polite but quizzical expression.

"You're sure it's not too much trouble?" she said, glancing at Leoni. "We could always pay you."

"Don't be silly, of course not. And yes, I'm sure. You're welcome. Like I said, I do have a spare room... and a couch." He glanced at John. "The shower works perfectly fine, and it's not attached to my bedroom or anything." His tone betrayed nothing at these words. "There's plenty of privacy, and it's a quiet, safe neighborhood. Not too far from here either. I have a squad car coming to pick me up nearby."

Adele sighed, feeling a slow sense of relief. To have her own room, in a quiet neighborhood, away from the festivities and chaos around them seemed like a treat too wonderful to pass up.

John, though, seemed even more annoyed.

Adele frowned at him. "You're welcome to take your chance at the hotel. You don't have to come."

The tall Frenchman scratched the back of his head, glancing from Adele to Christopher. Perhaps he was considering the prospect of her staying in an apartment in the city alone with the Italian.

"No," he said at last, shaking his head quickly. "Probably best for the case we stick together."

"For the case," Adele said nodding without batting an eyelid.

"For the case," John said.

Agent Leoni's lips formed a small smile, bordering on a smirk, but he strolled past the two agents, waving at them, and heading down one of the small streets. Perhaps it was just Adele's imagination, but it seemed like he'd chosen the smallest, most narrow of the streets to lead them, forcing John to turn sideways, and grumble as he followed along after the smaller Italian.

CHAPTER EIGHTEEN

Christopher's place in the city was *exactly* what Adele had pictured in her mind, not that she'd ever admit to either of her colleagues she spent any amount of time considering such things. It was neat, small, overlooking a quiet, manufactured lake on the outskirts of Treviso only a thirty-minute drive from Venice.

All the pictures on the walls were of animals or monuments and landmarks. Leoni didn't display photos of his family, nor did it show any of his achievements. A guarded, prim sort of décor.

Now, Adele lay on the couch which she'd managed to barter from Agent Renee, staring up at the ceiling fan swishing overhead. Her eyes traced the fan, falling down to the two yellow eyes staring out at her from a small little burrow made of cushion and cotton.

A cat. She wasn't sure why, but even this late at night, Adele found it telling that Leoni was a cat person. And even then, not a single strand of hair she'd managed to spot on the furniture or, God forbid, brushed under the chairs.

No—even with a cat, Leoni kept his flat immaculate. Vaguely, she wondered if he'd known he would be having guests. But as she thought more, she decided it was far more likely that Leoni simply lived like this.

She could just now picture his features twisting in a soft smile as he busied himself with vacuuming and dusting while the cat darted around his feet.

Certainly not the most usual of bachelor pads, but extraordinarily like the Italian.

Adele shifted, her head adjusting against the pillow she'd been provided and trying to find a comfortable position. She wiggled under the blankets, staring up at the still rotating fan and then blinked in the night, glancing across the room towards the old, carved wooden clock—an antique. Her eyes strained, aided only by moonlight drifting through the half open curtains by the jarred window.

She winced, staring at the small hands—past midnight. She'd been tossing for nearly an hour now.

Adele huffed, wondering if perhaps she ought to try and trade back with Agent Renee. He slept like a log, regardless of where they holed up. She groaned, twisting again, but as she did, she felt another sort of weight settling on her, equally as apparent as the blanket she'd been given.

She swallowed, staring at the fan again, feeling the two yellow eyes fixed on the side of her face...

Another woman murdered.

Fiorella Lettiere dead.

And nothing she could do to take it back. Perhaps it had been optimistic to think she'd be able to fall asleep knowing this...

Dead...dead...dead.

Three gone in a short matter of days, the killer clearly escalating, striking at the heart of Venetian youth and beauty. Not a tourist angle anymore—no. They were without a motive. The killer wanted *something...* But what?

Clearly depraved, clearly with a screw loose. What else could explain the masks? Could explain the stalking in the dark?

She sighed, her mind flitting back to the small apartment where they'd found Fiorella's corpse draped over her yoga mat, her neck cut, blood dried—only two hours old. The roommate had arrived only after the killer...

Had the roommate seen anything?

Adele huffed in frustration, wishing they'd been given the opportunity to speak to the witness. She understood shock could be a serious business, but at the same time, they needed to solve this case. The longer they waited, the more lives on the line.

They would have to speak to the roommate soon. Maybe tomorrow morning—at least, so she hoped.

Adele shifted again, pulling the comforter up by her cheek and trying to press her head deep into the pillow as if hiding in darkness.

But still, sleep wouldn't come in the quiet apartment.

She heard a sudden creak of a floorboard, followed by another. She went still, listening as softly padding feet—making as little noise as possible—moved from the hallway towards the kitchen. She heard the clink of a glass, a sudden swish of flowing water. The water stopped, and she heard soft sipping from the dark.

She turned, staring in the shadows towards where Agent Renee—in boxers and a t-shirt—was trying to tiptoe back towards his room.

The moment he spotted her, he went still like a deer in headlights.

"Restless?" she said, watching him, propping up on her elbow.

He blinked, frozen, wincing. "I—sorry," he murmured. "Didn't mean to wake you."

She shook her head. "Wasn't sleeping."

John took another sip from his glass and sighed. "You too?"

"Couldn't. Thinking."

"Lot to think about," John nodded, slowly, carefully, easing himself against the wall, reclining and watching her.

Adele sat upright now, her legs crossed beneath her, the blankets draping towards the hardwood floor. "Nice place," she said.

John grunted, unimpressed. "I'm more of a dog person myself," he said.

"Leoni's not that bad, John. You should give him a chance."

"A chance is exactly what I'm worried about," he muttered.

"Pardon?"

"Nothing," he said, shrugging and downing the rest of his glass in one long gulp.

Adele glanced towards the cat in its burrow, watching the yellow eyes still fixed on her; she shivered briefly considering the thought of *other* eyes watching... Always watching. She needed to keep on her toes, keep alert. Perhaps, partly, her insomnia wasn't just due to this case.

She'd seen too much, experienced too much in the last few months to not keep poised, ready at a moment's notice. This was a new place, a new location—new threats abounded. She winced, hoping that in part she was wrong.

She didn't have the time to sweep every hotel room or guest home for cameras and surveillance. Was she being paranoid? Vaguely, she thought once more back to the small package Robert had left to her. She'd hidden it in the closet, hidden it out of sight. More paranoia? Or just good old-fashioned grief? Would she ever muster up the courage to open it?

Adele closed her eyes, but gave the faintest shakes, just for herself. Fear was only paranoia if it didn't accompany a likelihood.

And the thought of a threat keeping tabs on her was far more than likely. It was inevitable.

"You're beautiful when you think, you know," John said.

She blinked, glancing up at him in surprise. For a moment, she waited for the stinging zinger to follow. But instead, he just watched her, his head sort of tilted as if trying to frame her just-so in the moonlight through the gap in the window.

“I—thank you,” she said, hesitantly.

“It isn't right what happened to you,” John murmured. “None of it.”

“I...” she winced, thinking of Robert, thinking of Foucault's harsh words. She shrugged. “It is what it is. I'm a big girl—I can handle Foucault.”

“Not that.” John pressed a hand against the back of his head but still didn't look away, something seeking, searching about his gaze which remained on her, his eyes tracing the slope of her nose, to her lips, to her hair, then to her eyes—holding, steady, unblinking.

Adele felt her stomach twist, but this time not due to unease, nothing to do with the case, with any thoughts outside, before or behind. She thought only of the moment now, watching the tall Frenchman, wondering.

He was always the more acerbic, more unruly of her partners. But she'd long known this was why she liked him.

He wasn't safe. Not at all.

Adele's job was to *make* things safe. To take monsters and put them behind bars...

Sometimes...

She hated to think in such terms...

But sometimes it was nice to have a monster on her side...

She stared at John, her eyes tracing his burn-mark, moving down to his fingers which curled around the glass he was holding. The same fingers so accustomed to his weaponry—to expertise as a war-maker in the field of death.

The killers she hunted were nothing compared to the reaper that stood across from her.

But that wasn't everything he was... He was also a protector, loyal to a fault, and indifferent to the bureaucratic pulls and vices. Perhaps that's why she liked him.

“It isn't right what happened,” John said, trying the words another way as if in a fitting room. “None of it. You were what, only twenty? Twenty-one when she died?”

Adele blinked again. He was coming from all angles tonight. First beautiful, now wondering about her dead mother. To her surprise though, maybe it was the late hour, or maybe just the view she had of a handsome Frenchman in his boxers, but she didn't feel offended.

She shrugged once. She'd spent enough time thinking of her mother's passing, she could find solid purchase on top of the scars... Just so long as she didn't press too hard and rediscover the festered wounds beneath. No... tonight was a night of scars. She felt nothing as she said, "About that, yeah."

"That's what I keep seeing with each of these girls," he murmured, shaking his head. "Each of them dead, on the ground. Each of them as young as you when your mother died. Beautiful, like you. Deprived like you by a cruel world." He spoke slowly, his voice raspy despite the water, his eyes hooded as if staring off into some far, unseen place. "It's not okay... I've seen what it did to you. I've tried to make it better. But there's no making it better, is there? It just is."

Adele shivered at his words, pulling the blanket a bit closer now. She stared up at him, listening, frowning as she did. She'd never considered John's reaction to these kills to have anything to do with her... Was that what he thought? Did he... *pity* her?

"No," John said, suddenly, watching her, though she hadn't spoken a word. "No," he said, louder, a bit more angrily now. "Don't do that bullshit, Adele. Don't shut down. Don't you dare. It's not like that. What—let me guess, you're thinking I feel sorry for you, is that it? That's not what I'm saying at all."

Adele just watched him, wondering how close she'd allowed the man that he knew her thoughts before they were voiced. As she considered this, she felt another jolt of fear. Too close, perhaps... Maybe not close enough... Sometimes it was nice to have a monster on her side for a change.

But not just a monster... A savior? A friend? A companion? All of it?

Psychoanalysis wasn't her expertise—probably a good thing.

She still just watched John, trying to keep up. Racing into a hail of bullets, or fighting for her life, covered in blood with John running to her aid was one thing. But to speak in the quiet of night in such slow, calm terms... It didn't suit her.

It didn't suit *them.*

"Are we a 'them?'" she said, still quiet.

John blinked. "Excuse me?"

She watched him a second longer, considering what she said, considering if it mattered. Not everything needed her input, or her reaction. John had his own mind, his own thoughts—she was happy to leave him to them. She couldn't cure everything or solve everyone's pain.

No...

Such talks didn't suit them... The two of them were born in action, bred in chaos. Always on the move.

And so, instead of speaking, Adele pushed off the couch, the comforter dropping to the ground at her feet. She strode towards John, practically scowling.

For a moment, he winced, one hand flinching as if to protect his face, seemingly thinking she meant to strike him. Adele ignored this, gripped his arm, hard, holding him and tugging it down so his fingers lowered from his cheek. They weren't much suited for words in the dark.

But action at night...

Adele smiled—a leering, predator's grin. Then, she leaned in, stepping on her tiptoes and sliding her hand up behind John's head, fingers in his hair, pulling him down and close.

She pressed her lips to him, hard, holding him in place and breathing softly through her nose.

John's breath was warm against her cheek and he didn't recoil. He didn't bend, nor did he duck—no part of him made any effort to aid her. He remained upright, head very slightly bowed. Adele remained on her toes, still leaning in, feeling her calf ache in a strange way.

Such an odd realization even as they shared breath.

His lips were surprisingly soft, given how hard his arms were, his chest. She leaned against him now, her eyes closed, her nose brushing his upper lip. Her cheek pressed to his as she twisted her head just a moment, and the moonlight through the window flashed through the space between their faces...

"Adele?" John whispered, pulling away briefly. "I—I didn't mean... I wasn't trying—"

She pulled him in again, sharing a deeper, harder, almost violent kiss, willing him to just shut up.

This time, it wasn't as long, and she stepped back, feeling her calf aching from being on her toes to reach the tall Frenchman. Her eyes lingered on his lips for a moment, along his chin, not quite looking to his eyes.

Whispers in the night were for others...

Not for them. At least not now and not yet. Maybe never.

"I... Well..."

"You get the couch," Adele muttered. She patted him on the arm, then brushed past John, marching towards the bedroom. She reached the first door on the left. For a moment, it seemed like John wasn't sure if he should follow or not.

She helped aid his decision, stepping in, without looking back and shutting and locking the door in one quick motion.

Now was time for sleep.

CHAPTER NINETEEN

Adele woke to the scent of coffee drifting through the quaint apartment, followed by a sudden pressure as the small, golden-eyed feline stepped across her head and down to her feet.

Adele winced, slowly shifting and glancing around, emerging from beneath the blanket of the bed she'd stolen from John the previous night. The cat had managed to slink through the open window, it seemed, along a narrow ledge. It rubbed against her cheek, and, wearily, Adele got to her feet, massaging the back of her neck and tilting her head to exhale at the ceiling.

The cat reached the door and began to stalk back and forth beneath the brass knob, mewling over its shoulder in Adele's direction. Adele sighed, and resisted the urge to roll her eyes as she kicked off the bed, dumping her blankets on the ground and, with stiff motions, approached the feline.

"You want out?" she muttered.

The cat continued to stalk, mewling even louder now.

Adele turned the handle and stepped into the hall, proceeded by the cat who scampered down the hall. Adele followed, still rubbing the sleep from her eyes just in time to spot the cat hopping onto the kitchen counter next to where Agent Leoni was standing, brewing a pot and, by the look of things, pouring himself a bowl of bland oats. Leoni was already fully dressed.

"What time is it?" Adele asked.

Leoni turned, his eyebrows rising. "Oh, good," he said. "You're up." He flashed a million-dollar smile and gently patted his pet's ears, scratching the cat under the chin before shooing it off the counter.

Adele glanced at the antique clock on the wall and her eyes narrowed. "Seven already?" she said, feeling a flash of irritation. In a defensive voice, she muttered, "I normally get my jog in before seven."

Leoni nodded, only half-listening as, still standing, he began working on his bowl of oats.

Adele felt an odd sort of competitiveness with Leoni. It took a moment for her to realize why: she had always been the most active in the mornings of anyone she knew. Normally, going for an hour or two run before eating a quick bowl of cereal and heading to work.

Now, seeing Leoni fully dressed, already pouring oats, she felt a flicker of a frown across her features. At the same time, she glanced towards the couch. John was still a giant lump beneath the blankets, a soft snoring sound echoing from the pile of pillows and comforters.

Adele smirked, feeling a bit better now. "Any news on the roommate?" Adele asked.

Leoni swallowed a spoonful of oats, then turned to her, nodding quickly. "Looks like she's out of the hospital," he said. He tapped his phone which rested on the counter next to the coffee pot. "Staying with her parents not far from here," he said.

Adele nodded. "Next stop?"

"Looks like."

"Got an appointment?"

Leoni shrugged. "They're sitting still until we can speak. Any time, honestly. Just waiting on sleeping beauty over there," he said, jerking his head towards John.

Adele tried to hide her chuckle. The phrase was a very Johnesque thing to say. Leoni's eyes were half-hooded as he took another sip of coffee and another spoon of oats. He hid his emotions well enough, but even a polite, professional agent like Leoni would have picked up on John's hostility by now, no doubt.

"Hey, you big lump!" Adele called across the room, doing her best to forget the brief interaction they'd had the night before. She felt a lance of embarrassment as she pictured the scene in her mind, pictured the quick pressure of his lips against hers, pictured—even—the soft rising and falling of his chest.

She winced against the invasion of vulnerability, and doubled down on the teasing, if only to cover the wound of affection with a veneer of mockery.

"Hey! John! You're shaking the foundation. Get up!"

The snoring paused for a moment, followed by a couple of grunts, then another couple of words that caused Leoni's eyebrows to rise.

"Is that any way to speak to a lady?" Adele replied.

"I wasn't speaking to Leoni," John's voice grunted from beneath his pillows.

"Funny. Leoni's standing right next to me."

Another grunt.

"Hey, we have a lead," Adele said, feeling by now that all sense of awkwardness had faded in the face of mild amusement and major annoyance.

John remained bundled up, pulling the comforter over his head, even tighter, it seemed to hold back the sound of her voice.

Adele sighed, but then stalked over, muttering darkly and poking at John's ribs with a sharp finger. Still no response. She reached out, yanked the pillow and tossed it across the room, before turning and heading back down the hall. “Gonna grab a shower,” she said to Leoni. “Let's leave in ten.”

The Italian agent flicked an amused glanced towards where John was trying to fling his blankets after Adele, but then flashed a quick thumbs up, returning his attention to his phone.

For Adele, some of her own amusement faded. She knew what came next would be crucial. Had the roommate seen anything about the killer? Had she perhaps been there in time to catch the murder?

Adele shivered at the thought, but pushed into the bathroom door, frowning as she did.

They were quickly running out of leads. Something had to stick, and soon, or the killer's rampage had only just begun.

CHAPTER TWENTY

A small, blue twostory just north of Venice welcomed the three agents as they exited Leoni's tinted-windowed sedan. Adele hesitated, frowning towards the small, glass-enclosed entry room. Three figures were seated around a thick, wooden table, their eyes staring unblinking through the windows, watching the approaching agents.

"Guess we're not invited inside," Adele murmured, approaching the porch-enclosure.

John, next to her, who still hadn't quite woken, or smoothed his hair for that matter, took the lead regardless, heading towards the two-story. He didn't bother to knock on the glass door, but instead said, "DGSI."

Adele recognized Drina Sargese, the roommate of the third victim, sitting between her parents, a blanket thrown over her shoulders, her tanned features fixed in a sort of distant gaze, watching them through the glass.

"May we come in Mr. and Mrs. Sargese?" Agent Leoni called over John.

The parents were both tall, apparent even as they sat in wicker chairs, their eyes set in wrinkle-free skin, despite their age. Adele supposed they might have had some professional help with some of their features. Something was just a bit *too* symmetrical, too perfect about their appearances. They couldn't have been much younger than forty, given the age of their daughter, but neither of them had a grey hair to be spoken of.

At last, the woman, who was wearing a shawl with braided tassels, beckoned towards them. She had Spanish features, and her eyes lingered on John but then slipped to Adele, and finally landed on Leoni.

One by one, the agents filed through the glass door, into the enclosed porch.

Two empty chairs also face the table. Adele took one, Leoni the other, and John, slow on the uptake was left to sit on a small red, wooden rocking horse, or remain standing. He opted for the latter, leaning against the glass door, shut now, and watching the three Sargeses.

"We were told you'd come an hour ago," said the woman in nearly perfect French.

Adele blinked, glancing at John, who was still frowning towards the rocking horse. Leoni, who'd been poised to speak first, it seemed, leaned back now, relaxing a bit and glancing towards Adele as if handing a baton.

“Apologies,” she said, quickly. “The drive was longer than we'd thought.”

“Drive? Not from Venice then?” the woman said, continuing in French.

Adele glanced towards Drina Sargese, the daughter, who was still staring off into the distance, the blanket still wrapped around her shoulders. She returned her attention to the matriarch and spokesperson of the small family.

“No ma'am,” she said, simply. “We don't intend to take up much of your time.” She glanced towards Drina. “But we had a couple of questions, if you can indulge us for a moment.”

The mother turned to her daughter and raised a perfectly stenciled eyebrow. The young woman didn't seem to notice this attention at first, but as all sets of eyes landed on her, she blinked at last, reacting finally, it seemed, to the sheer weight of watching.

She glanced around, spoke softly in Italian to her father, but then looked to Adele. Also in French, nearly as strong as her mother's she said, “I don't know anything...”

Her voice came soft and hoarse, and no sooner had she spoken, she looked away again as if hoping by speaking those words it would expel the agents from among them.

Adele nodded slowly, wondering just how direct she could be. Drina's fingers, which gripped the hem of the blanket over her shoulders, were trembling slightly. Adele winced and wanted to say something, anything, to assuage the young woman. Instead, though, she went quiet for a moment, allowing the odd silence to stretch.

She knew what it was to stumble upon the body of someone she was close with. Those images never left. Drina had no choice now but to be strong. Hopefully, others would come alongside and make it easier. But sink or swim moments in life were unavoidable.

Adele still wasn't sure if she was treading water herself or submerged entirely.

She blinked and cleared her throat. “I'm very sorry, Drina. If any of this is too taxing, we can come back later.”

“No,” the young woman said, quickly, shaking her head. “No,

please. I couldn't bear postponing. No thank you."

"Alright then," Adele murmured. "What can you tell me about that night? Anything at all could help."

"I said, I didn't see anything. Not really."

"What does *not really* mean?"

Drina winced, closing her eyes for a moment as if against a sudden headache, or a taxing memory. "Fiora and I were friends," she said, softly. "Not too close, mind you. Mostly, we lived together for the rent."

"I told her Venice was no good," her mother said quickly. "Told her not to spend time with a Venetian. Too many parties, too many festivals. Not enough study."

Drina frowned towards her mother, muttering something in Italian. This prompted a reaction from the father who scowled and shook a finger at his daughter but didn't speak.

Drina glanced back towards Adele. "Like I said, we weren't *that* close," she insisted, not looking to her mother, but clearly directing the words that way.

"Right," said Adele. "So you didn't see anything that night?"

"I arrived home after work... The door to our unit was open. I thought I might have heard footsteps *above* me. As I entered the unit, it almost sounded like someone, from a higher floor was passing back down the stairs." She shivered visibly, shaking her head. "I think the man might have been waiting for me. What if... what if he'd come in after me, too? What if—" Her voice cracked, and her eyes widened in horror.

Her mother and father both reached out, one hand on each shoulder, patting comfortingly. Drina shook again, whispering now, "But no... I didn't see anything. I just... I just entered and then... There on the ground..." She sobbed again, her head jerking down, staring at her lap now.

Adele sighed softly, nodding in a comforting sort of way and waiting a moment, allowing the girl to recover. John began to clear his throat behind her, but Adele glanced back and gave a quick shake of her head.

At last, Drina looked up again of her own volition. She seemed sad to see the agents still sitting there.

"I don't know what else to say," she whispered. "I don't know anything."

"You didn't hear anything?" Adele asked.

"Only the footsteps," she replied.

Adele paused for a moment, considering this. By all accounts, it had been a close thing. Drina had nearly stumbled on the killer. What did that mean, though? Perhaps he wasn't as careful as Adele first thought. Or perhaps he was *so* precise, he'd planned his attack within a short window, like a bloody heist.

She winced at this comparison and decided to change track.

"I don't want to keep you too long. Just one other, thing, your mother mentioned she opposed Venice..." Adele glanced towards the severe-faced woman who was nodding adamantly, her sculpted lips pressed in a thin line. Adele looked back at Drina. "She mentioned parties, festivals... Were you and Fiorella heading to any party in particular?"

Agent Leoni shifted nearly imperceptibly next to Adele. Drina, though, glanced up, swallowing. "I..." She swallowed. "I... no... No, not really."

Adele glanced towards the parents, noting the way Mrs. Sargese's shoulders sagged a bit in relief at her daughter's reply.

Adele frowned. "Do you all mind if I take a second with Drina? Alone? There are so many people here, it might be nice for us to have some breathing room."

Agent Leoni was already rising out of his seat before she'd finished. But Drina's parents were frowning. and her mother was already shaking her head. "Certainly no," she said. "Our daughter has been through a horrible experience. You can't expect us to—"

"It's fine," Drina said, quickly. She was watching Adele, a shrewd look in her eyes.

Her mother tried to protest again, but Drina shook her head quickly. "It's fine. I'm fine. Only a couple of minutes. It's fine."

Her mother sighed. She looked like she wanted to protest more.

Adele interjected before she could, "Truly, only another question or two. It just might be best for everyone if we give your daughter some space."

The mother looked ready to resist, but then Mr. Sargese rose from his seat, still having spoken nary a word. But he took his wife by the arm, and gestured towards the door, his eyebrows rising. Mrs. Sargese sighed, pulled her arm away from her husband, but then growled and turned, marching back into the house ahead of her husband.

Mr. Sargese looked over his daughter's head, his dark eyes meeting Adele's in a significant tilt.

"We're going to be fine," Adele murmured.

The father waited still, his hands on his daughter's shoulders as Leoni and John beat a retreat back through the glass door, out onto the lawn. The door creaked as it swung shut, and at last, Mr. Sargese turned, entering the house as well and closing the door, leaving his daughter and Adele on the glass-enclosed porch.

Adele waited for the sound of movement and footsteps to fade, before meeting Drina's searching gaze and saying, "There were no parties you were planning on going to?" She murmured. "None at all?"

Drina licked her lips, half glancing over her shoulder towards the house. But then, in a quiet tone, she murmured. "The *Compagnia dei Cielo* ball." She spoke so quietly, Adele had to lean in to hear. "Don't tell my mother," Drina added, quickly. "She doesn't approve of that sort of thing. Fiora and I were both going. Both excited to go."

She sobbed now, shaking her head, her eyes scrunching up, her nose bunching. "I guess that's not going to happen now."

Adele did her best to look consoling, but on the inside, her mind was whirring. Another victim from the same ball. The same masquerade party that would take place that evening. All three victims were connected to it now.

The killer was killing guests going to the masquerade. That much was now obvious, but *why?* And how was he choosing them? Randomly? Some other method? The guest list was already a no-go.

Still quiet, careful, Adele said, her throat dry all of a sudden, "Were you going alone?"

To her surprise, Drina gave a quick shake of her head. She paused, though, head half tilted as if wondering if she could take back the motion. But then she doubled down and shook her head again. "Not alone, no..." she said, quietly. "My boyfriend lives nearby—he was going to try and get some time off work to come."

"And Fiorella?" Adele said.

"Fiora was..." Drina frowned, troubled. "Dating someone. Someone much older—she'd hinted as much at least. But I'd never met the man."

Adele stared. Another secret lover. Just like Lorraine Strasser.

"Do you know his name?"

Drina shook her head adamantly. "No. Fiora was secretive about that sort of thing." She winced again, breathing quickly all of a sudden as if after a sprint. At last, though, finding a sort of hidden strength, she pressed through the sudden bout of fear, swallowing and speaking, "None of our friends knew who she was seeing. It was this big secret. I think Fiora liked it that way. Liked the attention."

"When's the last time she saw this mystery man?"

"That night, in fact. She'd gone on a date with him that very night. She'd bragged about it for a week. Apparently, he was very wealthy." Drina shrugged. "They went to *Ricardo's* on the Grand Canal. One of the more expensive restaurants in all of Italy. She wouldn't stop talking about it..."

Drina stared off, biting her lip, peering again into the distance through the glass around them.

"*Ricardo's*?" Adele murmured. "That's where she was for dinner. You're sure?"

Drina shrugged. "That's what she said. Like I said, I don't know who she was with. No one did. I... I'm tired, Agent Sharp. I'm sorry. There's nothing else I know."

Adele smiled at Drina, nodding quickly and pushing away from the table. "Get some rest. And..." She paused for a moment, one hand pushing back the chair, the other hovering somewhere near where she kept her business cards. At last, she pulled one out, and slid it across the table. "I know how jarring it must be... All of this. And I'm sorry." Adele winced. "If you need to talk..." She shrugged, tapping a finger against the card.

Drina didn't look up, but at least she didn't push the card away.

Adele nodded one last time, as if settling a matter for herself, and then she turned, pushing back out of the porch and rejoining Leoni and Renee who were waiting for her by the car.

Both of them watched inquisitively as she approached, their eyes fixed on her expression.

"Definitely another attendee of the same ball," she said, matter-of-factly, frowning as she did. Her feet tapped against the concrete sidewalk, and her hands jammed into her pockets as she rejoined her partners. "But also, apparently Fiorella, like Lorraine, had a mystery guy in the wings. Someone she was seeing on the sly."

Leoni frowned. "Think our first victim might have also had a secret lover?"

Adele shrugged once. "Worth checking out. Apparently, Fiorella and this mystery boyfriend were at a restaurant called *Ricardo's* the night she died."

Leoni whistled softly. "*Ricardo's*? On the Grand Canal?" He winced, shaking his head. "A very wealthy secret boyfriend in that case."

John grunted, though, already sliding into the front, driver's seat, even though it was Leoni's car. "Food is food," he muttered. "Killers are killers. Here," he clicked his fingers. "Give me the keys."

Leoni to his credit didn't even roll his eyes. He sighed softly, like a father maintaining patience with a rambunctious child, but then pulled his keys out and handed them to John's hand which was clicking over the top of the sedan.

Then, Leoni slid into the backseat, allowing Adele the front passenger side.

The door had barely closed, before John put the car in motion, squealing away from the curb. As he did, he muttered, "Directions towards *Ricardo's?*"

"Can't drive the whole way," Leoni replied from the back. "Parking lot outside Venice. Then have to take a boat."

"A boat?" John said, sounding scandalized. For a moment, it looked like his cheeks might have tinged green. "A damn boat?"

Leoni chuckled. "I mentioned *Ricardo's* is patronized by the wealthy, yes? Only access is by a boat."

John muttered darkly. Adele, for her part, stared through the windshield as they headed back towards Venice. Wealthy killers often had more means than others. Wealthy killers might have contacts too. *Compagnia dei Cielo* was patronized by influential sorts to...

Someone like this secret boyfriend? Someone who used their influence to gain access to a guest list?

She shivered at the thought, frowning now through the windshield as they moved away from the Sargeses' home and headed in the direction of the last-known location of their most recent victim.

CHAPTER TWENTY ONE

One home gone, ransacked and raided.

Six left, though. The painter reclined in the bubbling tub in the center of his living room, facing the balcony which overlooked Paris, in his fifth favorite spot... One didn't have the funds to travel, to remain low-key without some source of passive income, and for him, real estate had always made sense. The buildings themselves were like art, after a fashion. And he'd been careful—only ever killing one of his tenants over a dispute about rent. The tenant in question had been drunk at the time and insulted the Painter's eye... Such things now wouldn't have gotten under his pallid skin, but then... He'd been younger then. Police still hadn't found the body.

The Painter reclined in the hot tub, feeling the trail of warm bubbles against his sensitive skin. The lights were off, and the windows filmed with a tint, preventing too much sunlight from stretching into the apartment.

He winced, blinking his one good eye and exhaling slowly towards the ceiling as his head pressed against the back of the porcelain.

It felt nice to lounge, to think.

But his mind kept flitting back to the same thought...

She'd seen his face.

He gritted his teeth in frustration.

She'd *seen* his face.

She'd seen his face.

Damn it.

She was now trying to track those cameras back to him. His contact had come through, at least. Of course, the cameras would be a dead end.

He'd had plans in Paris, but now, it seemed, perhaps it would be best that he move again. Yes... No longer idling. One of his old acolytes, a man who he'd met once had gotten close to Joseph Sharp not long ago... Now it was the master's turn to succeed where the apprentice had failed.

The Painter smiled, swirling a finger around and around in the warm water, lifting it and watching the droplets tumble from the tip, one at a time, splashing back amidst the bubbles.

He'd intended to play some more while in Paris. Intended, even, to try and buy Robert's mansion through a proxy. He'd wanted the place to be the site of his final masterpiece.

But now... *She'd seen his face.*

He gritted his teeth, though not too hard—like his bones, his teeth were also quite brittle. No sense losing another over a little bit of misfortune.

Adele Sharp had gotten lucky. That was all—pure luck.

He winced, rising slowly from the tub, the hot water pouring down his body, splashing over the side of the basin onto the floor. Swallowing softly, he stepped delicately out of the hot tub onto a fluffy floor mat, feeling it soft beneath his toes.

He marched towards the windows overlooking the city, proudly standing facing the glass, and watching *his* city.

He hated leaving... But sometimes a cautious man had no choice. He hadn't made it this far, for this long without being cautious. He'd been careful, delicate, calculated. The police thought they had him pegged... But no. Even what they found was all charade, pretense.

The duplicity itself was the art. They would never find him.

And so, he couldn't allow his emotions to take control.

He placed his wet hand against the darkened glass, streaking his fingers down and leaving a trail of beaded moisture in a semi-circle outline around the apartments across from him.

No. He couldn't stay.

Which meant he'd have to expedite his next location... He'd already decided.

Joseph Sharp was next. Adele's father...

Yes, that would be the target. He would just have to check how expensive tickets to Germany were.

She'd seen his face, and it wouldn't be the last time.

CHAPTER TWENTY TWO

"The gondola is part of the charm," Leoni murmured over another series of grumblings from Agent Renee. Adele watched, mildly amused as the Italian agent used the paddle to carry them along the canal, edged against the buildings, heading towards the waiting dock of *Ricardo's*. The upscale restaurant seemed much like a greenhouse, made mostly of glass—glass ceilings, glass walls, glass doors. All of it, obviously, going the full mile to take as much advantage of the natural scenery as possible.

And it was quite beautiful.

With the sun above, winking through the buildings, reflecting off the water, Adele found her eyes leaving the two agents in their rented gondola, and flickering towards *Ricardo's* itself. The boat rocked a bit, though, and she glanced sharply back towards Agent Renee.

John had gone stiff again, his hands gripping the rail, his teeth clenched. He was staring directly between his knees, refusing to look into the water.

Adele tried not to smile, but it was difficult.

She'd seen Agent Renee run head-first into gunfire. Seen him fly a helicopter up windswept mountains during a snowstorm without anyone nearby to help. She'd seen him repel down a rope from a moving helicopter onto a chugging train.

But now, faced by a little bit of wet, he seemed frozen in panic.

She reached over from where she sat on the middle bench, and patted the tall Frenchman on the shoulder.

"Don't," he said, firmly. "I'm fine."

"You're green."

"It's the reflection off the water. I'm fine."

"Is the reflection off the water making your fingers tremble too?"

John looked ready to retort, but then, the boat rocked a bit in the wake of a passing outboard engine, and he cursed something fierce, glaring at Leoni.

"See—here, just fine," the Italian said, calmly. There was a soft bump of wood against rubber, and then Leoni danced off the back of the gondola, storing the attached oar, by twisting it and placing it alongside the wooden ridge. Then, he hopped onto the dock, tying off the front of the vessel to one of the mooring posts of the expensive restaurant.

Leoni glanced back at the rest of them. “Coming?” he said, innocently.

Adele exited the boat second, somewhat disappointed to have her feet back on land once more. The ride in the boat had been a nice change of pace. John took his time about it. Moving slowly, carefully. No sooner had he landed back on the dock, though, then his countenance shifted. His shoulders set, he puffed out his chest and he shot a glare from Adele to Leoni as if daring either of them to say anything about it.

Adele knew better than to tease John when he got like this.

Leoni, for his part, was too polite, she supposed, to do any such thing and was already moving, strolling along the floating dock towards a hostess standing just within the glass door to the glass building.

Leoni opened the door, causing the sun behind them to flash off the reflective material, and he bid a quick greeting to the hostess, who nodded in return, her eyes lingering on the handsome Italian when she thought he wasn't looking. Adele and John followed after as the tall Frenchman moved a bit more quickly away from the water than either of his colleagues.

“Pleasure to see you,” the woman behind the greeting stand said, smiling pleasantly and bobbing her head in a practiced nod. Her perfectly manicured fingers swept up, extending towards the tables set closest to the glass wall. “Table for three?”

She spoke English with a faint, charming trace of an accent. Likely, she was used to tourists and could peg foreigners with practice at this point. Her eyes moved towards John now, too, bouncing back to Leoni, then to John again as if she couldn't quite decide where to look.

Adele went entirely ignored. She frowned momentarily, and stepped in front of John, clearing her throat.

“We're here about a customer of yours,” Adele insisted, pulling out her phone and scrolling to the most recent photo of Fiorella Lettiere they had. She turned it, extending it towards the hostess, who was probably only mid-twenties herself. “Seen her?” Adele said.

The hostess sighed, seeming reluctant to look away from John, but when her eyes landed on the phone, she blinked and nodded once. “A—actually, yes. Why?”

“We're with DGSI,” Adele said. The woman's mouth began to open and Adele interjected, "Law enforcement. Interpol oversight. Look, this woman was here?"

The hostess' eyes were wide now, round and she was staring directly at Adele, her entire demeanor shifting. She swallowed, nearly audibly and blinked a few times as if dazed. "I—I... Umm, yes. Last night, actually. I remember. She was quite," the woman coughed delicately, "quite lovely in that dress of hers."

"Alright. Do you remember where they sat?"

The hostess waved the same perfectly manicured hand towards the table she'd been indicating earlier. As one, John, Adele and Leoni all turned, staring at the furniture. Like the rest of the restaurant, even the table was made of glass. Instead of chairs, two semi-circle benches—see through as well—though perhaps a sturdy plastic, protruded from the ground. Beneath the table, as if staring down a well or through a portal, one could see the swishing waters below. The whole spectacle was quite enamoring, but Adele's eyes were fixated on the indicated portion of the restaurant.

"Just there?" she said.

"Table three," the hostess replied.

Adele moved, ignoring the eyes of a couple of other customers who were sitting beneath direct sunlight facing the canal. A waiter, with a tray covered in more drinking options than she'd seen in most mini-fridges was tempting his table with the offerings, but also paused long enough to shoot the newcomers a curious glance.

Adele ignored it all, coming to a stop at the glass seating, her eyes narrowed as she looked around, scanning the location for anything of import. Of course, she doubted Fiorella and her secret lover were the only ones to have come here. But fingerprints weren't out of the question.

Still, fingerprints would take far too long, especially attempting to sort through all of them. On top of it, the roommate seemed to think the secret admirer in question was a wealthy one. Which meant...

Adele glanced back, towards the hostess.

Wealthy and egalitarian? She hoped not in this case. Perhaps old-fashioned manners and chivalry would help them find the guy.

She moved away from the translucent seating once more. "I'm going to need credit card information from that woman," she said, tapping her phone, "and her date. Do you remember anything about him?"

"He was much uglier than her," said the hostess without batting an eyelid. Then, she blinked, a hand half moving towards her lips as if worried she'd said too much. Her eyes shifted to John apologetically and then back to Adele. "I—I mean... Well, *she* was quite pretty." The hostess nodded towards the phone. "Which meant... And I don't know anything mind you, but it meant he was probably wealthy. Or some athlete. That's how it usually goes, isn't it?"

Adele shrugged. "Do you have the credit card information or not?"

"I... I one moment. Let me go speak with my manager."

The hostess held up another perfectly manicured finger on her opposite hand, and then turned sidelong, stepping away from the greeting stand and hurrying towards two swinging doors in the back of the glass restaurant. Adele considered following for a moment, but then decided to stay put.

Where would the girl run to on a practically floating restaurant anyway?

A few moments later, the girl returned, accompanied by a man wearing a scowl and a white chef's hat. The man was muttering beneath his breath, a pile of receipts clutched in his fingers as he approached.

"This is my manager," the girl said, quickly, extending a hand in the same way she'd done to display the tables. "He has what you need." Then, just as quickly, and seemingly grateful to escape the focal point of attention, she moved back behind the podium like a soldier behind a bunker.

The man in the chef's hat was puffing breath, his cheeks red from a hot kitchen. He glanced around the three agents and then pointed at Adele. "Law enforcement?" he asked. His English was much harsher and more grating than the hostess'. Adele decided sticking such a man in the kitchen was probably a wise move.

"Yes," she said, simply. "We're looking for credit card information from one of your customers."

Leoni pulled out his identification, flashing it towards the manager, who barely glanced at it. The man shrugged, muttering to himself and glancing at the roll of receipts he had in one thick fist. He began to methodically and quickly, with sharp movements, flick through them, grumbling as he did.

He paused, raising an eyebrow. "Table three?" he said.

Adele nodded.

The manager chef continued sifting through the receipts. For a moment, he paused and asked something in Italian to the younger woman across by the doors.

"At eight," she called back. "Enrico was on shift," she added.

The manager sighed, pulled a long receipt from the pile, examining it like a banker checking a euro note. For a moment, as he paused his flurrying fingers, like a magician with a deck of cards, Adele was given a brief glimpse at the *numbers* on the bottom of the receipts. Her eyes bugged. One of the bills was for nearly a thousand euros. Another, as he flipped it over—she nearly gasped—was for more than five thousand.

Suddenly, the beautiful view of the canal, and the restaurant's atmosphere felt a bit more jarring than when she'd first stepped off the gondola.

The manager, at last, clicked his tongue, pulling out one of the shorter receipts from the pile. "Here," he said, quickly. "Let me check, one moment." He paused as he spoke, clearing his throat briefly and then stepping sideways until he was out of view, blocked by the hostess' silhouette from the other customers who were watching curiously. Loudly, he declared, "I'm afraid we can't provide client information!" He said it loud enough for the rest of the patrons to hear. Then, just as quickly, before Adele could even frown, he handed the receipt in question to Leoni and shrugged. "That's what we have." He tapped a finger towards an order number at the bottom of the receipt and murmured something to the hostess.

Quickly, she looked behind her stand and Adele listened to the soft clacking of keys, suggesting there was a registration computer back there. A second later, she nodded, turning the computer and the manager jerked his head towards it.

"Information for payment, there. Please take what you need," he said in a much quieter voice, "Then leave. Thank you." Just as abruptly as he'd come, the man turned and left, swift of heel.

Adele watched him go, frowning, but then noting a quiet gesture from Leoni, she joined both him and the hostess behind the stand. Leoni's finger pressed to a clean, wiped-down computer screen hidden behind the wooden stand.

"There," he murmured. "Card number and name."

Adele leaned in. "Paul Krupp," she murmured, then glanced towards Leoni.

He already had his phone out, though, and she could hear the quiet dial tone past his cheek. Everyone waited for a moment, standing in stray beams of sunlight reflected through the glass walls above. At last, Adele heard a faint voice on the other end, and Agent Leoni spoke quickly in Italian. She couldn't quite understand the words, but she gauged the pause followed by Leoni leaning in. The Italian nodded once to himself, waited a second as the voice on the other end spoke and then, he began to read the credit card number.

Leoni said something again, and this time, Adele could easily make out the name. "Paul Krupp."

She faintly heard more murmuring on the other end. Leoni frowned, leaning back from the computer screen and, despite whatever he was hearing, he took a moment to nod in polite gratitude towards the hostess.

The younger woman smiled at the acknowledgment from the handsome man, and cleared her throat delicately, watching Leoni's every movement. The Italian agent spoke a bit longer.

Adele could feel her patience wearing as everyone waited, watching... At last, though, the Italian glanced towards her and made a wiggling motion with his fingers. In English, he murmured, lowering the phone briefly, "Number?"

"What?" she said.

"Your phone number?" he asked.

Adele rattled it off and listened as the digits were translated into Italian. A few seconds passed and then, her phone vibrated a single time. She glanced down to find an attachment from an unknown caller.

"Get it?" Leoni asked.

Adele clicked the attachment and a file suddenly opened. It looked like a combination between a passport and a driver's license, with some additional information thrown in. She blinked, then nodded, reading the name at the top of the file. "Paul Krupp," she murmured. "Forty-five years of age. German citizen. Yes—I got it."

Leoni thanked his contact then hung up, turning towards Adele.

She was already scanning the document from the unknown number, frowning as she did. She felt all too aware now of the attention from the hostess and the other patrons. With a surreptitious nod, she moved back towards the glass door to the restaurant and out onto the dock. Leoni gave another murmur of gratitude to the hostess before following them back out into the breeze.

The door was still swinging shut, the soft flutter of wind lifting her blonde bangs as Adele frowned, her eyes glued to the information in front of her. "Well then," she muttered. "That's not a coincidence."

John seemed happy to be distracted by anything save the inevitability of another boat ride. "What?" he said, quickly.

"His travel records," she said, looking up. "He comes to Venice every year. During the festival."

"We don't have records of any other kills from previous years," John pointed out.

"No... Not that, but also..." Adele trailed off, scrolling down the document towards bank records. "He's a major benefactor of the festival," she said, frowning. "I have at least five deposits totaling nearly half a million euros over the last six years..."

John frowned. "Deposits? To whom?"

"*Compagnia dei Cielo*," Adele said, looking up, her eyes wide. "Specifically, it seems, according to the transfer notes, in service of funding the masquerade ball."

Leoni crossed his arms next to John, and both men watched her closely. "The same ball all three of our victims were going to attend?"

"The one and the same," Adele replied, looking up now. "The first day of the ball is tonight," she said. "He'll be there, no doubt."

"That ball is tonight?" John asked, frowning. "Why does that strike me as ominous?"

Adele shook her head, lifting the phone again and then pausing. "Mr. Krupp also has records of staying at the same hotel, every time he's here."

"Where?" John and Leoni said simultaneously.

"The *Fauna Hotel*," she murmured, reading the bank statement again. "In fact... it looks like he's checked in there now for another three days... Think if we pay his room a visit he'll want to entertain guests?"

John grunted. "I don't think he has a choice. He went on a date with one of our victims the night she died. He comes from money, knows the festival well..."

"He's from Germany," Leoni added. "And our second victim was German."

"And Lorraine was also dating a mystery man," Adele murmured, nodding slowly. "Could have been the same guy..."

"German millionaire turned serial killer?" John asked. "Think it's likely? How come he's been visiting the festival for six years and only now started killing?"

"We don't know that," Adele murmured. "Maybe he hid his murders better before. Now... though... our killer is sending a message. The masks, the women all on the same guest list of the same masquerade ball—which he happens to be a benefactor of? That's a touch too coincidental for my taste."

Leoni was already moving towards the gondola they'd rented. As he brushed past Adele he said, "Which hotel was it?"

"The *Fauna Hotel*."

"That's not far from here. We can get there by the canal."

Adele glanced to John, whose face was greenish again. She patted him consolingly on the arm and began to help Leoni untie their vessel.

As she did, she considered their options. Mr. Krupp was involved. He had to be—too many connections, too many little threads leading back to him. He'd dated the third victim in secret. The second victim was also seeing someone in secret—possibly the same man. Why all the secrecy? Just a little Venetian romance? Forbidden love? Or could it be something more sinister? Could he be the killer? Circumstantial evidence wasn't enough to indict. But it was enough to arrest.

She could only hope he was at his hotel, rather than preparing for another kill.

CHAPTER TWENTY THREE

Adele heard the clap of footsteps on the stairs as, flanked by her two colleagues, she hurried up the final flight to the penthouse of the Venetian hotel. The buildings in Venice weren't as tall as she was accustomed to, neither were the hotels, and so after six brisk flights, they were already stepping into the hall towards the door at the far end.

"This one?" Leoni said quickly, his voice low.

John had his weapon in hand, his shoulders set as he moved quickly down the hall, framing the door across from them.

Adele nodded quickly. "Concierge said East penthouse. That's the one." She also spoke soft, low, but her voice strained with a sudden spurt of adrenaline.

"And he's here, we're sure?" John murmured back.

Adele shook her head. "Concierge seems to think so. Mr. Krupp hasn't left his room. Remember, he's a suspect, not a killer."

"Not that we know of," Leoni said.

"Yet," John added.

Agent Renee seemed pleased to once more have his feet on solid ground and he took the lead, hurrying towards the Eastern penthouse. The long windows, tinged with red and green swirls overlooked the canal and the city, staring down at the hundred little islands of the Venetian lagoon. For a moment, Adele was distracted by the view alone, but then, Agent Leoni stepped past her and she was jarred back into focus, her eyes fixed on the sealed door at the end of the long hall.

John reached the door first, large fist raised, gun in his other hand. He pounded his hand on the door. "DGSI!" he called. "Open up!"

Leoni's back pressed to the opposite side of the door frame and Adele had stepped against the hallway's wall, out of the line of potential fire from the penthouse doorway itself.

"No room service!" A voice shouted back in German. "Go away!"

"Law enforcement!" Adele called, in the same language. "Open up!"

She heard a pause, and then a string of German curse words. "Go away!" the voice yelled. "I'm busy!"

John glanced at Adele and she nodded again. He pounded his fist against the door a third time. Adele heard the sound of an exhausted sigh and a rattling sound, then the door opened briefly. A brass chain secured it shut, and, judging by the sound, Adele guessed he'd just placed it.

A thick eyebrow arched over an intelligent and annoyed eye staring out into the hall. "What?" the man demanded.

But before he could proceed, Agent Renee—doing Agent Renee things—slammed the bulk of his form against the door, snapping the brass chain easily and sending the man inside tumbling back with a howl.

Adele allowed herself a moment of frustration, wondering if John was *trying* to get Foucault to come down on them both. Still, she supposed what the Executive didn't know couldn't hurt him. Leoni stared, blinking and giving a little sniff of surprise. Adele shrugged, then followed her partner quickly into the penthouse of the Venetian hotel. The room was twice the size of Lorraine Strasser's. The walls were windows, again making use of the views of the city and the canal. She spotted a small in-room bar, with a row of bottles on multiple shelves.

The bed frame seemed to hover off the ground as if levitated by magnets. The room itself smelled of sweat and room service. And Adele spotted a small trolley with the remains of what looked like an expensive steak.

The man in question was cursing and spluttering, wearing a woolly white bathrobe as he pushed back to his feet, grumbling in frustration and murmuring dark words in German. He pushed one hand off the ceramic bowl of an in-suite Jacuzzi in the center of the room itself. A couple of blue towels were bunched up, damp and abandoned on the floor. The room, Adele realized a second later, also smelled of weed.

She fixed her eyes on the man she recognized from his file as Paul Krupp.

Still blustering and growling, he finally regained his feet, jabbing a quivering finger in Agent Renee's direction and uttering a series of words that John—thankfully—couldn't understand.

"What's he saying?" John muttered.

"He's politely wondering why you slammed his door into his chin," Adele replied in French, quiet and allowing interpretive license.

Paul Krupp was finally settled, his finger still pointing at John, his jaw jutting defiantly. The German millionaire had a weak chin with bristles. His eyes were lovely, though, like twin black opals, reflecting a strange amalgamation of blues and orange, as if the colors were mismatched, or perhaps he was wearing contacts.

He was average height and, judging by the proportions of his fluffy white bathrobe, of average build.

He wasn't ugly, as the uncharitable suggestion of the hostess at *Ricardo's* had implied, but judging by the silver in his hair and his average features, something a bit more akin to personality or bank account was likely what had attracted someone so young and beautiful as Fiorella Lettiere.

"I'm sorry for the intrusion," Adele tried, hoping to at least correct some of the swirling ill will.

Krupp touched gingerly at his chin, turning his glare from John to Adele, who was speaking in his language. "You know German?" he said, his voice much deeper than his physique might have suggested. A smooth, velvety voice, like rich chocolate now that it wasn't shouting through a penthouse door.

"Yes, sir," she said, quickly. She glanced towards John whose weapon was at his side now, aiming towards the floor. Behind her back, her fingers twitched in a sort of waving motion. Her attention mostly on Krupp, she did note John react to her movement and slowly holster his weapon.

Krupp, to his credit, didn't exude fear as most might at having their room intruded by three armed persons. Instead, he seemed angry, his eyes flashing.

"Do you know who I am?" he demanded in that rich, smooth voice of his.

"Paul Krupp, yes?" Adele asked.

He blinked. "What is this about?"

"We have some questions about your whereabouts last night," Adele said quickly, standing awkwardly in the doorway that her partner had busted.

"What about last night?" he demanded.

"Were you in contact with Lorraine Strasser?"

She watched his reaction firmly. But the man didn't even blink at the name. His face remained impassive, almost reptilian. Not even a blink. The sort of face used to hiding emotions. Perhaps a banker, or a lawyer, or a poker player.

"I don't know that name," he said, stiffly. "But I do believe you need to speak with my lawyer."

Adele frowned. "She was a German too."

"No clue who that is." Again, the man didn't even blink. But his tone was too dead, now—too impassive. He'd just been hit by a door; he'd been furious seconds before. Now, though, he seemed calm, cool, entirely indifferent. But the absence of an emotion was just as telling as the presence of one.

He had shifted seamlessly into a defensive mode, betraying nothing...

"Are you sure?" Adele said. "I can show you a picture."

"I don't need a picture. I don't know these women."

"You were seen with one of them, last night. You paid for her meal, in fact. And now she's dead."

At this, the man's face flickered. A frown creased his brow, and he glanced sharply towards Agent Leoni who was also watching him.

"Dead?" He swallowed once, his eyes fluttering, like a camera lens, adjusting, calculating and making a decision. At last, he shrugged. "I wish I could help you, agents. I don't know what you mean. You need to speak with my lawyer.

Adele gritted her teeth, taking her turn for frustration now. She pulled handcuffs from her waist, approaching the middle-aged man. "Turn around," she said, firmly. "Paul Krupp, you're under arrest."

***

The Italian precinct North of Venice smelled like Executive Foucault's office used to—expensive cigars mixed with cheap cigarettes covered by air freshener. Even the interrogation room they found themselves in, which Leoni said carried the more friendly title of "interview room" at this particular precinct, had the stale odor wafting on the air, likely introduced by the black vent set just below an ancient camera which looked older than Adele.

Her focus though remained on Paul Krupp. The German millionaire took a posture she was long familiar with. Wearing his white bathrobe and leaning in his folding chair, he made it seem like a king on his throne. All that was missing was his scepter and armed guards.

Though the latter had already been phoned and would be arriving soon enough from a local, high-end law firm Leoni warned them about.

Now, though, they had a brief window to themselves before the lawyer arrived.

Adele cleared her throat where she sat just off from the suspect. John sat on her side of the table, on the far edge, watching Krupp with hooded eyes. John had a dangerous look in his gaze that unsettled Adele. She knew better than to ask him to wait outside, but the way he sometimes got, especially when young women were concerned was unnerving. The last thing she needed was for Agent Renee to knock out their suspect before the lawyer arrived. They'd be lucky to escape Italy if that happened. Foucault would have both their jobs, especially after his warning at the start of the case.

Thankfully, Leoni—who also seemed a good judge of human nature—had surreptitiously maneuvered to the wall between the suspect and John, leaning against the cold concrete, and watching the scene where he stood.

Krupp kept shooting unnerved glances towards John, but he kept his lips sealed tight, breathing only through his nose, like a child refusing to spit out a marble he was chewing on.

Adele rubbed at her temples briefly, rolling her shoulders. No one spoke in the still room, and she didn't break the silence either.

Instead, she beckoned with her fingers towards Leoni. He approached, handing her three photographs he'd printed for her before entering the room.

One by one, like laying place mats, Adele set the photographs of Rebekah James, Lorraine Strasser and Fiorella Lettiere in front of Mr. Krupp. She watched his eyes as she laid them down and his gaze flitted away from John to acknowledge the photos. He swallowed briefly, staring, but didn't flinch, didn't blink.

The three young women smiled out from their head shots—all of them having aspirations in the theater or modeling had ample photos to choose from.

Adele tapped her fingers above each of the smiling faces staring up at Krupp. Leoni took this cue and leaned in, producing three more photos. He laid them each on their respective counterpart and stepped back.

John's fist tightened where it rested on the table. Krupp actually blinked now, a gasp for anyone besides the poker-faced German.

The three new photos displayed the coroner pictures of the woman's heads—each of them with their necks slit, their eyes closed, their flesh cold.

Adele just watched him, not saying a word, allowing the photos to speak for themselves. Mr. Krupp continued to stare, no longer glancing in John's direction at all. He opened his mouth, briefly, letting out a soft little sigh.

He looked towards the door sharply, all of a sudden, as if willing his lawyer to arrive. Then he looked back towards the photos, blinking now and, by the sound of things, tapping his foot hurriedly against the ground.

Adele crossed her arms, still quiet. Thankfully, Renee also kept his lips sealed, and Leoni satisfied himself with the role of spectator.

She watched Krupp, allowing the sheer weight of the six faces in the room, staring at him, to be pressure enough.

The German looked around, glanced down at the photos and winced again. His facade was crumbling now, whether from guilt or grief, Adele wasn't sure. One way or another, though, it seemed clear he knew the subjects of the photos.

"H—how did it happen?" he said at last, breaking the long silence.

Adele took her time, allowing his own words to remain heavy on the air, to stand for themselves. "They were killed by an unknown assailant," Adele said, softly. She tapped a finger over Fiorella's photo. "She was with you last night." She tapped another finger over Loraine's lifeless photo. "She was also seeing someone in the city..."

This last part was a hunch alone—she had nothing to tie Lorraine Strasser's secret boyfriend to Krupp save the connection of the masquerade ball. And also their deaths...

For a moment, the words remained heavy on the air, right where Krupp had placed his own, but then, heaving a sigh as if collapsing under the pressure of it all, he exclaimed, "I didn't kill anyone! I—I cared for them! Truly—I did. I was quite fond of both Lorraine and Fiorella!"

Adele blinked, refusing to betray the sudden jolt of excitement.

CHAPTER TWENTY FOUR

Apparently, the pressure of three murders was too much to allow the German millionaire to wait for his lawyer. Adele knew men like this were used to getting what they wanted, *when* they wanted it—understandable perhaps, given how money opened doors for everyone with a heartbeat—and were not used to waiting for anything. Least of all lawyers, or peace of mind.

But now, peace of mind was distant at best, chased away by the sightless gaze of three dead women.

"So you admit to knowing both of them?" Adele said, carefully, speaking German.

John was frowning, likely only catching a word or two of his non-native tongue. Leoni knew German perfectly but remained silent.

"We were acquaintances, yes," Krupp said, delicately, sniffing once and shrugging. "Lorraine and Fiora were friends—that's all. To see them like this..." He wrinkled his nose and looked away. "Please—I don't want to look at them. Such a shame."

"You don't seem too broken up about it," Adele said, softly.

Krupp looked back at her, frowning. "Would you like me to cry? I could do that for you. But I'm being honest, agent. They were friends... Acquaintances. Temporary companions, nothing more."

"Were you sleeping with them?" Adele said without batting an eyelid. "I can't help but notice they're quite young... You're what, forty-three?" She knew the actual age but wanted to knock him off guard even further.

"Age is a number," he spat back. "It's not like they didn't have fun too."

"So is that a yes? Were you sleeping with them?"

Krupp muttered beneath his breath for a moment, glancing to the door again as if looking for an exit now. "Move the pictures," he said through gritted teeth. Then, adding, as if it took all his willpower to do so, "*please.*"

Adele nodded to Leoni, who stepped in, carefully, respectfully, placing each photo on top of each other, and then lifting the stack, stepping back to lean against the wall once more.

Krupp stared pointedly away from where the Italian reclined.

"I noticed when I was going through your records," Adele said, quietly, "That you have a wife back in Berlin. Does she know about your... acquaintances?"

Krupp's demeanor changed all at once, the blood practically draining from his face to match the coroner photos. "You—you didn't tell her, did you?" he said, his voice straining. "I—hang on. Don't—she doesn't need to know. I didn't kill anyone! I didn't! I couldn't. Why would I? Two gorgeous women in Venice that let me sleep with them whenever I wanted in exchange for a few small gifts and some meals?"

Adele refused to wrinkle her nose. "So you were sleeping with them? That's how you saw them, then, is it? As high-end hookers? Did they see it the same way?"

Krupp snorted. "Like you said, they were young. They wanted some fun just as much as me. I'm not the bad guy here."

"Unless you killed them."

"I didn't."

Adele's eyes narrowed. "I'm not sure I believe you."

Krupp's lips pressed into a thin line again, but this time in a sort of expression of pain. He closed his eyes for a second, gathering himself. Then, in a calmer voice he said, carefully, "I come to Venice for the festival... It's a sort of break—a relief from my life back in Berlin. It's stressful, doing what I do. My wife—as you've so kindly brought up—doesn't..." He swallowed. "Doesn't appreciate the *needs* a man like me has."

Adele tried not to gag. "Needs? Is that what it is? So you come here from Germany every year for the festival to sleep with young women, is that right? Luring them with money?"

He glared at her. "I don't *kill* anyone."

Adele pointed back towards the photo stack in Leoni's hand. "And what about Rebekah James? Did you know her too?"

"That third photo?" he said, shaking his head quickly.

Leoni leaned in with the head-shot of the pretty American, holding it in front of Krupp's face. The German man barely glanced at it before shrugging and shaking his head. "Don't know her—never met her."

"Look longer," Adele said. "And try to be more convincing." She could feel her own temper rising at the cavalier way in which Krupp was simply dismissing these two women who he'd wined and dined for one purpose only. She highly doubted either of them knew about Mrs. Krupp, or the other lover in Venice. She wanted it to be Krupp—she wanted him to be guilty.

But as he looked longer at the photo of Rebekah, again there was no recognition on his face. He shrugged. “No clue who that is,” he said, firmly.

In English, Leoni said, “Ms. James' friends didn't mention anything about a lover here,” he said.

Adele winced, but leaned back now, unfolding her arms, and placing her hands against her legs, holding them still. Briefly, she allowed her mind to trace back to their interview with the American woman's friends. They'd said Rebekah had a boyfriend back in the States—someone she loved. They seemed to have thought it impossible she'd cheat on anyone...

But secret lovers weren't secret if everyone knew about them. Perhaps Rebekah's friends had been duped. Perhaps she'd also been seeing Paul Krupp behind closed doors.

But there was no evidence of it.

“When were they killed?” Krupp said suddenly, his eyes wide, his eyebrows high. “Yes, tell me, when?”

Adele frowned. “Why?”

“Because,” he said firmly, “I've been with each of my,” he coughed delicately, “acquaintances every night I've been here. We've gone to theaters to restaurants—we've been seen! There should be bills. Credit card statements,” he said suddenly, nodding fervently now. “Have you checked credit cards? Have you thought of that?”

“Interesting idea,” Leoni said, hiding a smile from where he leaned.

But Krupp seemed unwilling to let this thread go. He was nodding firmly now. “Yes,” he said, insistently. “Five days ago, when I first arrived, I was at a small production of *Othello* and then had drinks at a local place. The next day, I was...” He paused, but then looked at Adele directly in the eyes, “Making passionate love with Fiora in my hotel. We didn't leave for nearly six hours. You can ask room service.”

“One order of room service doesn't prove anything,” Leoni said, quietly.

The Italian seemed to realize the same thing as Adele. Six hours in a hotel room on Tuesday would mean that Krupp couldn't have been out and about, lurking Venice to kill Rebekah—the same woman he claimed to have no connection with.

“It wasn't just one order, though,” Krupp said, delightedly. “Definitely wasn't.” He was wagging his head up and down now, as if excited. “We ordered every hour.”

"Ordered what?" Adele said, allowing her distrust to seep into her tone.

Krupp replied without batting an eye. "Chocolate, whipped cream and cherries. Every *hour.* The caterer will remember me—I promise that."

"Why?" Leoni asked.

Krupp winked at the Italian like a couple of old pals sharing an inside joke. But Leoni didn't smile back. Krupp shrugged, though as if to say *your loss,* and said, "Because she was a round, but pleasant little thing. I asked her to join us." He shrugged again. "She declined. But still, she'll remember me. Just ask her about the man..." he coughed again. "Covered in chocolate. She'll remember."

Adele shared a look with Leoni. "And this was Tuesday?" she asked, firmly.

Krupp nodded, bobbing his head again, the relief practically emanating from him—he seemed to be able to read the disappointment in her tone. He was acting too confidently, too certain for this to be a bluff. What would be the point? They'd be able to check within the hour if he was lying.

As if sensing he'd made his case, Krupp doubled down again, declaring, "I have pictures, too. Timestamped. But yes, it was Tuesday. All night. Is that when that poor woman died? The one I don't know? Because there is no way I could have killed her. I was with Fiora the entire time."

"Ms. Lettiere is dead," Adele said, quietly.

"I... Yes, I suppose she is. But still, the room service will remember me. Credit card bills—hotels keep those for room service. Yes, I was there—they'll remember." He seemed a little more nervous now... But then nodded to himself, as if, it seemed, to convince himself more than Adele.

She watched him closely, frowning as she did. He had the demeanor of a sleazeball, or a rat. But a rat fleeing a sinking ship. A rat who knew he hadn't stolen the cheese.

She hated the possibility that he might be telling the truth. That his deviancy might be the very alibi that cleared his name. Rebekah James' friends hadn't mentioned anything about a secret lover—they seemed to have thought it extremely unlikely... Still, Adele wasn't ready to give-in just yet.

She looked to Leoni and said, "I'll wait here with John. Do you mind checking with the room service? Six hours... If there's even a chance he's lying..."

Leoni sighed but nodded. In English, he said, "I'll do that as long as you look through those photos."

Then, before she could protest, he moved towards the door with haste, as if fleeing a crime scene himself.

Adele sighed, softly, glancing out into the hall as Leoni lifted, looking in the direction of the Sergeant who was safe-keeping Mr. Krupp's personal items, including his phone. A phone filled with horrific photos.

Yet... if Mr. Krupp was telling the truth, then found somewhere in chocolate and whipped cream and depravity, she'd also find his alibi.

Which meant they had the wrong man. The killer was still out there...

She sighed, pushing slowly to her feet and tapping John on the shoulder to rise as well. She looked Krupp directly in the eyes and said, "I hope you're lying." She didn't need to say it, but it felt good to do so. She turned on her heel, with John following close behind, watching as Leoni left the precinct out the front, and then moving towards the sergeant who had Mr. Krupp's phone.

CHAPTER TWENTY FIVE

The final weekend of the festival had arrived, and with it the *Compagnia dei Cielo* masquerade ball would dawn in final culmination.

He smiled to himself, considering what came next. He hummed softly in time with the music from the stage, his legs crossed over the top of the seat in front of him, his arms spread across the empty seats on either side of him.

He watched the stage as the singers practiced for the ball itself. He'd strode in with a nametag and a stolen workman's hat. It was amazing how a little effort opened even the most sealed doors.

He hummed along with the star's part, reciting it from heart.

He watched a woman in a flowing gown cross the stage, her bare feet tapping against the wooden boards. He listened as a man replied in music to the harmonizing query. Question, answer, question, answer—every good musical composition had questions and then left the listener satisfied with an answer.

And so what would the next question be?

And who would provide the final answer?

He smiled at the thought, his arms still spread behind him, his eyes still fixed on the stage. He continued to hum as he played the scene in his mind's eye, allowing the thoughts to spread, to expand with the music itself, to fill his imagination full and complete.

Tonight was the culmination of the festival and the first day of the grand ball. And then, they would have their answer to the questions he'd posed up until now.

The guest list had practically been given to him. Everyone involved in any way with the festival was able to get their hands on it.

Sometimes, it felt like people were willing participants in his creations.

Questions demanded attention.

If he'd done everything right, it meant all eyes would now be on the ball.

And then...

He hummed a bit more, waving a finger beneath his nose lazily like a conductor.

...Then *she* would die. The final answer to it all.

They were all the same after all...

CHAPTER TWENTY SIX

Adele stood outside the interrogation room nearly two hours later, wishing she could scrub soap across her eyes, but also staring in frustration towards where Leoni was nodding, and repeating his findings. "I'm sorry," he said, softly, in response to her disbelieving look. "But it's true. Two separate staff at that hotel recognized Mr. Krupp. One of them filed a harassment complaint which the hotel has promised to look into. It isn't him, Adele. He was at the hotel during the time of the first murder."

Adele practically collapsed against the sealed interrogation room door, refusing to glance back and hoping desperately Krupp couldn't hear them from within. She'd let him stew in it a moment longer. A man like that...

She shivered, shaking her head.

Sometimes, it was hard to remember it wasn't her job to right every wrong in the world. She couldn't possibly do that. A small, vindictive part of her wanted to at least let Mr. Krupp's wife know, back in Berlin what her husband was up to in Venice.

But again, it wasn't her place. Not to mention, the lawsuits she'd open herself up to would likely permanently crease the Executive's brow in a frown as deep as they came.

No... No Krupp was a bad memory.

She winced, picturing the photos and the time stamps on his phone. Far too much chocolate and whipped cream, for her liking. But at least, mercifully, it had disguised some of the *actions* in the pictures themselves.

Worse, though, if such a thing were possible—the timestamps corroborated what Leoni was now telling her. And what Krupp had said.

Not guilty.

He couldn't have done it. He had slept with two of the victims—he'd admitted as much. But he couldn't have been there to kill Rebekah James.

"Maybe he has a partner," Adele said, hearing how desperate her words sounded even as she spoke them.

John was standing by Leoni, his gaze flicking towards Adele and staying on her. Over the last hour, she'd filled him in on the translation of Krupp's words. To her surprise, he seemed less angry than he had before. John was unpredictable in these things. It almost seemed to excite him to think the killer was still out there, where John could get at him. Rather than safe behind bars in a police station.

She shivered. Hopefully he wasn't feeling too trigger happy, one way or another.

"So what now?" Renee said, crossing his large, muscled arms. "It's not that sleazeball, so who is it?"

Adele shared a look with Leoni, as if in that final glance, he might change his words and provide some brief glimmer of hope that the German millionaire was the actual killer. But Leoni just shrugged, wincing and shaking his head apologetically.

Adele pushed away from the interrogation room, door, stalking—more than walking—towards the twin doors at the end of the hall which led out into the afternoon.

"Tonight's the culmination of the main portion of the festival," Adele said, softly. "The first week ends, and with it, most of the festivities."

"The ball too," Leoni added, walking briskly to keep pace as they moved together towards the doors.

"Yes, the ball too. Clearly, the killer is pointing towards the ball. Whoever it is—he's careful, not stupid. He knows he's guiding us towards the masquerade ball. The *Compagnia dei Cielo* are well known enough," Adele said, quickly, "He'd know the kills would attract attention. All three were on their guest list."

Leoni paused, holding out a gentle hand, his fingers grazing her arm but causing her to turn, looking him in the eye.

"Maybe he wanted us to release that to the press," Leoni said, quirking an eyebrow. "Maybe it was part of his plan. Perhaps he's frustrated we sat on that."

Adele shook her head. "The media still doesn't know the identities of the victims. Foucault wants to keep it that way. I don't see how informing the public will help anything."

Leoni frowned. "Not informing. Warning. If the killer is targeting that guest list—then others will be in danger too."

"This masquerade ball..." Adele murmured, "How big is it, exactly? Ticket sales are in the hundreds. But the night of?"

"At least a few hundred," Leoni said, without hesitating. "It's one of the more lucrative and most exclusive balls in the city during the end of the first week. It's the culmination, the climax of the festival itself."

"Well... You're right," Adele said, turning back to face the doors and reaching out a hand. She paused, though, her fingers against the metal L, her eyes peering through the glass, but her posture frozen for a moment as she considered. "It would be a warning... The killer is going to strike at this ball next. It seems obvious—everything has been leading up to this. He wants us to know where he'll kill next."

"So what do we do?" John chimed in, again, an eager edge to his tone—it seemed—at the thought of getting another shot at the real killer.

Adele kept her gaze through the doorway, her mind spinning, thinking, placing pieces together. "Everyone will be in masks, dancing... There will be noise and music and revelry..." She trailed off.

"We won't be able to find him in all that," Leoni murmured. "We'll have no way. He might kill someone in front of our eyes without us being able to stop him. The masks alone will make it impossible to narrow down potential suspects."

Adele nodded once and then pushed the precinct door open, stepping out into the street. Leoni was right. The killer was planning for this. He'd practically laid a trail of breadcrumbs to the doorstep of whatever he planned next.

But... They would only lose if they agreed to play the killer's game. She couldn't allow that to happen. No. The masquerade ball was the target, the disguise and the means and opportunity all rolled in one. Someone's life was forfeit if they allowed it to proceed.

Which meant one thing. They would have to stop the ball. They had to shut it down completely.

***

It was nearing evening by the time they managed to reach the *Compagnia dei Cielo* offices for a second time. The car ride, parking, then the brisk ten-minute walk, led by an eager John Renee, brought them back to the old, wretched office space. Now that Adele knew how ornate and pristine the structure was on the inside, she wondered if perhaps the external dilapidation in contrast was some sort of artistic statement.

She had never much understood the theater sorts.

Now, Harmony—or Ms. Herrera—was waiting outside the door to

the office space, flanked by two new lackeys Adele didn't recognize. Both of them had pristine physiques but wore brightly colored Venetian masks covering their faces.

"Well?" Harmony called out across the street. She was, to Adele's surprise, no longer wearing her ridiculous snowflake and icicle dress, but now was clad in flowing, black gown with pieces of stained-glass, it seemed-sewn into the fabric itself. She no longer had hair, suggesting, Adele thought, it had been a wig earlier, but now was completely bald save a single patch of hair buzzed in the shape of a swirling circle with reds and blues dyed through the odd symbol.

Adele met Harmony's scowling gaze. "Ms. Herrera," she said.

"Harmony!" The woman snapped.

"Yes, Harmony. Director," she added, clearing her throat and coming to a stop in front of the woman. "I need a moment of your time."

Ms. Herrera shook her head fiercely, though, causing two matching stained glass fragment earrings to swish. She gestured from side to side towards both of her escorts. One of them had his arm hooked through hers, the other was waiting, his elbow crooked, it seemed, to do the same on the other side.

"I'm quite busy," Ms. Herrera said, testily. "I'm sure you don't know, but the ball—*my ball*—is about to start. And while fashionably late is always my mode of introduction, I have to be going. So if you don't mind... On the phone you said it was urgent. Well?"

"We've had three dead now," Adele said, stiffly. "Three," she added with emphasis. "The killer is targeting your ball."

Ms. Herrera sniffed, shaking her head and causing the stained-glass fragments of her dress to reflect the dipping sunlight.

"The ball starts in an hour," Harmony said, firmly. "There's nothing we can do. I'm sorry to hear about these women. But most people of import are going to be at the *Masque Cielo*. I'm sure it's a coincidence."

Adele shook her head. "I'm afraid not," she said. "We think," she glanced towards Leoni if only to strengthen her case with corroboration before returning attention to Ms. Herrera, "that the killer is targeting your guest list. Young women—beautiful, successful... He's going to continue, Ms. Her—" she caught herself, coughed and said, "Harmony. He's going to continue."

The woman wrinkled her nose, a gesture that did not suit her perfectly applied makeup. "It sounds like you're describing your job to me. And it sounds like you're doing poorly at it. I still don't see why you called ahead to leash me like some hound."

"We didn't leash you," Leoni interjected. "I called as a courtesy. But while it is our job to find this murderer, we need your help."

"Oh? What do you want?" Harmony seemed more willing to hear the words coming from Leoni.

Adele, though, said, flatly, "Cancel the ball, call it off. Postpone it. Whatever you need to, until we can find who's behind these murders."

At this, Harmony actually snorted laughter. She shook her head side to side, bending over and snorting again. She glanced open, her eyes practically shimmering with tears from mirth. "You're—cancel? Good one." She said, scathingly. She laughed again, this time clearly forcing the sound, a harsh, grating guffaw. "Is that all?" she asked, firmly. "Hmm?"

"I'm serious," Adele countered. "Your guests are in danger."

"Is that what you think?" Herrera snapped. She now had both her arms looped through the arms of her escorts on either side, her neck straightened, her multi-hued earrings swishing. "I'll have you know, half of the higher-ups in most law enforcement will *be* at the ball. I personally invited them. Understand?" She said, firmly. "We have private security. The guests are near drunk by now, no doubt. Can you imagine canceling? We'll have a drunken riot in the streets. No, Agent Sharp, I'm afraid I will *not* be canceling anything without a direct judge's order. And as it happens, there will be three judges at the event. Maybe you can ask one there."

Adele stared, feeling her frustration mounting. She glanced at Leoni who shrugged. "Without a judge's order," he murmured, softly, "We can't bend her arm."

Adele looked back at Harmony. "If you go through with this, someone's going to die."

Harmony shook her head, and began to move, walking slowly, escorted on either side, heading towards the nearest waterway, where a sleek, black speedboat was waiting with a masked driver and another passenger in a flowing gown.

For one moment, Adele felt a wild urge to reach out and stop Ms. Herrera. But what then? Leoni was right. Without a judge's order, she couldn't force a private enterprise to close down, especially not one with deep pockets and connections like *Compagnia dei Cielo*. On top of it, Ms. Herrera was possibly right... Canceling such a large event so close to its beginning might see drunken tourists and would-be guests rioting in the city...

She breathed softly, giving a small shake of her head as John glanced at her. The three of the agents stood outside the old, crummy building, watching its beautiful occupants reach the waiting boat. Adele heard the chug of an outboard motor, watched as Ms. Herrera folded her dress delicately beneath her, and settled in the cushioned portion of the vessel. Then, the sleek, black speedboat, with its five occupants, moved very slowly away from the dock, out to the main waterway.

Harmony didn't look back a single time.

“Someone's going to die at that party,” Adele murmured.

“She won't shut it down,” Leoni replied quietly. “And we won't have enough time to get an order.”

Adele nodded slowly, showing she'd heard. They couldn't shut down the masquerade ball... But the killer was still on the loose, still targeting someone. Which meant they still had a job to do.

But if they couldn't shut down the ball, it meant they only had one option left.

“What are you thinking?” Leoni asked, noting the look of resignation on Adele's face.

She sighed once, looking away from the water and glancing back in the direction they'd come. “I'm thinking,” she said softly. “If she refuses to shut it down... We're going to have to attend that ball ourselves.”

Leoni cleared his throat, then he reached into his pocket and pulled out a single slip of golden paper with silver writing across the top in Italian.

Adele turned, staring at the man. “What's this?”

Leoni extended the golden slip to her. “A ticket,” he said, softly, “to the masquerade ball.”

Adele reached up, her fingers grazing the delicate slip of paper—though it felt more like thinly pressed aluminum than anything else. Even the ticket, the way it flashed and shimmered as she turned it to try and make out the Italian words seemed an elegant thing.

“You bought a ticket?” she asked, softly.

“I...” he coughed delicately, “I, in fact, was planning on attending anyway. As it is, I only have the one.”

Adele blinked in surprise, looking back up at Leoni. “You're sure?”

He shrugged. “They might not shut down their party for the sake of a life, but I'm more than happy to forgo a night of revelry if it means we can catch this murderer. I'm sure. We both know you're better at this sort of thing. Computers, information, flying planes,” he smiled, “all me. Finding a needle in a haystack though...” He tipped his head towards her. "I'm happy to concede that role. But," he held up a finger, "I only have the one ticket. Which means..." He glanced towards John, and shrugged apologetically, "You and I, big fellow, are going to have to run surveillance. Unless of course, you'd like to get all prettied up, John."

Renee snorted. But then paused at these words, as if realizing something and glancing sharply at Adele.

She frowned. "Wait, hang on, prettied up?"

Leoni smiled now, mirroring Harmony's own sound. "You better believe they won't let you in looking like that, ticket or not. Haven't you been listening? This is the most exclusive ball in Venice. And that ticket only gets you so far. We don't have a warrant, and they'll have their own security, meaning we can't enter without a judge's order. Too late for one of those." He smiled, patting her on the arm and turning to lead them away. "No, no," he murmured, "you can't go in like that."

"I don't have a dress," Adele protested, feeling her stomach twist. "Or a mask," she added. She frowned at Renee. "Stop grinning."

"I'm not grinning," he said while grinning.

She frowned even more now, crossing her arms. "I don't have anything fancy in my suitcase."

"Well," Leoni said, hands in his pockets now, eyes ahead as he continued to walk. "Good thing I know a guy on short notice." He looked back, doing his best, it seemed, to suppress a grin of his own. "Are you coming, or what?"

CHAPTER TWENTY SEVEN

Michaelangelo's Masks was practically empty as Adele stepped through the front door of the now familiar shop. She glanced around the cramped space, at the various pieces of art arranged on the walls. Again, she felt confronted by a leering crowd as the masks behind the glass counter stared down at her, eyeless faces fixated on her every movement.

She cleared her throat hesitantly, glancing around the small space. Behind her, through the closing door, caught by its spring, she could still hear the sound of the festival, increasing in volume. Evening had fallen now, the masquerade ball itself would start within the hour. They were running out of time before the killer would most likely make his move.

She winced at the thought, trying to consider what came next. The killer had left a trail of breadcrumbs in the form of bodies, leading them to the *Compagnia dei Cielo*'s ball. But what was his plan? Who was he after now?

Adele shivered slowly, shaking her head and stepping further into the nearly empty store. The sounds of the festival goers behind her echoed with laughter and applause and music and voices. She could hear conversations—too loud—prompted, she guessed, by the early consumption of alcohol. Even from here, through the window facing the canal, she spotted the motion and movement of various boats with performers preparing for the final parade of the last night of the festival. Everyone had likely already bought their masks, hence the empty shop.

Not that Adele was complaining. She didn't need any spectators for what came next.

"Angelo?" she called into the shop and cleared her throat. "Excuse me, Angelo!"

She heard a clearing throat, and then a face popped up from behind the glass counter, eyes bleary and red, staring out at Adele over the translucent service. The well-fed shopkeeper's eyes widened in delight and he gave a little wave, which accompanied a small hiccup.

"*Polizia*!" he declared. "Mask?" he added as a quick afterthought.

Adele nodded once. “Mask, yes, actually. This time. And...” She swallowed, trailing off, “You don't happen to have a dress somewhere too, do you? Any old thing will do.”

Now, Angelo was paying full attention. The redness of his cheeks and nose seemed due to a bottle clutched in one hand. The full-length workdays were finally being rewarded, it seemed, in the tradition of the other festival goers outside the shop.

He waved his bottle around a bit, indicating a back room. “Dress? Mask?”

“Yes,” Adele said, nodding abruptly. “Sorry, but quickly, please. I have payment. Just give me that guy there,” she said, nodding to a pale mask at the bottom of the display. It was simple, unadorned, and unpainted.

But Angelo snorted shaking his head wildly. “This? No. No for you? No-no!” he wagged a finger beneath his reddish face. “I give you better.”

Adele gritted her teeth. “More expensive too, I'd guess?”

He laughed off the comment with a shrug and a snicker and then turned, reaching out for another mask. Adele saw it and she felt her shoulders slump. She sighed and said, “Angelo, really. I'm in a hurry. Just give me the plain one please.”

But the mask maker seemed adamant now, offended even. “You no like? You say ugly?” he asked, shaking his head at her. “Go! Go then. No mask. I artist!” He waved his bottled around like a cudgel. “Angelo masks! Art!” He declared with a bellow.

Adele sighed. She didn't have time for this. Already, the clock was ticking. “Fine,” she said, firmly. “Just get me a mask and a dress. Please hurry.”

She could feel her own anxiety mounting, watching as Angelo, delicately removed the indicated face wear off the wall. She sighed in resignation, staring at the flamboyant thing, then watching as the mask maker hurried into a back room, declaring over his shoulder. “Dress! Match to dress! Mask, yes!”

The words made sense, but how he'd assembled them didn't. Still, she supposed she was at Angelo's mercy if she wanted to get into the ball. Leoni's ticket was now folded neatly in her wallet. She had the entrance slip, now she simply had to play the part.

It didn't suit her to pretend to be something she wasn't, but sometimes, it took a sheep in wolf's clothing to find a killer.

“Hurry up!” she called into the back room.

Angelo appeared almost on cue, as if he'd been waiting for the words as a sort of introduction. He held out a dress in front of his wide frame, his ample belly on either side of the cloth, jutting out like an eclipse. "Will fit," Angelo declared. "Trust me. It fit." He nodded, waving a hand towards Adele. "Come, come, try!" he said. He pointed towards a changing room at the back of the shop, behind a thin curtain.

Adele stared at the dress, then glanced at the mask. She sighed again. "Fine," she muttered. "How much do I owe you?"

***

The *Compagnia dei Cielo's* ball would take place in the Plaza theater, in the heart of Venice. Already, outside, as she made her way carefully through the rows of onlookers, she spotted men and women dressed in all manner of beautiful ensembles, each and every one wearing some sort of mask. Two rows of guests moved slowly through the wide-open doors to the magnificent theater.

Now Adele understood the acting company's fascination with felines. The giant, marble lion on *top* of the theater, a statue overlooking the crowds illuminated with flood lights held the bearing of an onlooking guardian, surveying its subjects and protectorates beneath its marble claws.

The looping architectural design of the theater itself was patterned with etchings in marble and ivy, and more statuary and stained glass. A mural of multi-colored tiles spanned the entire length of three columns facing the Grand Canal and reflecting back the rising moon.

Even outside, the theater seemed otherworldly. Fluttering ribbons and silk, likely lifted by hidden fans, extended out from flagpoles, like vibrant, multi-hued beams of sunlight stretching to the sky. A fog machine, again unseen, had created wafting vapors, extending from behind the giant marble lion's mane. The tendrils of grey mist fell onto the crowd bellow, swishing overhead as if to further disguise the mask wearers.

This would only make their jobs harder, yet Adele couldn't help but take a moment to simply stare at the presentation. Entranced by the combination of the falling night sky, the fluttering ribbons and silk, the giant statue, the old theater, the crowds of beautiful humans in beautiful garb against a backdrop off a postcard of the Grand Canal. Along the water, the first flotillas of performers, illuminated by colorful spotlights, began to move. The cheers of the crowds further down the streets could already be heard on the air. Laughter and applause and singing also echoed across the mist from the hidden fog machines.

Adele blinked, trying to focus.

She moved quicker than the other guests trailing towards the queues outside the doors. One thing she'd refused: high heels. A woman had to put her foot down somewhere. And down or up, high heels would make it impossible to maneuver. Especially in this ridiculous get-up.

She sighed softly as she neared the entrance, placing the mask she'd been given over her face now, feeling her arms chill in the mist where the dress left them exposed. She wished she'd had a chance to tan a bit before.

Focus... She thought to herself.

She scanned the crowds outside the old theater, and then her eyes landed on Agent Renee and Leoni who were waiting for her by the water's edge. Both of them wore their normal clothing—a neat, tidy suit for Leoni, and a sweater and slacks—with a mustard stain—for John.

As she drew near, though, Leoni nudged Renee, pointing towards Adele.

John turned, frowned, but then his expression slipped as his eyes landed on her. His gaze did a quick once-over as if unable to resist the motion. He blinked and stared at her mask with the effort of a man attempting to avoid being caught glancing at anything else.

The dress was modest enough, but tighter than Adele might have liked. No room for the gun in her dress, so she'd been forced to stow her phone and firearm in the small, purple purse she'd been provided, now looped over one wrist.

John continued staring at her, slack-jawed as she neared.

"Agent Sharp," Leoni said, still smiling in that lupine way of his. He nodded politely. "You look lovely," he said.

John's mouth closed a second later, and he paused long enough before swallowing to maintain at least some dignity.

"I get it," Adele snapped, "The mask is stupid. Let it go, we're here for a job." Her face was already itching beneath the thing. She'd wanted the plain white face-wear, but now, she'd been cornered into wearing this *thing*. It wasn't exactly...ugly. In fact, Adele might have thought it beautiful on someone like Ms. Herrera, or even one of the victims. It just didn't *suit* her. It was too—artistic. The single peacock feather out of the top looped back down against a crystalline mesh over her cheeks. The white porcelain of the mask itself was streaked with ribbons of purple and blue and green to match the delicate feather. The dress, at least, was a simple blue affair—with, thank God—straps.

"It's not stupid," John said, reflexively. "You look like an angel." The moment he said it, he blinked, and glanced off, shaking his head. "I mean... you look okay."

Leoni glanced between the two of them, still grinning, but then he nodded in the direction of the theater. "I think you'll fit right in," he said, softly. "Agent Sharp—remember, we'll be out her keeping surveillance. Keep us apprised of anything. Are we clear?" He had a more serious look in his eyes now and John was frowning at the words, looking at Adele again with a note of concern in his gaze.

Adele waved a hand briefly. "Yes," she said, simply. "I will. Keep an eye out here. If you see anything..."

"We'll call you," Leoni said. "You do the same." He flashed a thumbs up. "Good luck."

The way John watched her left Adele unnerved briefly. For a moment, surrounded by all the beauty, the spectacle, talent from around the country, the music and sounds and statues—despite it all—it almost seemed as if Renee only had eyes for her in that moment.

What a peculiar thought.

Still, she shrugged off the emotion rising in her chest and moved in the direction of the theater's entrance. No time for romance now... They had a killer to catch.

CHAPTER TWENTY EIGHT

Inside, the theater was even more stunning than outside. Again, a low fog hung over the room. The lights above came from chandeliers, but the crystal baubles glowed with multi-colors, casting reflective patterns across the theater like the glinting of diamonds and opals and sapphires.

Adele swallowed as she spotted a woman and man, both dressed in white outfits and white masks, floating along the ceiling, like angels. She couldn't spot the wires as the trapeze artists danced about, near the chandeliers, moving between the illuminative devices with practiced choreography.

More servers moved throughout the room below, dressed in the same pure white outfits and white masks. By the stage, a man in a black suit was crooning softly, his voice moving through the room like the mist.

Small little sparking lights, like glow-bugs also hovered across the mist. Adele frowned, uncertain if these were actual lightning bugs or some sort of technology using the mist as a reflective surface. She couldn't quite make it out as she moved between the other partygoers.

The floor itself had been cleared of any seating, and rather resembled a giant frozen lake. Some sort of gloss was spilled across the floor, giving the ground a watery, icy look. Giant lily pads—green carpets with a reflective sheen—patterned the ground, leading towards rows of tables, a dance floor with pirouetting dancers, and a small circle enclosure with a lion-tamer and two bright-eyed, golden-maned lions.

Laughter filled the area. Hundreds of guests moved throughout the room, some watching the would-be angels floating on the ceiling, others reaching out to try and touch what seemed to be lightning bugs floating in the mist. Others only had eyes for the lions and still others were pointing towards a row of acrobats in the dark recesses of the stage, preparing, it seemed, to make their entrance.

Everyone wore masks, everyone wore dresses, suits, beautiful clothing. No one stood out in that everyone did.

How on earth could she find a killer in all of this?

For a moment, as Adele stepped off a lily pad carpet onto the glossy, water-like floor, she spotted trails of silver beneath the strange varnish, like streaks of moonlight or starlight against a tapestry of sky. One moment, the floor seemed an expansive frozen lake, the next like the night itself.

She shivered, again, the emotion prompted by nothing to do with the case.

For a moment, she felt herself drift as if transported into a fairy tale. Flowers, bright yellow, vibrant orange, green, pink, purple and crimson all lined the walls behind the tables. It all seemed so... strangely wonderful. She'd never seen its likeness before.

For a brief moment, Adele paused in the stream of guests, moving from the entrance through the room. Some immediately joined the dancers, swirling, spinning, dresses flowing, gloved hands pressed in interlocking fingers as the music thrummed around them.

For a brief moment, Adele felt her guard slip. She wanted to close her eyes, to drift away. Briefly, she wondered what it might be like to attend an event like this without the worry of catching a serial killer. To her own surprise, as she watched a tall man and a smaller woman dance across the floor, she thought of John.

Immediately, beneath her mask, she felt her cheeks heat up, and she swallowed. She thought back to that kiss in Leoni's apartment. Thought back to the look in his eyes, the warmth of his lips.

She shivered, standing there—this time not only due to the sleeveless nature of her garb.

She'd missed John.

For a moment, she half-glanced to her side as if looking for the tall Frenchman. It would have been something indeed to walk into a place like this with Renee. Granted, he probably would have hated everything about it. But then again, the way he'd been staring at her, unable to look away, perhaps he wouldn't have been able to hate the spectacle, as his attention would have been already captured.

She allowed herself a small smile, grateful again for the mask. These things were really quite useful given their proper place.

She'd nearly allowed John to drift... Nearly chased him away herself. She wanted to frown now, the smile slipping. No—she couldn't let that happen again. She was determined as she stood in this strange, otherworldly old theater. Determined not to let him slip again, she needed to know where this all ended, where it took them.

She closed her eyes, behind her mask, brushing gently to the side as another group of guests moved past her, laughing and oohing and aahhing as they did.

Focus... She needed to focus. She could consider John later. The ball was lovely, but even hidden in the most beautiful scenes, one could find ugliness beneath.

Adele moved towards the dance floor, watching as one of the white-clad angels flitted above, dancing upside down, as if walking on one of the chandeliers. The woman was quite beautiful, even with the mask.

As Adele looked around, she could feel a rising current of worry. Everywhere, she saw youth and beauty. Beauty and youth. She watched as another couple danced by, laughing. She turned, examining a young woman adjusting her mask next to the lion's cage. She frowned and regarded an older gentleman helping someone who could have been his daughter step towards one of the tables with the silver seats.

So many potential victims. All of them young, all of them beautiful all of them at this masquerade ball.

So who would the killer choose? Another one of the trapeze artists moved overhead, but this time, instead of an angel, the acrobat twisted, presenting the left-side of their body, the opposite portion... And Adele realized the outfit was split down the middle. White and pure on one side, red and black on the other. A devil or an angel?

Someone was watching over this party, just like she was. She looked around, her eyes flitting from one masked face to another. Would the killer use a knife again?

Would he be so bold? She glanced towards a terrace, where one of the acrobats was adjusting a thin wire to his outfit. She began to move, slowly, towards the stairway curling up the back of the room, hidden in shadow.

The terrace would present a better vantage point. Yes—that was the move. The terrace.

***

John crossed his arms where he leaned against the dock mooring post, staring at the old theater, and frowning as the last of the guests trickled in past the three security guards collecting tickets.

"You sure you don't have another?" John grunted, his eyes still ahead.

"Ticket?" Leoni guessed. "No, I'm afraid not."

The mist was thinning against the sky now, and John's eyes kept darting to the enormous marble lion placed above the theater. He wondered how long it had taken them to get the sculpture up there just for a stupid party.

Not so stupid, though, he thought to himself. Not if it meant he could see Adele like *that.* He resisted the urge to whistle beneath his breath. Something about that mask, that dress, the confident sway of her hips against the close-fitting cloth. The way her eyes had sparkled beneath the blues and greens and...

He swallowed, shaking his head as if trying to dislodge a spell.

"Damn," he muttered.

"Pardon?" Leoni asked.

John looked over to the smaller Italian. Leoni didn't lean against a post, but instead stood with his arms crossed, his suit sleeves, somehow, practically unwrinkled despite the posture. The Italian agent kept his eyes fixed on the doors, his attention unwavering.

Other members of the public were beginning to push in, it seemed, behind the partygoers. These tourists and revelers also wore masks, but none seemed nearly as well-dressed as the masquerade attendees. John watched a group of young men and women, each of them drinking something, laughing, clinking bottles together and singing a song along with music echoing from the theater.

The crowds of revelers following the parade of spectacles on the water were also moving, slowly, along with the floating scenes of artistry. They were getting louder as they drew nearer, moving along the docks, over the bridges and following the canals.

He watched a group of older women crowd past Leoni, standing on their tiptoes as they peered up the water way, waving silk handkerchiefs towards a man paddling a red boat. On the boat, a woman in a translucent bubble spun around and around, sparklers flashing above the strange sight. Behind them, a metal dragon had a masked man riding it, juggling red balls above the dragon and, occasionally, stopping to feed the balls to the dragon which would prompt a burst of blue fire.

John looked away as the loud older woman called and hooted trying to get the attention of the boat paddler, who glanced over and then flashed a crooked grin, waving merrily towards the docks.

John sighed, stepping away from the mooring post and moving to the other side of Leoni. He stood next to the smaller man, acknowledging the theater.

"So we just wait out here, is that it?" John asked.

Leoni shrugged. “See anything worth checking out?”

“I did earlier,” John muttered.

Leoni turned his eyes away from the theater to give John a long look.

Renee glanced back. “What?” he snapped, wishing he was standing anywhere but in the presence of the handsome Italian.

“Do you dislike me for some reason?” Leoni said, softly.

John blinked. He cleared his throat. What sort of damned tactic was this? Asking a direct question? About John's *feelings* no less? The bastard.

“No,” he lied.

Leoni smiled slightly. He looked away again, glancing back towards the theater. “I'm not going to pursue Adele, John. She was clear with me. And...” He paused and shrugged. “After seeing the way she looks at you, I'm not about to intrude.” Leoni patted John on the arm, gave a little sigh, and then began to walk towards the theater entrance.

John stared after the Italian, blinking in surprise. He hastened to catch up, swallowing and saying, “Hang on. The way she looks at me? What do you mean?”

Leoni strolled towards the theater, but said, “If you don't know, I won't tell you, Renee.” He looked at the tall man. “I said I wouldn't pursue her. But if you're dumb enough to bungle it, then that's on your head.” Leoni flashed a wicked little grin and then patted John on the arm again, a bit more roughly this time.

Before John could consider this, and before Leoni could speak to one of the guards outside the theater, John's phone began to ring.

He frowned, fishing the device from his pocket. “Adele?” he said, quickly.

A pause, the sound of music and laughter, and then, over the background noise, Agent Sharp's voice. “John? Look, is Christopher with you?”

John frowned, glancing towards the Italian. “After a fashion.”

“Well, I think I have a lead. I might need backup.”

CHAPTER TWENTY NINE

Adele's eyes fixated on the young woman she'd spotted from her vantage point on the terrace. Below, the woman in question was laughing a controlled, crystalline sound, designed to resonate and allure more than communicate any sort of mirth. The woman in question was followed by a gaggle of seven young men, all of them fawning over the masked lady.

Her gently sloped neck gave way to a strapless dress with three diamond-like buttons down the bosom. Her mask itself was perfectly transparent, as if made of blown glass, allowing onlookers to glimpse her stunning features beneath the glass. It was a strange juxtaposition between the distortion of the glass itself, but also the obvious beauty of a celestial nose, sharp cheekbones and small chin beneath full lips. The woman had blonde hair, similar to the second victim: Lorraine Strasser. She was moving through her crowd of onlookers, nodding in greeting to anyone who tried to catch her attention.

Obviously some sort of local celebrity.

The belle of the ball stood out from the others, receiving more than her fair share of jealous glances as she passed, moving, with her entourage, towards the lion enclosure.

"That's gotta be it," Adele murmured, watching from the terrace, her phone pressed against her dress from where she'd gone through the embarrassing but necessary effort of retrieving it from the small purple purse that also carried her gun.

She watched the woman trace through the crowd, wondering if, perhaps, anyone else was watching with equally close scrutiny. The killer was here, somewhere. In hiding? In plain sight? Behind one of the many masks? Was he also watching this beautiful young creature carve her way through the dance floor?

It would be the crown jewel in the murderer's achievement. A belle of the ball as the culmination of his killing spree.

Would he do it with so many witnesses hanging on the blonde woman's every word?

Adele frowned, her eyes tracing the men introducing themselves to the lady. Did any of them look suspicious? No signs of hidden blades she could spot from up here. Could one of them be the killer?

Adele needed a closer look. She began to turn, but at just that moment, a voice suddenly echoed out in the room, vibrating from the direction of the stage.

She turned, glancing towards where Ms. Herrera was standing on the platform, her arms wide as if to embrace the room.

"Welcome!" Harmony declared, a small mic against the smooth slope of her mask. "It is a delight to see all of you here with us today. *Compagnia dei Cielo* bids all of you a humble greeting! My name is Harmony, and I will be the Master of Ceremonies for this evening."

A small cheer and scattering of applause met these words.

Behind the mask, Harmony's lips twisted up. The tall woman, with her nearly sheared head, dipped in a small bow, causing the stained-glass pieces dangling from her ears to flash in the many lights throughout the room. Her dress similarly reflected back the glow.

"Of course, the entertainment for the evening has only just begun," Harmony's projected voice echoed through the hall. She spoke firmly, powerfully, with an obvious stage presence. Everyone stared up at the Master of Ceremonies, waiting—it seemed—for another opportunity to applaud.

Adele, though, redirected her attention towards the young belle. She was looking towards Harmony as well, but seemed mildly irritated, now—judging by her hand on her slender waist—by the redirection of her many suitors' attention away from her.

Adele began to move now, trying to keep her attention on the young belle, while also moving quickly towards the stairs. She needed to get closer.

Harmony's voice continued to echo over the old theater, but Adele ignored the sounds now, focusing on the curving stairwell in the back of the theater, leading down from the balcony seating. She hastened back towards the glazed lake-like floor, hurrying now, through the attentive crowd towards where the young, blonde woman was standing near the lion-enclosure.

Adele winced, wondering what might happen with a quick nudge or a push. But the woman, her hand still on her hip, remained standing.

A commotion did erupt, however—instead of coming from the belle, it was coming from the stage.

Adele frowned, looking over the heads around her towards where Harmony seemed to now be speaking to someone in the audience closest to the stage.

“I'm afraid I don't understand...” The Master of Ceremonies was saying, still in English for the sake of the tourists, her voice hoarse. She leaned in.

Then, Adele watched, horrified as a hand snaked up from the audience, latched around the back of Ms. Herrera's neck and yanked the woman bodily off the stage. A scream went up from the crowd. People yelled in horror and surprise.

Adele cursed and broke into a sprint, shoving through onlookers and hastening towards the sound of the commotion now accompanied by yelling and physical motion.

Damn it. Not another young woman, then. The killer was after Harmony. Of course, it all made sense now. Who better to target than the head of the *Compagnia dei Cielo* themselves—maybe this had been the killer's goal all along!

Adele elbowed past a man, knocking a wineglass flying. “Sorry!” she yelled, before breaking through a gaggle of women who were too distracted by one of the trapeze artists to notice the commotion towards the front of the room. She pulled her phone from her purse, cursing, already dialing John's number as she raced forward.

Adele heard another shout, more commotion and then a scream—this time, by the sound of things, coming from Harmony herself.

CHAPTER THIRTY

A tangle of limbs, vibrant jewelry and flashing pieces of stained glass were hard to parse out as Adele tried to close in on the two struggling figures. Over her shoulder, she spotted John and Leoni hurrying towards her through the masked gawkers, accompanied by the security officers from out front.

Ever her nemesis, a high heel went flying past Adele's face, the dislodged strap nearly whipping her in the eye. She winced, reflexively lifting a defensive hand as she moved in to separate the struggling entities.

"Adele!" a loud, booming voice echoed behind her. She waved towards Agent Renee, gesturing at him to join her.

But as she stood over the two struggling forms of Ms. Herrera and the unknown assailant, she realized both were still moving, both kicking beneath the trapeze artists above.

"Stop!" she snapped, feeling her heart hammer, but allowing her thoughts to catch up with her fear.

Harmony was gasping and scratching long, painted nails across the cheek of the small man on top of her.

The man in question wasn't familiar to Adele. His mask had been knocked off in the tussle, and he had bright, reddish features, not quite unlike those of Angelo's back at the mask shop.

Adele leaned, grabbing the short-statured man, and ripping him by the collar of his suit off the Master of Ceremonies.

The leader of the *Compagnia dei Cielo* remained on the ground for a moment, gasping, and trying to recover herself. Part of her dress was torn, and there was a bruise forming just beneath her eye, which was also exposed from an askew mask.

Adele knew enough Italian to understand what the man was screaming, trying to struggle from her grasp and reach towards Harmony. "You whore!"

"Stop that," Adele snapped, shaking the man roughly. His hands were empty. No knife. She quickly held him with one hand, while her other darted towards his pockets.

At the same time Agent Renee came barreling through the crowd, shoving gawkers roughly aside, and reaching Adele a second later. A hand the size of a glove descended on the small fellow's other shoulder, holding him in place like an anchor on a ship.

The small man turned, and actually had to crane his neck to meet John's towering glare. The fellow squeaked and stuttered something in Italian. Agent Leoni sauntered through the crowd behind John, like a small boat traveling in the wake of an icebreaker.

Leoni said something softly, and then reached down to help Ms. Herrera back to her feet. She accepted his hand, gasping, and cursing in Italian, muttering a series of expletives.

"Marlowe," she said at last, growling, "you idiot. You're going to jail for this." She spoke in English, and Adele wasn't sure if this was for her benefit or John's.

Adele looked away from the small man she had in her grasp. Again, she hadn't turned up any weapons from the frisk.

"You know this man?" she said, waving towards the assailant.

Harmony sniffed, reaching up delicately and probing at the bruise beneath her eye. All of a sudden she seemed to realize the attention levied on her. Ever the performer, she tilted her chin just so, allowing the lights to catch her mask as she readjusted it on her face. With an air of wounded dignity, she sniffed again, and with an imperious wave of her hand, she gestured towards the man, "A talentless hack," she said, firmly.

The man struggling in John's large grasp seemed to understand her English well enough. He spat back in the same language, "Whore. Thief. Coward. You wouldn't know talent if it came up and tweaked that big nose of yours!"

Harmony snorted back. She was making shooing motions towards the guests crowded around her. But at the same time, she couldn't seem to resist a parting shot. "Big nose? I suppose for someone as small as you everything seems large. Your stature matches your skill as an actor; I was right to fire you the first time. The second time was just for fun."

The man tried to tear away from John, wanting to lash out again.

Adele though, stepped between the assailant and his target. She turned towards the fellow, who had a nose like a beak, and eyebrows too close together. "What do you think you're doing?" she snapped. "That's assault," she added, pointing towards the stage where he had dragged Harmony from.

Marlowe looked at Adele, his features still tinged with the effects of alcohol. He sniffed and coughed and glanced off sheepishly like a child scolded by a headmaster. "She's evil," he said, snapping. "She still owes me," he added, waving a finger at the master of ceremonies. The same finger eventually jutted skyward, towards one of the trapeze artists who was continuing, resiliently, the dancing pattern across the ceiling.

"That was supposed to be me," he snapped. "She promised. You promised!" He added, shouting towards Harmony again.

The tall woman's eyes flashed with something akin to guilt, but just as quickly she shook her head, and clicked her tongue. "Agents, you saw this. He attacked me. Arrest him."

Before she received a response, as if assuming her word would just be followed to the letter based on the delivery alone, she turned, facing the onlookers nearest to the front of the stage, and spreading her arms as if to embrace them. "Please, don't let a little bad behavior distract you." She gestured towards the tables, which were now being laden with silver platters, the odor of scrumptious food now wafting through the room. "Aha, dinner is served. Please, this way. This troubled man is going to be taken from here. And no, thank you, I'm quite all right. Thank you very much."

Still speaking moving back and forth, translating herself between Italian and English, likely for the sake of any tourists in the crowd, she moved towards the platters of food, along with the majority of the gawkers and onlookers.

Adele, for her part, shook the shoulder of the small assailant. "You attacked her because she fired you?" The man just stared at her, sullen and frustrated. He muttered something in Italian, and Adele turned sharply towards Agent Leoni. "Can you keep an eye on him," she said, quickly.

The small man's hands were already behind his back, and there was a sound of a *click* as Renée cuffed him.

Adele was already glancing around the crowd, some of the faces still turned towards them, the others attracted by the promise of food. She couldn't see the young woman she spotted earlier.

"Where is she?" Adele said, softly to herself. "Where is she?" she repeated a bit louder this time.

"Who are you looking for?" John said, leaning in.

"A girl. A young woman. Looked like the sort of person our killer might target."

John frowned, glancing around, and trying to follow Adele's sweeping gaze. "Do you think he got her in the confusion?"

Adele hesitated, and then pointed. "There, see, by the drinks. I think that's her."

She moved in that direction, but then paused. The young woman looked safe enough. If indeed it was the same blonde-haired beauty from before. Still, there were no other crowds, no onlookers, no cries of further violence. The room was settling once more back into a swing—the music, the spectacle glossing over the random act of violence. Agent Leoni still had a hold of the suspect.

"Can you keep him," Adele said. "Get him somewhere quiet, question him."

Leoni dipped his head.

"And John," she said, turning towards the large Frenchmen. "See that girl over there, can you keep an eye on her?"

Renee frowned. "What are you going to do?"

Adele's mind was racing as she stood by the front of the stage, glancing after Harmony, whose tall form still stood proud amidst the gathered audience.

Three murders. All of them on the guest list for this particular ball.

And yet something didn't sit right. Where was the killer? Not this small, drunk man, surely. There never would have been a better distraction than this sudden attack. And yet as far she could tell, the killer was still in hiding. Which meant what, exactly?

Was he even coming?

For a moment, frozen in place between the two agents, she closed her eyes, thinking. Her fingers trailed absently towards the mask, touching the cold, smooth surface.

And then she froze. Her mouth opened, just a bit.

She frowned, thinking back to the mask maker. Thinking of that sales pitch the first time she had visited his story.

"Seventeenth-century masks," she murmured, softly.

"Excuse me?" Leoni said.

Adele glanced at the man where he stood, seeming awkward without a mask of his own surrounded in a sea of covered faces. She looked around and closed her eyes again, thinking. "Those masks. The ones the victims had. Angelo, the mask maker, said they were seventeenth-century French aristocracy."

"Yes?" Leoni said, phrasing the word as a question.

Adele felt a shiver along her spine. "What if we're at the wrong ball?"

Neither of her partners blinked. She could feel her own mind racing, thinking desperately. Maybe it hadn't been a trail of breadcrumbs at all? Maybe the bodies from the guest list of this ball had been exactly intended to damage the ball. Maybe, even, the killer had hoped it would close the ball. She had been close to doing that very thing hadn't she? If Harmony had been more cooperative, they would've postponed the ball entirely.

What if that's what the killer had been anticipating?

Seventeenth-century French aristocracy.

All three of the masks had been similar. The ones around them were more ornate, some of them translucent, some of them with entire head coverings. Many of them beautiful, but all quite different. The masks on the victims, though, had all followed a similar pattern. Coloring was different, yes, and some etchings were strange, but in general, according to the mask maker, they were all from the same time period.

"What do you mean?" Agent Leoni said. "A different ball?"

"What if he was trying to shut down this one? Or, what if he was just trying to throw us off the scent?" Adele could hear her heartbeat pounding now. "What if this was a ruse? He's not here," she said this last part breathlessly. "I don't think he's here."

Now, she turned towards the small man in Leoni's grasp; she gripped him by the lapel, looking him square in the face. "Marlowe," she said, firmly, "you're in trouble. Did someone set you up to do it?"

The man blinked, his features still reddish. "She fired me," he said, softly.

"Did someone put you up to attacking her?" Adele said, firmly.

The man just shrugged, glancing off. In Adele's mind she wondered how much it would've taken for someone to coerce an unhinged, fired actor to assault his perceived source of grievance. Had someone maybe slipped him some money? Riled him up over beers at the bar? Maybe she was overthinking it.

"You're familiar with the area," she said, shaking his suit and causing his frame to rattle. "Seventeenth-century French aristocracy. Any other balls that follow that?"

The man winced, shrugging once, but then pausing. "I didn't mean to hit her."

Adele held her tongue. "Are there any other parties like that?" she insisted.

The native Venetian shrugged again, but then glumly said, "There are all sorts of balls. But yes, there's one old, stodgy sort. It's not nearly as popular as this one. I wouldn't act for them even if they paid me."

"There is one? Where?" Adele said, firmly.

The wounded actor glanced off to the side, and after a muttered encouragement from Agent Leoni, he looked up, and said, "They're hosted out of *Ricardo's*. It's a restaurant—"

But Adele was already turning, moving. "John, just keep an eye on that girl. Leoni, the suspect is yours."

Both of them called after her in perfect synchronization. "Where are you going?"

In answer, though, Adele stalked away, ripping the stupid mask off her face, and tossing it onto one of the tables, where it clanged against a silver platter. "Following a hunch," she called over her shoulder. She picked up pace, grateful again she hadn't worn high heels, hefting her purse, and keeping it close to hand in case she needed the firearm kept within.

What if the killer had been playing them all along? What if he wasn't at this ball at all. The masks. The masks were the clue. They had to be. Which meant she was already running late. For all she knew, the killer had already claimed his prize.

CHAPTER THIRTY ONE

He watched her across the room. The restaurant on the water had often served as the space for the Seventeenth century styled masquerade—*Danza dell'aristocrazia.*

. They weren't as flashy as some of the other parties during the final week of the festival, nor were they as populated.

Something like sixty people meandered through the room, all of them dressed appropriately for the time period, powdered wigs, and big hooped dresses for the ladies with neckerchiefs and long sleeves for the men.

As for himself, as he moved slowly, walking along the glass wall which faced the canal, he adjusted his suit. His barrel chest protruded against a tight, silver-buttoned jacket.

He wore a simple mask, pale and ghostly, again appropriate to the time period.

Behind him, he could hear stringed instruments coming from *Ricardo's* small performer stage. He could smell the food, wafting on the air from the direction of the kitchens. He allowed himself a small, contented smile, all the while staring through the glass at the small boat which had just arrived, docked near one of the mooring posts. A woman stepped out, followed closely by an older man and woman.

Her parents had come with her.

He stared through his mask, his face beneath becoming rather fixed as well. Why had she brought her parents? They didn't need to see what came next.

He shivered, shaking his head and glancing off through the glass.

He turned, nodding politely at a group of guests crowded around one of the small tables, with the swishing blue waters visible through the translucent floor.

He moved until he was on the far side of the room, his arms crossed over his barrel chest, his eyes hooded.

She hadn't known he would be here. Of course, if she had, she never would've come. But the invitations had worked, as he knew they would. The invitations for a month, dropped off, not by the postal workers, not even by an event organizer. Hand-delivered, personally, assuring just this moment.

So what if she had brought her parents? Like a little girl, a child, needing the hand holding. So what?

He would continue with the plan anyway. She deserved what happened next.

And so, he lay in wait, watching, moving with the flow of the gathered guests. It felt like being a bottle on waves, swishing back and forth, but through his mask, his eyes fixed on her. He gestured towards one of the waiters, and the man approached, quirking a quizzical eyebrow behind a thin mask.

"Her drinks," said the man, "make sure they're filled. Sherry," he added. "She likes sherry, and..." he added, catching the waiter's arms and holding him tight. The man frowned, his wrist going rigid. "Don't tell her it's from me, just keep them coming."

The waiter looked hesitant for a moment, but then the large man slid a €50 note into his pocket and patted him on the chest.

The money seemed to assuage any sense of hesitation, and the waiter nodded happily, turning on his heel to fulfill the request.

Now it was a waiting game. He wasn't the sort to accost someone out in the open, no. He preferred to approach when they least expected him.

His teeth gnashed behind his mask. He was the composer, and this was the composition. All of them were the same after all... The whores. Rotten to the core. Every single one. The way they had bled out beneath his fingers, only a practice for this true culmination.

Hadn't she been the one who'd started it? Hadn't she been the one who sealed their fates?

He glared towards where she was laughing at the table, accepting the brought drink without question, and already taking a sip. He'd spent enough time with her, watching her, even talking with her, that he knew her habits. In fact, they'd gone on a date once before, nearly two months ago.

She shouldn't have treated him like that. Shouldn't have laughed at him. He had thought it was a date. But she had said she thought it was an interview.

He wanted to smash his fist against the wall, but instead remained with his arms crossed, watching as the glass was emptied and another was brought out.

The girl and her parents were settling at a table, next to some people they seemed to recognize despite the ensembles.

"Come here my love," he said softly. "Come on." He spoke with the gentle, coaxing tones of a master wrangling a hound. "Come here," he said, now through gritted teeth, his voice muffled by the mask. Freedom be damned, witnesses too. Some things were more important than self-preservation. Self-respect for one. But more than that... sending a message. Besides, no one would suspect him. They'd already missed it three times. Just one last one—one more time. That's all he needed.

The second glass wasn't emptied nearly as quickly, but it had the effect he'd known it would. She had never been one to hold her drinks. And now, he watched as she excused herself from the table with her parents, her perfect blonde hair swishing above the mask. Even from here, the sloped angle of her cheekbones was obvious. She had always been gorgeous. Gorgeous and cruel.

He waited, watching as she approached, passing by him towards the powder room. She didn't even recognize him.

This back portion of the restaurant was the only part not covered in windows. The darker concrete allowed for the privacy of the guests. The walls were painted green with a crimson stripe and had tasteful portraits of Venetian scenery lining the corridor that led to the bathrooms. Two candles spluttered in brackets, exuding the faint aroma of apples.

He waited until he heard the footsteps pause, and then he turned around the corner as well, stalking towards where her small form stood.

She was glancing from side to side, navigating the restrictions in her peripheral vision due to her own mask. She wore a flowing teal dress that spilled all the way to the ground and long pale gloves. She looked positively... *scrumptious*.

She finally seemed to decide which of the doors was to the lady's powder room, and she pushed in; as the door began to swing shut behind her, the man stuck out a hand, catching it.

She didn't ask, didn't react. Suggesting again, she hadn't seen him.

He slipped quietly in behind her, where she approached the sink, and glanced in the mirror, reaching up and slowly removing her mask to reveal her young, eye-catching features.

He stared from the side, catching the smooth angle of her jawline, the perfect counters of her nose and cheeks, and the composition of her facial structure, allowing her long eyelashes to flutter in the mirror. She seemed a moving sculpture like from some museum.

He could feel his stomach twisting as he stared at her, allowing the door behind him to ease shut completely now, without a sound. He reached back with his fingers and twisted the lock on the door. It clicked quietly.

For a moment, he stood there, watching her, his head slightly tilted, so he could stare at her through the gaps in his mask—he could hear his own labored breaths now echoing in the still, quiet space.

"Hello, Mona," he murmured quietly.

The young woman in front of the mirror yelped, dropping her mask and whirling around. Her foot stamped into the mask where it had fallen as she tried to reorient.

She stared at the man in the powder room with her, the blood fleeing her cheeks all of a sudden. She stammered a couple of times, staring at his outfit, staring at the golden name tag on his lapel, clearly confused.

He took two quick steps towards her now but didn't reach out to touch—not yet. He towered over her, his shadow swallowing her like some whale at night.

Beneath the glow of the fluorescent lights above, her long eyelashes fluttered, and her porcelain features scrunched in a frown, her smooth brow just furrowing as she tried to make sense. Her eyes glanced towards his golden name tag, designed to trust someone with such a simple apparatus.

Then again, he *was* involved with this ball. A master of ceremony, in fact, hired two years ago. Long before he'd met Mona. Long before she'd cursed him with an askance glance and a tilted smile of those full lips.

He realized he was still breathing heavily.

"I—I, am I in the wrong room?" she stammered, shaking her head and glancing over his shoulder. Of course, she didn't know the door was locked, not yet.

This was always the most delicious part. The way the mind churned in search of some hope, some unlikely release from the reality of the situation.

He smiled behind his mask, enjoying every moment.

"Not laughing now, are you?" he said. "Are you Mona?"

Her eyes widened and she took a hesitant step back, her blue dress dragging over the crushed mask on the ground. She reached out a steadying hand against the cold sink, blinking and hesitantly shaking her head.

"I'm sorry, do I know you? This is the woman's room—I think. Are you in the wrong room?" her eyes glanced towards his name tag again. But some of the trust and confusion was now leaving her cheeks along with the blood. Pale and scared.

Just how he liked them. All of them. They were all the same.

"No more laughter, hmm?" he said, repeating the phrase he'd rehearsed so many times leading up to this moment.

"I don't understand," she said, her voice trembling. He was so close now, and she began to inhale slowly, sucking air as if preparing to scream, just in case. She was still uncertain of the danger she was in. So stupid—all of them were. Their stupid, pretty faces. Princesses protected by daddy and money. Protected by a world fawning over symmetrical flesh and bone. Nothing besides a gift from birth. And yet they flaunted it like it made them special. Not effort, not work, not character—no, stupid beauty and youth. Nothing they'd earned at all.

He felt his hand clenching at his side, his teeth gritting. The pompousness of it all. Little more than a spoiled brat driving around a BMW their daddy bought for them, thinking somehow it made them special. But no—pure genetics. Pure luck.

So why had she ensnared him so? Why did she turn so many heads? A sculpted face, like some artistic declaration from existence itself. A masterpiece of art slipped into by sheer chance... Just like those masks he'd left behind. Of course, everyone would be too stupid to realize the origin of those masks. His masquerade ball was nothing to most Venetians. Nothing to the beautiful *things* in the city.

Well, he'd shown them. He'd claimed them as unwitting participants in his own ball.

In the same way he was about to do with Mona.

Yes. When it all ended, even their ghosts would dance to his tune, subject to *his* masquerade. The ultimate underdog story, starring him against the fashionistas, the theater types, against expectation, pomp and ceremony. His hands had claimed their lives for himself. The masks had claimed their beauty, hiding them in anonymity. Anonymity under his authority, under *his* masquerade ball. Besides... He smiled. They weren't laughing now.

"You... shouldn't... have laughed," He said, breathing heavily now, panting like a dog with a bone between his teeth.

He reached up, lowering his own mask and staring at her now. He caught a reflection of himself in the mirror. He had never considered himself an ugly man. The surgical scar above his lip from where his cleft pallet had been worked on still displayed beneath an attempt at a mustache. His eyes were perhaps a bit deeper than he would have liked—perpetually giving him a look of tiredness. His cheeks—well, he stored fat in his face. Nothing he could do about that.

But he was a large man, too. Tall, proud. That's what these little whores wanted, wasn't it? A man's man—beauty to tame a beast?

Well, this beast wouldn't be tamed.

She gaped, staring at him... "I... I'm sorry, do I know you?"

He felt like he'd been slapped, standing before her, mask clutched in his hand, peeled from his face like the skin of some fruit, revealing the juicy flesh beneath... But now?

Do I know you?

His temper rose like a tide. He yelled in fury, backhanding her across the face and sending her stumbling beneath the sink, her head cracking against the porcelain with a dull *thunk.* She yelled in pain, scrambling to try to regain her feet, but he closed in, his large frame and barrel chest jutting out like some barricade, his shadow swallowing her whole.

"Stay there!" he spat. "Stay on the ground, Mona! I'm warning you!"

She whimpered, staring up at him. She began to draw breath, but his hand shot out, gripping her throat. His large hand fit entirely around her slender neck, and he gave a soft little squeeze. Any breath she'd been trying to summon suddenly fled in a wheezing gasp.

"None of that," he muttered, darkly. "Scream and I squeeze. Understand?"

She was crying now, tears streaking her makeup, spreading it down her cheek, removing her second mask as well. Even beneath this one, though, she was a natural beauty. A lure in the dark. A light on cold roads beneath glinting moonlight. The sort of distraction to lure travelers to their demise. She knew what she was doing.

"You all know what you're doing," he spat, growling deeply. His shoulders heaved. "You know—you know!" He screamed. "How dare you not remember me? How dare you!"

"I'm sorry!" She spluttered. "Please... Please what—what do you want? Help!" She tried to yell, but he clapped a hand over his mouth now. His other hand reached into his belt, pulling out the small knife... a knife he'd used three times before.

"All the same," he muttered again, his breath ragged, heavy. "All of you, the exact same... You laughed. When I thanked you for the date... You *laughed.* Said it wasn't a date! What did you think? I paid for the meal and everything!"

Now, suddenly, her eyes widened in greater horror. Recognition dawned across her perfect features. Mona shook her head, desperately, her golden hair shifting about beneath the sink. Something about beauty crammed in such an undignified location gave him a jolt of vindictive satisfaction. It was like watching a crumpled daisy struggle and twist.

He found he was smiling now, his hand still around her throat.

She tried to choke out a response, her eyes wide, but fixed on his face. She hadn't seen the knife yet. Just another little delight, unwrapping a birthday gift one ribbon at a time.

He released his grip just enough so she could choke out. "I'm sorry. I—I remember now! Yes. I thought—I'm sorry. I didn't mean to laugh!"

His eyes narrowed over his leer and he bent his head, dropping to a knee and looking her in the eyes. "Didn't mean to?" he whispered softly. "I suppose I understand." He caressed the slope of her neck with his large hand, running a thumb along her windpipe until she gagged. "Yes... We all do things we don't mean to. I didn't mean to hurt Rebekah. Or Lorraine. Or Fiorella..." he shook his head sadly. "Didn't mean to at all. Didn't mean to slit their pretty little throats and allow them to bleed out as I watched. I liked it when they gasped the final time. You can see the moment when the light fades, you know? When it disappears from their eyes. It's like a spark." He shook his head slightly, staring off into the distance, watching, for a moment, a memory seared into his brain.

He supposed, perhaps, if he was being charitable, he might understand why she hadn't known it was a date. He'd contacted her agency—another little model-wanna-be. He'd posed as an employer, interested in an actress for a fake photo shoot. It had been simple enough, using his ties to the festival.

How could he not? He'd seen her headshot passed around with some of his coworkers. He'd seen her beauty—it had snared his eye and he couldn't look away.

He shook his head slowly... Perhaps if he was being generous, he could understand why when she'd met him at the restaurant, she hadn't realized it was a date. She'd brought a portfolio with her work, been smiling, wearing a suit, all professional, all polite.

She hadn't known then, had she? They were meant to be.

So what if it had taken a little deception to get here there? So what? When he'd told her, at the end of the evening he could still remember the conversation...

"Do you remember?" he whispered, his hand still outstretched, the knife still just hidden behind his back. "Do you? Hmm? Do you remember what I said?"

"I'm sorry," she was gasping, crying still, shaking her head. "I'm sorry! Please, I'm sorry. We can go on a date, whatever you want! Please, I'm sorry!"

His face twisted in rage... "You *things* will say anything won't you? Just to escape justice? Hmm? I asked you what you thought of the date. You stared at me, then laughed. You said you didn't realize I'd thought this was a date. You looked at me like I was trash. Like there was never a chance someone like *you* would look at someone like *me.* You laughed. And then you left. I heard you after, you know. When you paused and called your agency. I heard you yelling, upset. Saying that you'd been set up. Is that what you think of me? Some ugly nuisance? Some *weird creep.* Remember those words? Hmm? Not laughing now are you. The weird creep is scary when you're alone, isn't he? Hmm? Laugh again, Mona. No—look at me. Don't cry. Damn it, LOOK AT ME!" He said in a fierce, but controlled tone, his voice reverberating. "Laugh. Do it Mona. Laugh for me. Now."

Her eyes were wide, they flicked past his waist and then froze. She'd spotted the glint of the knife. Her lips were trembling where she rested, crumpled beneath the sink.

"Oh, yes," he said. "Hmm. Things don't look very nice right now, do they, Mona? Hmm? Laugh for me. Laugh, I said!"

CHAPTER THIRTY TWO

Adele didn't bother with a paddle this time, and instead sat in the back of a small speedboat, tapping her fingers rapidly against the metal of the side, waiting impatiently as the boat guide headed towards the dock outside the glass-structure of *Ricardo's* restaurant. The festival around them was in full swing. Twice, now, someone had thrown flowers towards the boat, and a red rose had landed in the vessel, which the boatman had lifted and tucked behind his ear, waving towards the masked audience on the side of the water.

Fireworks were exploding all across the city, and music and dance and spectacle filled the streets and bridges along Venice's canals. But Adele's eyes remained fixed on the glassy structure of the looming restaurant ahead of them.

"I'll pay after," she said, quickly. "Sorry, look—just stay here. No time—no don't tie off. Wait!"

The boat tapped delicately against the rubber guards against the side of the wooden docks. Many other small watercrafts lined the jetty outside the restaurant. Inside, she could see figures moving about, bright lights, people in strange, old-fashioned outfits and masks to match the victims. This was it.

This was the ball. It had to be.

"Come on, come on," she muttered, poised now as the boatman guided them in. Before they'd come to a full halt, she jumped from the vessel, her feet tapping against the jetty. She then raced forward, her dress fluttering, her shoes slapping against the wood, her purse clutched in one hand.

She stood out, no longer wearing her mask, but now wasn't the time to worry about tickets or decorum.

Two doormen raised their hands as she approached, like some sort of guardians, their masks expressionless as they tried to intervene.

"Police!" Adele snapped, shoving one of their hands away.

The doormen were hesitant though and tried to block her path. One of them grabbed her arm, yanking a bit too hard.

She snarled, pulling her gun—not pointing it, but pulling it. Both doormen immediately backed away, letting go and allowing access.

Adele kept the gun pointed down and said, a final time, "Sorry. But police. Move!"

They stepped fully away from the door, and she shoved through, into a much smaller, cozier masquerade ball than the one she'd left. Here, people in strange garb were dancing in time with live stringed musicians at the back. Food was being served and small groups were gathered around translucent gaps in the ground, watching the water beneath and laughing together.

Adele's eyes danced around the room, her breath heavy, trying to find something *anything* that stood out. Behind her, she could see the two doormen muttering quickly into cellphones, likely calling for police.

Good. She thought. Back up.

Where was he? Had she made a mistake? A hunch was only a hunch... But the mask maker had been clear. The masks were from *this* ball. Seventeenth century something or other. She'd forgotten now. It didn't matter either way. The killer had a message; he'd wanted to share it. But he'd also gone out of his way to kill guests from the other ball—a competitor. Much larger and better funded judging by the looks of things inside the small, glass restaurant.

Still, through the windows, displayed against the city, the scene of the buildings on either side of the canal, the lights and spotlights from the passing floats and the fireworks in the distance gave even this small gathering an eerie, otherworldly appearance.

She breathed heavily, mask-less—attracting more than a few curious glances.

"You," she said, pointing towards a passing waitress with a golden name tag. "Is anyone missing? Hey, stop, police!"

The young woman in question only picked up her pace though, shooting uncomfortable glances towards the doormen, then Adele, and then towards the customers she was serving.

Adele huffed in frustration, approaching a table with young partygoers. Some of them wore powdered wigs and odd neckerchiefs. "Hey," Adele said, waving her hands to catch their attention. Masks turned towards her, like barn owls on a branch. Their conversations quieted as they stared at her. She tried again, slowly, speaking English just in case anyone understood. "Is anyone missing? Any of your friends? Anyone you've seen?"

Blank stares. She growled and tried French. But this didn't help either. A couple of the younger women at the back of the group were giggling now, whispering to each other and Adele exhaled in frustration, turning to face the rest of the restaurant. She spotted the band playing, violins and cellos mostly. She watched as five or so couples danced around the clear floor, moving in time with a slower music than had been allowed back at the *Compagnia dei Cielo* ball.

She needed to think.

If the killer was back at the other ball, then John and Leoni would have to handle it. They were more than equipped. But the three victims had nearly shut down that ball. The masks didn't match. It was like the killer was speaking, his language clear and obvious.

Not everyone could communicate in the native tongue of psychopaths and killers. Especially seeing as the words were more subconscious, psychological, than voiced and reasoned. But it all made sense to her. It did. She had studied the language—she could speak it.

And whoever the killer was had been playing a game. He thought he was clever—smarter than the rest of them.

So where was he now?

Cautious. He'd always been cautious.

Adele watched the two doormen behind her, still yammering into their phones, both of them glaring at her through the glass, but standing close enough to the dock they could jump in case.

Now, some of the partygoers had spotted her gun and were whispering.

"Polizia," Adele said quickly. "Polizia!" She repeated.

Some partygoers calmed a bit at this, but others still kept a watchful eye on her, nervous now in their motions. She exhaled in frustration, forcing herself to think, to ignore the eyes on her, ignore the attention. She wished more than ever she hadn't been forced to wear a stupid dress now.

Still, she needed to think like the murderer.

Had he lured his next victim somewhere?

She hesitated, but then shook her head, her eyes moving away from the glass corners, the walls staring out at the city.

No. He killed under the cover of night, wearing a mask. This was not a bold man. He was a coward. Someone who preferred his actions hidden from plain sight...

Which meant what?

She breathed slowly... And then, her eyes turned from the glass, the walls, the crowds, the witnesses. They settled on a single dark hall at the back of the restaurant.

The bathrooms?

He didn't lure his victims. He sprung when they were vulnerable.

Her eyes remained fixed now on the dark hall, the only space in the restaurant not girded with some see-through material. The only space for privacy.

Privacy, the place for the intimate, but also the depraved...

She picked up her pace now, marching forward. She reached the hall, past a row of paintings, ignoring the artwork, her eyes dancing from a door with a male figure. She pushed it open. “Hello?”

The bathroom was empty. She frowned, turning to the other door. She reached out and tried to enter.

Locked.

Her heartbeat pounded; she could feel eyes still watching her down the hall. In her form-fitting dress, her purse in one hand, her gun in the other, Adele's eyes narrowed, and she rapped the purse-clutching fist against the door. “Hello? Hello!” She said, louder.

No response. Then, a sound. Was that a whimper?

“Hello?” she called, more urgently.

She tried the handle again. Still locked.

CHAPTER THIRTY THREE

Adele backed up, her shoulders slamming against the wall. She breathed deep, thanking her lucky stars she'd refused high heels and then, with a yell she rushed forward, slamming her foot *hard* into the weaker section of the door.

These bathroom doors weren't thick oak, but rather flimsy and serviceable. It cracked beneath the pressure and she kicked again, her ankle jarring, wincing but feeling a flush of relief as the door slammed open and she stumbled forward, her gun still clutched in one hand.

The scene before her curdled her blood.

A *large,* very large fellow stood over a small, bleeding woman. The man had a knife, which was pressed to the woman's neck. She was twitching and gasping, moving still. Alive, then. But blood had begun to trickle down her throat.

"Stop!" Adele yelled. She fired, twice.

But the big man had been alerted by the shattered door and he dropped on top of his victim, going flat and twisting suddenly, using the woman in the teal dress like a shield.

Adele cursed, her bullets slamming into tiles above the sink, chipping flecks of ceramic and sending them scattering across the ground.

"Don't move!" Adele yelled. "Don't you dare!"

The large man had odd features, a scarred lip and deep, ghoulish eyes. He was easily as tall as John, and wider—though partly due to a poor diet, it would seem.

Still, he dwarfed the woman clutched in his grip, like some sort of sea monster grasping at a silver fish.

He snarled in her direction, spitting Italian words she couldn't understand. But the gesture of his knife now against the woman's bleeding neck was obvious enough. His eyes blazed at her, and he flung a mask in her direction which she dodged, by sidestepping. The face covering slammed against the wall behind her.

"Let her go!" Adele said. "Or next bullet is for your head."

If he understood her, he didn't show it. Instead, he seemed caught between a decision, glancing down at the shivering, trembling woman in his grasp, then back up at Adele, his eyes still blazing with fury and anger.

He stared at her features for a moment, his eyes sliding across her face, down her nose to her cheeks. For a moment, Adele felt gross like she was some sort of prized hog being examined at a butcher's shop. The man seemed to see something in her he didn't like and gestured wildly with the bloody knife. Moving it from her to his victim, screaming more words she couldn't understand.

Now, she heard footsteps behind her, hurried, rapid footfalls. She glanced in the mirror, spotting the two doormen had pulled up and were now staring in horror at the scene in the bathroom.

"Stay back," she demanded, aiming the words over her shoulder, but her eyes and barrel still pointed towards the threat.

He was staring from her to his clutched prize, further enraged, somehow, by Adele's arrival. Why, she couldn't say. But she knew that sort of leering, ogling look. A look she'd received before. Some called her an exotic beauty, others called her all sorts of other, colorful names. Hating her before she'd ever so much as said a word due to appearance alone. Getting ahead in a profession in law enforcement had always come with obstacles due to facial symmetry alone.

Again, Adele hated she'd worn the dress.

"Let her go!" she demanded, voice rising to fill the space. Seeing, in the mirror, the two doormen behind her frozen in place as if unsure what to do.

The large man on the ground was shaking his head though, clutching the gasping, trembling form of his new victim against his chest like some security blanket. One large, hairy arm wrapped around her slender waist, holding her tight against him. His other hand kept the knife against her windpipe. She was still bleeding—a superficial cut, though, Adele realized.

She aimed, carefully, trying to gauge the likelihood of a successful shot.

The man wasn't calming down. He was becoming more agitated under Adele's watchful glare. For a moment, she wished Leoni had come with them.

She needed someone to translate. Then again, perhaps that would only make things worse. The man, the gorilla of a fellow, was getting more and more agitated, his wide, deep set, ghoulish eyes flashing with some demonic rage. His knife was pressing harder and harder against the woman's skin.

She knew that look. He was going to finish what he'd started and damn the consequences.

As if finally deciding something, the man ripped his gaze away from Adele, looking down at the victim in his lap. He stared at the side of her cheek, his eyes flashing with strange longing, and then the knife began to cut, to finish the job.

She didn't have a shot. No time to think.

She yelled, fired at the ceiling, just to buy time, and the man flinched, the knife going still, and at the same moment, Adele lunged, covering the distance. Again, grateful she didn't wear high heels, her dress fluttering around her as she lunged in, knee first.

A dress or not, as she surged over the top of the girl, the gunshot distracting everyone for second, she had a spare moment to lash out, her knee catching the man solidly in the side of the face.

She had thought it might stun him. She had seen the angle, timed it perfectly.

But as she crashed over, against the ground, gasping, it felt like she'd slammed her knee into the side of a boulder.

The man was still upright, shaking his head, dazed, and it was Adele on the floor. She still had her gun in her hand, though, and she aimed straight towards him. With a snarl, though, the man, who had been little more than distracted by a knee to the forehead, spun around, his thick skull glinting beneath the florescent lights. He flung the victim towards Adele now, shoving her, hard. The pain seemed to have jarred him into a more reasonable course of action. Or, at the very least, one bent on self-preservation. He shouted in fury and stamped a foot, almost like a child, but then, as Adele tried to disentangle from the victim on top of her, he turned and bolted.

Like an American linebacker, he slammed into the two doormen, sending both of them reeling back. One of them went head over heels through the swinging door of the men's restroom.

Adele, quickly, extricated herself from the victim, glanced down, staring. Yes, only a superficial cut. She was still breathing. Adele quickly ripped at her dress. It took her second, but she tore off a piece of the cloth, careful to use a clean portion, and then pressed it to the woman's neck. She pointed at the second doorman who was still trying to recover.

"Keep pressure," she demanded, miming the motion with her hand gesturing hurriedly at him with her gun.

The doorman tentatively entered, glancing up the hall towards the fleeing form of the killer, then back towards Adele. She gestured now with her off hand, lowering the gun. The man hesitantly approached, and then, quickening, nodded, showing he'd understood, and dropped to a knee, placing his hand firmly against the young woman's throat. He kept the cloth in place.

Adele mimed a phone call with her pinkie and thumb, and said, "*Polizia!*"

The Italian nodded back quickly.

Now, certain the young woman would be taken care of, Adele turned, and broke into a run, racing back out into the hall. An older couple were coming nearer, their faces creased in extreme worry. The man tried to stop her, asking her something in Italian, but Adele brushed past him. She heard the groggy groan of the second doorman who'd been sent bodily through the men's bathroom. She paused just in time to watch the large killer, barreling through the final portion of a small group of guests, sending powdered wigs flying and masks scattering as he raced back outside through the glass door.

Adele gave pursuit, her gun lowered, her finger against the trigger guard, careful not to let loose an unintentional shot.

She heard the sound of a motor and yelled in frustration as she realized the man was commandeering the boat she'd rented.

As she also exited the restaurant onto the dock, she spotted the speedboat turning, rocking wildly beneath the large frame of the enormous killer. He had a knife, brandishing it towards the driver, but the boatman seemed to have his wits about him, and he lunged, jumping over the side before the large man could catch him.

For a moment, the large man floundered on the water, rocking back and forth.

Adele aimed; the knife flashed. But the large man spotted her just in time and dropped, ducking low.

Adele cursed. She couldn't aim lower. Behind him, crowds had filled the rails, were watching the procession of the floats along the river.

Adele's heart hammered, watching as the large man, likely native to Venice, began to guide the boat himself, heading back up the water, fleeing.

She glanced wildly around and spotted a gondola. She would never be able to catch him like that, but if she reached the shore to run along the walkways, perhaps she could catch up before he reached the far bridge.

She could hear the chug of the motor as she landed inside the wooden boat and began to paddle, doing exactly as Leoni had when they'd first arrived at *Ricardo's*.

It didn't take long for the front of the wooden gondola to jar against the sandstone side of the walkway opposite the canal. She moved quickly, hastening towards the nearest rail, and then, stowing her gun back in her purse and looping the bag over her shoulder, she reached up, climbing.

To her surprise, a couple of helping hands reached over. The festival, still in full swing, had the Venetians and the tourists giddy. Two older men who'd helped were nodding, smiling at her from behind their own masks, and flashing thumbs up.

She thanked them with a nod of her own, but was already moving, hurrying through the crowds, shoulders brushing against shoulders, ducking under a juggler throwing flaming bowling pins over his head and catching them behind his back.

She apologized quickly as she nearly tripped over a busker's guitar case, and then found the railing, watching as the killer, and his small speedboat, made his way up the canal.

Because of his size, and perhaps, in part, due to his inexperience with this particular watercraft, he was moving slowly.

"Stop!" she yelled.

The killer didn't look back. She continued to move, following the same waterway, pushing through the crowd, through the festival goers, yelling even louder, "Stop right there!" but it didn't matter.

The words fell on deaf ears. What was the point of shouting? He was clearly determined to try and escape.

So she saved her breath, jogging now, cutting in and out of the crowd, wishing desperately she'd called one of the other agents for backup.

Now, as she moved along the rail, she saw a particularly large gathering of people. She cursed, knowing that if she tried to move through them, she'd lose the speedboat which was heading towards the bridge. So, instead, she jumped onto the railing itself, walking across it like a balancing beam, hurriedly, moving quickly, doing her best not to look over the edge at the water. She reached the other side, jumping back onto the bridge itself. Below her, she spotted the killer's boat, moving just beneath, water spreading out as white waves on either side.

She aimed, this time towards the liquid.

She waited as the boat crossed beneath her, it would emerge a second later on the other side of the bridge. She would have a clear shot.

"Stop!" she tried a final time.

The tip of the boat emerged, she braced, aiming, preparing to end it now if she had to.

And then the boat emerged.

But there was no killer.

She frowned in frustration, glancing sharply the other direction. And then she spotted him, clambering desperately over a railing on the opposite side of the bridge from where he had abandoned the boat. He was wet, suggesting he'd taken a dive.

She cursed, wheeling around, and though this part of the dock had fewer pedestrians, she still didn't have a clear shot. The man broke into a sprint, aiming towards one of the small alleyways that Venice was famous for. She gave chase, fear trickling along her back with pulses of adrenaline, watching as the man's enormous frame slipped into the small alley, and he sidestepped, scraping his belly against the wall.

She aimed again, but he disappeared around the corner just before she could fire, she cursed, and then paused. Was it smart to follow him back there?

If he was waiting around the corner with a knife, or another weapon, she'd be a sitting duck.

The crowds around this portion of the city were smaller, the festival goers sparse. There would be fewer witnesses. Exactly the sort of space the killer might like.

Breathing slowly, she began to inch through the alley, gun raised. It wouldn't give her plenty of time. But it would give her enough space in case he was waiting in ambush.

Fewer people, fewer witnesses.

But fewer people meant open ground to run. A second later she heard the clatter of footsteps.

He wasn't waiting, he was bolting.

She cursed, stepping out of the alley, and breaking into a run herself. She spotted him, moving up the pathway between large buildings on either side, heading away from the canals, away from the water.

If he reached the vehicle, she wouldn't catch him. She had to get to him first.

She burst forward.

The man was large, heavyset, dangerous, and muscled. But this meant he was also slower. She raced, gaining, and now he was glancing frantically over his shoulder, gasping and wheezing, clearly not meant for large bursts of exertion.

His face was reddened, his eyes bulging. The knife was still clutched firmly in his left hand.

She aimed, gun rising, and shouted, "Get down! Get down now!"

The man paused for a moment, breathing heavily, relieved, it seemed, to have an excuse to stop moving.

He was gulping and gasping, desperate, trying to gain air. For a moment, she wondered if this was perhaps how his victims had felt, unable to breathe, their necks slit, gurgling on their own blood. For a moment, she thought to fire.

But for now, he wasn't a threat. He still had a knife, but he was far enough away, nearly twenty paces, but she had him in her sights.

There was nowhere left for him to go. No alleys to escape into.

"Get on the ground, now!" she yelled.

The man slowly turned, his knife still clutched in one hand.

"Get on the ground!" she yelled again.

He was breathing heavily, his large chest heaving and falling.

"Careful," she said, sternly. "I *will* shoot you."

She wasn't sure if he understood a single word, but at the very least, he would understand the gestures with the weapon. He didn't stare at the gun though; his eyes were fixed on her face. Again, she felt an oily, gross feeling as he stared at her, examining her like an item.

He said something softly, shaking his head.

She gestured with the gun, firmly, aiming towards the ground. She stepped in, closer, now only ten paces away.

"I *will* shoot you unless you drop," she said firmly.

The man just continued to stare at her, and his tongue actually reached out and licked his lower lip. He swallowed once, and closed his eyes, inhaling through his nose as if savoring something delectable.

His eyes opened again, and some of the redness had faded from his cheeks. He glanced over his shoulder, but he was still breathing heavily.

"Nowhere left to go," she said, quietly.

It was a strange thing to confront a killer who couldn't speak her language. He didn't seem to understand the words she was saying, and the few mutterings he gave she couldn't comprehend. But the language she had spoken, the language she understood to come and catch him was universal among psychopaths and serial killers everywhere. The language of blood, of graves, and bones hidden deep, was a language she knew, and he knew. The language of unspoken words and subconscious thoughts, a language of brokenness and hidden secrets. A language formed in depravity but released in brutal action. And this was a language he was fluent in. Not a language she enjoyed, not one she'd come up with, but one that she had to know to do her job.

And yet somehow, in those thoughts, in the brief exchange between his half glances, and muttered comments, she knew, in part, the despair he was feeling. This knowledge that whatever he'd enacted, whatever he'd wanted was falling apart around him. He had failed. She had seen to it. Nothing gave her greater delight. The wind behind her had picked up, passing through the streets between the buildings, carried over the sea, and tinged with a salty odor. The cool breeze against her skin raised the hair on her arms, and for a moment she felt the chill of wearing her dress.

She kept her gun pointed, but didn't move closer, and didn't back away. Sometimes, in moments like these, patience was all that was required.

If he thought it through, and came up with another plan, she would respond. But for the moment, she knew he was trapped. Now, he just had to realize it himself.

His eyes flashed; he stared at her, and fireworks exploded behind him all of a sudden, illuminating the scene and accompanying the bathing moon.

He muttered something else, a word she couldn't understand. And then he spat off to the side reached up, and with a quick, swift motion slit his own neck.

The knife clattered first, falling from suddenly rigid fingers. It flashed with red and silver where it hit the ground. The body followed, toppling to its knees first, blood down his neck and throat, gurgling, a desperate sound.

She cursed, instincts taking over and broke into a sprint. She dropped by the man's side, quickly pressing her beautiful dress to the man's bloody neck, trying to stop the flow. Already, his eyes were shut, already, crimson stained his throat, the ground. He twitched, then stopped moving.

Adele cursed, trying to keep pressure, but already feeling the warmth seep through the thin cloth of her clothing. She stared, trying to bind the wound, trying... desperately... futilely... watching, refusing to look away. He had stared at her like she was some sort of item, a slab of meat. And now, bleeding, like a stuck pig, like something else found in a butcher's shop.

Her hands were stained, her dress too. No more pulse, no more movement at all. Adele breathed heavily, holding a hand to the fabric against his neck. No one to witness his death. No one to mourn his passing, fireworks overhead as if the city itself were celebrating.

She stared at his corpse a moment longer, exhaling slowly, and then, despite every instinct, every part of her wanting to just leave him there, she reached into her pocket, one hand still pressing her dress to his neck, and pulled her phone to called for paramedics.

CHAPTER THIRTY FOUR

Adele shivered where she stood in the shadow of one of the balconies, watching the police move about the crime scene. She stared at the shape beneath the white tarp which had been dragged over the corpse.

Dead.

So many things seemed to end that way. She glanced up at the skies—the fireworks had faded now. The festival was still ongoing but had moved to other parts of the city and diminished in intensity with home-bound spectators, exhausted from the night's culmination.

In the same way, perhaps, the killer's own crescendo had finally come to a conclusion, ending beneath a white sheet on a cold, blood-streaked sidewalk.

She watched where Agent Leoni was discussing in grave tones with some of the Italians. Watched as John approached her, frowning as he neared.

"You look cold," the tall Frenchman said, coming to her side and leaning against the wall beneath the balcony as well. He didn't face her, but rather preferred to stare off in the same direction as she did.

"You try wearing a dress," Adele murmured. "It's hardly meant to be warm."

"I'll take you at your word," John said. He glanced at her, his dark eyes peering down where she shivered. "If I had a coat, I'd offer it to you."

"If you did, I'd probably say no," Adele said, flashing a small, weary smile to show she was kidding. She turned her attention back to the body, shivering as she did. Agent Leoni had stepped away from the gathered police and looked around. The handsome Italian spotted both of them and began to approach, moving with surefooted steps through the Venetian streets.

"Sometimes these things end bloody," John said. "Give yourself a break. You need food and sleep. I hear *Ricardo's* is a nice place."

Adele glanced at him, scowling. "Not funny," she muttered. "Besides, I'm not really in the mood for Italian."

John's eyebrows flicked up a bit. He winked. "How about French?"

he said, innocently.

She elbowed him in the ribs, soft enough to be playful, hard enough to shut him up.

Agent Leoni now stepped beneath the shadow of the terrace above, glancing between the two of them. "They identified him," he said with a nod.

"He dead?" Adele asked, if only for further confirmation.

"Yes, I'm afraid."

"Well, others aren't anymore. I suppose it's a fair trade," Adele murmured.

Leoni blinked, tracing the words, but then said, "His name was Abele De Rose. A part-time opera singer and a patron of that masquerade at *Ricardo's*. One of the masters of ceremony. Looks like he had a bit of a vendetta against *Compagnia dei Cielo*. We have a police report of threats made. Nothing ever came of it."

Adele breathed slowly, nodding. "Two birds with one stone, then. Killing the ball's guests as a vengeance, and killing the young women as..."

"Jealousy, most likely," Leoni said, soft. "The other young woman, a Mona Santarossa is going to make a full recovery. Thanks to you."

"Jealousy," said Adele, shaking her head. "What a stupid reason..."

"You'd be surprised what people would do for jealousy," Leoni said, shrugging. "Good job, though. Both of you."

John didn't grunt, this time, but instead said, "And you." He reached out a large hand, and shook Leoni's, standing beneath the terrace, both of them looking each other in the eyes as Adele watched.

She half-frowned at the exchange. Was it her imagination, or were they being friendly all of a sudden? John said, "Thanks," with a simple nod.

Leoni returned the gesture. "And to you, Agent Renee. It's been a pleasure." The Italian gave Adele a warm smile and a nod, and then turned, moving back towards the gathered police, moving with his usual slow, careful pace as if plotting out each step with caution, watching the very cracks in the ground as he moved away.

Adele watched him retreat, but then turned away to glance at John.

"I think I am tired," she murmured. "Not sure I'm up for a drive to the city."

"We still have that rat-infested horror hole," John said, nodding. "We could always stay there and take our chance with the lice."

Adele smiled, then exhaled slowly. "I'm sure they'll have clean sheets." She glanced back towards the body beneath the white cloth, shivered once, and then turned away, limping slowly from where her foot had crashed into the bathroom door back at *Ricardo's*. John sidled next to her, and her hand slowly slipped around his shoulders, using him for support as the two of them moved away from the crime scene, away from the corpse and back out into the city.

CHAPTER THIRTY FIVE

Adele heard John moving about the kitchen. She glanced over her shoulder from where she stood near the raincoat closet of her small French apartment. Back in Paris, now, the next afternoon, she was glad to be off the flight, glad to leave that horrible hotel behind them.

It was as awful as they'd been told. She scratched at her neck in annoyance, perhaps out of little more than concern, but part of her wondered if the promises of lice had been a bit more than accurate.

Still, she was glad to be back at her place.

And glad, somehow, that John was here too.

“Ready to go over that report?” he called from the kitchen.

“Yeah, one second!” she called back from where she stood by the closet, staring at the sealed door.

She shivered briefly, listening as her partner moved about the kitchen, heard the sound of a whisk as he began to stir the eggs he'd promised to make. A *killer* omelet, he'd said. She wasn't so sure. Especially after seeing him reach for the pickles in the back of the fridge.

She winced, but still felt a flush of gratitude, stepping past where both their suitcases rested by the front door.

The taxi drive to her place had given them an opportunity to split up, to separate. It had been John who'd asked if she wanted to spend the afternoon going over their report to Foucault.

John who'd asked, but Adele who'd said yes.

She didn't want to do work, but she also didn't want John to leave. A strange thought, perhaps. And yet she'd made up her mind. She'd give it a chance. Besides, free omelets were always a perk.

On top of it, while she'd rather get a nap, take a shower, or make sure she didn't have lice from that stupid hotel, she also found that simply having Renee around was worth the sacrifice of the creature comforts. At least for now.

The killer was out there. The man who'd been taunting her for nearly a decade. She wasn't about to give up the chase now. No, rather, instead of hiding, it was her turn to go on the offensive.

She was going to find him... She could feel it. She still needed to ask Foucault about that camera—to see if his contacts had any leads. One way or another, she'd seen his face. She knew what the killer looked like.

Where would he go next? Into hiding? Stay nearby in Paris, keeping an eye on her?

She shook her head, hearing John humming in the kitchen, listening to the sound of a saltshaker and, what she desperately hoped she was wrong about—the popping of a cap from a bottle of beer.

"John," she called over her shoulder, one hand extended towards the raincoat closet. "You're not putting beer in the omelet, are you?"

A pause. "Umm. No?"

"That sounds like a question. What about pickles?"

"Adele, just trust me, okay?"

She sighed and wanted to retort. But she supposed a beer and pickle omelet was a small sacrifice to pay for having Renee over at the apartment. Only PG—she was determined. At least for now. But having him around made the difference.

The difference for what exactly?

Courage, she supposed. Courage enough to look at what Robert had left her. Did she want to know? She shivered, one hand resting against the handle to the closet.

But then, still listening to John behind her, strengthened by absolutely nothing more than the sheer sound of him, she slowly slid open the closet.

There, in the back, the brown parcel she'd received nearly a month ago. She'd left it, untouched, untended.

She'd intended to leave it there forever. But sometimes, things hidden in the closet were of little value unless exposed to the light.

She swallowed again, shaking her head slowly and then reaching out.

She pulled the package to her and carefully, meticulously, like unwrapping a Christmas present, peeled the tape away. She moved over to the sofa, sitting down and unwrapping the box, listening as John now whistled and then paused long enough to take a swig of something behind her.

She didn't roll her eyes as her gaze was now glued to the box on her lap. She opened the flaps, fingers—to her surprise—shaking from the motion. She swallowed, feeling a lump in her throat and then opened the box completely, staring inside.

She frowned, reaching in and pulling out a single manila folder.

On the front, was a small note which read. *My love is yours forever, my dear. Trust your instincts.*

She frowned. That was it. A simple, two line note on the front of the folder. She wasn't sure what she'd been expecting. Robert had always been a sentimental sort. But then again, he also knew the truth of the saying: actions spoke louder than words.

And so, with hesitant, careful motions, she peeled open the manila folder, and froze.

Robert's actions were, indeed, far louder than any words.

She stared, her mouth open, at the multiple photos of a small man moving through sliding glass doors. A man she recognized.

She leaned in, staring, lifting the photos and shifting through them. She glanced at the back of the photo, reading a quick scribbled note. *Agence D'enquête Privée.*

Had Robert hired a private investigator?

She shivered, staring.

In one of the photos, the small man was staring at the camera, his eyes catching the light, one of them far brighter than the other, like a reflective piece of glass. He was small, frail standing against the steps as he did.

But also, he had hair. Thin, curling hair, and eyebrows too. This photo was taken before he must have shaved them, then.

"Robert, what did you stumble on?" Adele whispered softly, wondering now if her old mentor had touched a stove too hot to handle. Why hadn't he told her what he'd found?

She flipped another photo. The only other one with writing on the back. It read, "*Suspect? Outside Adele's, watching. Followed. Thought you'd be interested where he went, Robert.*"

The handwriting was cramped, blocky—not Robert's. The private investigator's?

She turned to the final photo and then went suddenly still.

The man was entering a building and now, the title of the structure was visible over his diminutive form. She stared, unblinking, trying to make sense of it.

A police precinct in Paris.

The man was entering the sliding doors, entering a police station...

She shivered, remember now back to the copycat killer who'd captured her father, more than a year ago now. She remembered how he'd taunted, whispered and hinted...

Something about the killer's connections had given him an

advantage. Now, it all was starting to make sense.

Was her mother's killer a policeman?

Impossible...

But maybe...

She shivered, wide-eyed, staring at the photo and shaking her head.

“Adele?” a voice called from the kitchen. “Do you like mustard on your eggs?”

She swallowed, her throat dry, her fingers still all of a sudden. She flipped the photos over a second time, but then forced her eyes away, looking up and out the window, facing the city. She watched through the glass, eyes on the horizon, past Paris itself.

Slowly, she closed the lid to the box, tucking it gently against the armrest. Robert had hired a private investigator. His parting gift to Adele, helping her with the thing she cared most about. Robert always knew what to do.

She shivered, shaking her head side to side. He'd hired someone who'd followed the killer to a police station. What did it mean? Had the small man been making a report? Was he on the force? Did he have friends there? It would explain so much if he had those connections.

She leaned back, resting her head against the top of the headrest, feeling a slow chill down her spine. Robert, even from the grave, was helping.

“Thank you,” she murmured at the ceiling, feeling tears suddenly in her eyes.

“I went ahead and added mustard!” John called. She heard the soft clink of plates against the kitchen table. The scrape of a chair. “Trust me,” her friend called, “these are to die for!”

Adele blinked, feeling a tear trickle down her cheek. She glanced towards the box on the couch, wanting to reach out, to rip it open, to stare at those photos and memorize every pixel. She wanted to go through each one with a fine-toothed comb...

Trust your instincts.

She would do that... All of it. She was more determined now than ever.

But, listening to John prattling behind her, listening to the clink of plates being set, she supposed it wouldn't be the worst thing in the world to wait until after brunch. No, perhaps a little bit of patience would go a long way.

Besides, those pictures weren't going anywhere. They were hers. Not Foucault's, not the DGSI's. They were hers. The killer had made a mistake. She was closing in. He would feel the same icy shiver down his spine now. He didn't realize how close she was.

She reached up, wiping angrily at her face, wiping her tears away and then rising, sniffing once. With almost an air of disdain, she purposely looked away from the brown box with the pictures.

They could wait, at least for a moment.

Mustard, beer and pickled eggs were waiting. More importantly, though, the chef was waiting, watching her over his own plate, waiting politely for her to join before tucking in. She met his gaze where he was grinning across his breakfast creation, watching her approach with excitement.

One way or another, the killer was on his own. Alone, isolated. Adele didn't have to be. She had others to rely on, to count on. Others who would help. Others like Robert. Like John.

If she had to lie about some stupid eggs, it wouldn't be the worst thing in the world.

Her smile was rather fixed as she approached, smelling the creations from the plate. But as she met John's own grin, his eyes flashing in delight and some mischievousness, she found her smile became a bit more eased.

"Thanks," she said, quickly, looking determinedly away from the small brown box against the arm of the couch.

"Well?" John said, gesturing at the food. "Thoughts?"

She glanced down. "No pickles," she said, suddenly, relieved. The omelet had cheese and onions and mushrooms. And in fact, smelled quite good. She looked up. "No mustard either."

John winked, grinning. "Gotta keep you on your toes, Agent Sharp. So, about that report..."

She listened vaguely as he trailed off, running over the details of their case in Venice. John had been on particularly John-esque behavior over the last few days. This case seemed to have brought out some of his more furious tendencies. She thought back to their conversation in the old theater. He'd been about to tell her something... It had seemed important.

Now, though, there he sat, smiling, winking. Back to his good-natured self. She felt a chill along her arms accompanying a note of worry on John's behalf.

But perhaps now wasn't the time. No... She couldn't solve every case.

She watched him—a man in her apartment. He'd even made her

breakfast. Without pickles.

The chill faded and she smiled, feeling a flicker of warmth through her chest.

The killer would have to wait. At least for a moment. After breakfast, though, she'd hunt him. And she wouldn't stop until he, too, was a lump beneath a white sheet.

***

"Would you like some juice? Oh—oh, so sorry, sir. I mean, what can I get you?"

The painter leaned back in the airplane seat, looking up at the stewardess from beneath his hat. He hated it when people mistook him for a child, but then again, it had often been his greatest weapon. He smiled sweetly, allowing his features to arrange like an artwork themselves.

"Water is fine," he said, softly. "*Merci.* Say, how much longer is it until we arrive?"

The stewardess turned towards her cart, pouring the water into a glass with ice. He watched, frowning at the ice. It would hurt his teeth. He wasn't thirsty anyway, at least not for water.

He glanced towards the window of the plane, across the empty seats between him and the side of the plane. He'd purchased all three seats of course—he hated flying with others. Besides, a man from his means needed *something* to invest in.

And invested he was.

"Only another hour until Berlin," the stewardess said pleasantly, placing the cup on the upright table.

The Painter nodded once, and leaned back, glancing out the window, allowing a small smile to curve his lips.

Germany—it had been a while.

He wondered what Adele's father was doing now. Soon, very soon, he wouldn't have to wonder at all. Very soon, neither would Adele.

The cat was out of the bag. She'd seen his face.

Now, like many of the great artists of old, he was on a timer—a contract was due, a masterpiece and commission waiting for completion, an excited audience on the edge of their seats waiting for the grand revelation.

Soon, very soon.

He continued to smile and reached into the small cup, removing the ice cubes, and placing them gently on the seat next to him. Sometimes, it was just nice to watch something melt. Then, he took the plastic cup and sipped softly, enjoying the view of the sunlight coming through the open window.

So very, very soon.

NOW AVAILABLE!

<u>LEFT TO FEAR</u>
(An Adele Sharp Mystery—Book 10)

"When you think that life cannot get better, Blake Pierce comes up with another masterpiece of thriller and mystery! This book is full of twists and the end brings a surprising revelation. I strongly recommend this book to the permanent library of any reader that enjoys a very well written thriller."
--Books and Movie Reviews, Roberto Mattos (re Almost Gone)

LEFT TO FEAR is book #10 in a new FBI thriller series featuring Adele Sharp (the series begins with LEFT TO DIE, book #1) by USA Today bestselling author Blake Pierce, whose #1 bestseller Once Gone (a free download) has received over 1,000 five star reviews.

As bodies turn up dead in ports around the Mediterranean, FBI Special Agent Adele Sharp—triple agent of the U.S., France and Germany—is the only one who can navigate the thorny jurisdiction issues between all the countries.

She is also the only one brilliant enough to enter the mind of this psychotic killer and hunt him down.

Why is he criss-crossing the Mediterranean? Why is he leaving a victim in each port? Is water his common theme? The vessels he uses? Or something else entirely?

Time is running out, and if Adele makes a wrong choice, the life of the next victim—or her own—may just depend on it.

An action-packed mystery series of international intrigue and riveting suspense, LEFT TO FEAR will leave you turning pages late into the night.

Blake Pierce

Blake Pierce is the USA Today bestselling author of the RILEY PAGE mystery series, which includes seventeen books. Blake Pierce is also the author of the MACKENZIE WHITE mystery series, comprising fourteen books; of the AVERY BLACK mystery series, comprising six books; of the KERI LOCKE mystery series, comprising five books; of the MAKING OF RILEY PAIGE mystery series, comprising six books; of the KATE WISE mystery series, comprising seven books; of the CHLOE FINE psychological suspense mystery, comprising six books; of the JESSE HUNT psychological suspense thriller series, comprising nineteen books; of the AU PAIR psychological suspense thriller series, comprising three books; of the ZOE PRIME mystery series, comprising six books; of the ADELE SHARP mystery series, comprising thirteen books; of the EUROPEAN VOYAGE cozy mystery series, comprising six books (and counting); of the new LAURA FROST FBI suspense thriller, comprising three books (and counting); of the new ELLA DARK FBI suspense thriller, comprising six books (and counting); of the A YEAR IN EUROPE cozy mystery series, comprising nine books); of the AVA GOLD mystery series, comprising three books (and counting); and of the RACHEL GIFT mystery series, comprising three books (and counting).

An avid reader and lifelong fan of the mystery and thriller genres, Blake loves to hear from you, so please feel free to visit www.blakepierceauthor.com to learn more and stay in touch.

BOOKS BY BLAKE PIERCE

RACHEL GIFT MYSTERY SERIES
HER LAST WISH (Book #1)
HER LAST CHANCE (Book #2)
HER LAST HOPE (Book #3)

AVA GOLD MYSTERY SERIES
CITY OF PREY (Book #1)
CITY OF FEAR (Book #2)
CITY OF BONES (Book #3)

A YEAR IN EUROPE
A MURDER IN PARIS (Book #1)
DEATH IN FLORENCE (Book #2)
VENGEANCE IN VIENNA (Book #3)
A FATALITY IN SPAIN (Book #4)
SCANDAL IN LONDON (Book #5)
AN IMPOSTOR IN DUBLIN (Book #6)
SEDUCTION IN BORDEAUX (Book #7)
JEALOUSY IN SWITZERLAND (Book #8)
A DEBACLE IN PRAGUE (Book #9)

ELLA DARK FBI SUSPENSE THRILLER
GIRL, ALONE (Book #1)
GIRL, TAKEN (Book #2)
GIRL, HUNTED (Book #3)
GIRL, SILENCED (Book #4)
GIRL, VANISHED (Book 5)
GIRL ERASED (Book #6)

LAURA FROST FBI SUSPENSE THRILLER
ALREADY GONE (Book #1)
ALREADY SEEN (Book #2)
ALREADY TRAPPED (Book #3)

EUROPEAN VOYAGE COZY MYSTERY SERIES
MURDER (AND BAKLAVA) (Book #1)
DEATH (AND APPLE STRUDEL) (Book #2)
CRIME (AND LAGER) (Book #3)

MISFORTUNE (AND GOUDA) (Book #4)
CALAMITY (AND A DANISH) (Book #5)
MAYHEM (AND HERRING) (Book #6)

ADELE SHARP MYSTERY SERIES
LEFT TO DIE (Book #1)
LEFT TO RUN (Book #2)
LEFT TO HIDE (Book #3)
LEFT TO KILL (Book #4)
LEFT TO MURDER (Book #5)
LEFT TO ENVY (Book #6)
LEFT TO LAPSE (Book #7)
LEFT TO VANISH (Book #8)
LEFT TO HUNT (Book #9)
LEFT TO FEAR (Book #10)
LEFT TO PREY (Book #11)
LEFT TO LURE (Book #12)
LEFT TO CRAVE (Book #13)

THE AU PAIR SERIES
ALMOST GONE (Book#1)
ALMOST LOST (Book #2)
ALMOST DEAD (Book #3)

ZOE PRIME MYSTERY SERIES
FACE OF DEATH (Book#1)
FACE OF MURDER (Book #2)
FACE OF FEAR (Book #3)
FACE OF MADNESS (Book #4)
FACE OF FURY (Book #5)
FACE OF DARKNESS (Book #6)

A JESSIE HUNT PSYCHOLOGICAL SUSPENSE SERIES
THE PERFECT WIFE (Book #1)
THE PERFECT BLOCK (Book #2)
THE PERFECT HOUSE (Book #3)
THE PERFECT SMILE (Book #4)
THE PERFECT LIE (Book #5)
THE PERFECT LOOK (Book #6)
THE PERFECT AFFAIR (Book #7)

THE PERFECT ALIBI (Book #8)
THE PERFECT NEIGHBOR (Book #9)
THE PERFECT DISGUISE (Book #10)
THE PERFECT SECRET (Book #11)
THE PERFECT FAÇADE (Book #12)
THE PERFECT IMPRESSION (Book #13)
THE PERFECT DECEIT (Book #14)
THE PERFECT MISTRESS (Book #15)
THE PERFECT IMAGE (Book #16)
THE PERFECT VEIL (Book #17)
THE PERFECT INDISCRETION (Book #18)
THE PERFECT RUMOR (Book #19)

CHLOE FINE PSYCHOLOGICAL SUSPENSE SERIES
NEXT DOOR (Book #1)
A NEIGHBOR'S LIE (Book #2)
CUL DE SAC (Book #3)
SILENT NEIGHBOR (Book #4)
HOMECOMING (Book #5)
TINTED WINDOWS (Book #6)

KATE WISE MYSTERY SERIES
IF SHE KNEW (Book #1)
IF SHE SAW (Book #2)
IF SHE RAN (Book #3)
IF SHE HID (Book #4)
IF SHE FLED (Book #5)
IF SHE FEARED (Book #6)
IF SHE HEARD (Book #7)

THE MAKING OF RILEY PAIGE SERIES
WATCHING (Book #1)
WAITING (Book #2)
LURING (Book #3)
TAKING (Book #4)
STALKING (Book #5)
KILLING (Book #6)

RILEY PAIGE MYSTERY SERIES
ONCE GONE (Book #1)

ONCE TAKEN (Book #2)
ONCE CRAVED (Book #3)
ONCE LURED (Book #4)
ONCE HUNTED (Book #5)
ONCE PINED (Book #6)
ONCE FORSAKEN (Book #7)
ONCE COLD (Book #8)
ONCE STALKED (Book #9)
ONCE LOST (Book #10)
ONCE BURIED (Book #11)
ONCE BOUND (Book #12)
ONCE TRAPPED (Book #13)
ONCE DORMANT (Book #14)
ONCE SHUNNED (Book #15)
ONCE MISSED (Book #16)
ONCE CHOSEN (Book #17)

MACKENZIE WHITE MYSTERY SERIES
BEFORE HE KILLS (Book #1)
BEFORE HE SEES (Book #2)
BEFORE HE COVETS (Book #3)
BEFORE HE TAKES (Book #4)
BEFORE HE NEEDS (Book #5)
BEFORE HE FEELS (Book #6)
BEFORE HE SINS (Book #7)
BEFORE HE HUNTS (Book #8)
BEFORE HE PREYS (Book #9)
BEFORE HE LONGS (Book #10)
BEFORE HE LAPSES (Book #11)
BEFORE HE ENVIES (Book #12)
BEFORE HE STALKS (Book #13)
BEFORE HE HARMS (Book #14)

AVERY BLACK MYSTERY SERIES
CAUSE TO KILL (Book #1)
CAUSE TO RUN (Book #2)
CAUSE TO HIDE (Book #3)
CAUSE TO FEAR (Book #4)
CAUSE TO SAVE (Book #5)
CAUSE TO DREAD (Book #6)

KERI LOCKE MYSTERY SERIES
A TRACE OF DEATH (Book #1)
A TRACE OF MUDER (Book #2)
A TRACE OF VICE (Book #3)
A TRACE OF CRIME (Book #4)
A TRACE OF HOPE (Book #5)

www.ingramcontent.com/pod-product-compliance
Lightning Source LLC
Chambersburg PA
CBHW030617310726
48979CB00003B/761